LADY DEATH

SAM RAVEN
BOOK THREE

BRIAN DRAKE

ROUGH
EDGES
PRESS

LADY DEATH

PROLOGUE

NUMBER ONE GOAL: DON'T DROWN.

Sam Raven swam slowly, taking his time with each stroke. He had a bomb on his back. The weight slowed his movement a little, but he didn't want to rush. There would be time to hurry later. Multiple enemies waited on the shore. If he took his time, he might be able to reduce the number before the really heavy fighting began.

He lifted his head above the calm water. Another 100 yards, maybe. The chill of Markermeer Lake in the Netherlands bit through his wetsuit and was hard to ignore. It reached deep inside him.

Stay focused.

The target yacht was still anchored at the jetty. He swam a little harder to increase speed, creating more ripples in his wake.

He needed to plant the bomb first, then slip onto land for his secondary target. The house, 50 yards from the jetty contained five people who needed to die. Five people taking a rest from a killing spree, who had thus far evaded authorities. Raven didn't intend to let them get away. Tonight, they'd learn the meaning of the word *payback*.

He reached the rear of the yacht and treaded water long enough to slide the backpack off his shoulders. Unzipping the pack in the water, he removed the bomb, two blocks of C4 and a timer enclosed in a thick plastic bag to keep the water out. He didn't have the option of a magnet to hold the bomb to the yacht's fiberglass hull, so he'd rigged a loop of nylon rope to the bag. He'd hang the bomb on one of the rear propellers.

Taking a deep breath, he dropped below the water's surface. The mini light on his goggles shined a small circle on the belly of the yacht. He was closer to the left prop, so he slipped the nylon loop around a blade, tied a knot to make sure it held, and pressed the timer. The display's greenish glow filled the dark water.

Five minutes.

He figured the five terrorists also had a vehicle at the house. He planned to remove the option from their escape plans as well. The house was in the middle of nowhere and they'd have nowhere to run except into his bullets. The city of Hoorn was miles away, but the bright lights of the city were visible in the distance.

For Raven, it was another night in his war without end, and he was a man made for war. Once he'd worn the uniform of the 82nd Airborne and 5th Special Forces Group. Later he'd traded his officer patch for the anonymity of the CIA Ground Branch. Now he was freelance. No uniform. No home.

It wasn't the life he'd wanted. Raven had seen the worst the world had to offer and escaped for a quiet civilian life. Then fate dealt a cruel blow with sudden tragedy, and vengeance became his new mission. The only link to his past was the sterling silver locket around his neck. He never talked about what was inside, but it motivated his crusade. He pursued the world's predators, those who created victims and heartache, to deliver justice one bullet at a time.

Like tonight.

Raven reached shore and stripped off his flippers and wetsuit. Beneath, he wore a skintight black combat outfit. Shedding his goggles, he reached into his pack for web gear and weapons. He shrugged on the assault vest and buckled it at his waist. A Nighthawk Custom Talon .45 autoloader went into the holster on his right hip. Spare magazines and grenades stuffed the pockets of the vest. His main weapon was a Colt M4 Commando in 5.56mm. The M4 Commando's 11.5-inch barrel gave him a weapon the size of a compact submachine gun size with rifle-caliber punch. A suppressor extended from the barrel to make it a silent killing tool.

Lastly, he removed from the pack a pair of combat boots and laced them tight.

He studied the one-story house. To the right as he faced it, a line of trees created a dividing line between the house and the adjacent empty plot. The nearest neighbor was two miles away. To the left, empty space, cleared of trees and debris, until it met a section of tall grass.

Raven ran for the grassy lot, dropping prone within the tall strands. He began a slow crawl until his body was parallel to the house.

He peeked through the grass. Lights highlighted the exterior. They didn't turn off, so they weren't activated by motion. More lights burned inside. The kill team was up late. Planning their next hit? It wasn't out of the realm of possibility. Whatever they were doing, their time on earth was nearing its end.

Raven flicked off the safety on the M4 Commando as he examined the Jeep parked in front of the house.

No lights in the driveway. The front of the Jeep faced the road. If there were motion lights, they'd catch him before he reached the vehicle. If alarms were attached to the motion lights, the kill team would respond before he had a chance to disable the car.

Easy problem to fix. He grinned.

Three minutes till the bomb detonated.

All he had to do was wait.

Former officers of Iran's Quds Force made up the kill team. The Quds Force was one of five branches of the Islamic Revolutionary Guard Corps. Quds were responsible for military intelligence gathering and special ops, and their officers were well-trained, but some felt unappreciated. Colonel Farzim Radan was one such officer who decided to earn more money as a terrorist-for-hire.

Radan had taken four of his fellow officers with him, adding his girlfriend Pari Mehrnia to the mix as well.

And the team had kept busy.

In recent weeks, they'd assassinated two off-duty US sailors in Madrid and set off several bombs throughout Israel. US intelligence had dubbed them the "Radan Unit" and put them at the top of the presidential kill list.

Western intelligence was racing to eliminate the unit and end their killing spree. Raven lucked out. He found them first. He had sources who wouldn't talk to the CIA or Mossad, the proverbial friends in low places.

Now he was at their back door.

And he had no intention of letting them escape.

A door opened and closed. Raven scanned the area. His pulse quickened. Had he tripped a sensor in the grass? He tried to pick out movement in his peripheral vision but saw no one. Nothing indicated a response team heading his way. Whoever exited the house remained in shadow too.

Terrific.

Two minutes.

Raven tucked the M4 Commando to his shoulder. He fired once. The Jeep's rear tire popped loudly. He fired a second round. Another tire gone.

Flicking the Colt's selector switch to full-auto, Raven broke through the grass. His boots crunched on dirt. The hair on the back of his neck prickled.

Raven dropped and rolled forward. A loud burst of automatic fire crackled, zipping overhead and smacking into the dirt. Raven rolled onto his side, lifting the suppressed M4 and returning fire in two quick bursts of his own. The gunner, bathed in the outer light, stood in the open. He sprinted for the trees on the side of the house. Raven fired another burst and missed again.

Raven scrambled to his feet and ran to the Jeep. No motion lights snapped on. He grabbed a grenade from his vest and dropped it at the garage door. Taking cover at the front of the Jeep, he waited for the explosion. The grenade detonated and sent pieces of wood flying. Raven plucked another grenade from his belt and tossed it into the garage. The blast filled the empty space and blew open the door into the house.

Another blast shook the ground and lit the night sky with a bright orange flash. *Bye-bye yacht.* Raven grinned as he slapped a fresh magazine into the M4.

He left the Jeep. A gunman met him mid step. Another gunner filled the garage doorway. They both zeroed their weapons on Raven's face.

———

THE PAST FEW days had been full of activity for Colonel Farzim Radan and his team. They'd taken refuge at the Hoorn house thinking a few days rest would serve them well before resuming work.

Radan shifted on the bed to let Pari Mehrnia sit up and slide off the bed. Naked, she went to the dresser for her cigarettes and lit one. Radan lay on the bed and admired her trim body in the glowing night light near the door.

"I don't like being here," she said. Cigarette dangling from her lips, she climbed onto the bed and sat against the headboard. She blew a stream of smoke at the ceiling.

Radan remained on his back. He put his hands behind his head.

"Another day won't hurt."

"They're going to find us."

"You worry too much."

"You don't worry enough. One of us has to keep this group alive." She took another drag.

Somebody knocked urgently on the door.

Radan and Pari exchanged quick looks. She pulled the sheet over her as Radan rolled off the bed and pulled on a pair of shorts. He opened the door. "What?"

Heydar Abbasi, former captain in the Quds Force, stood in the hall. He held his Krinkov automatic carbine at the ready. "Somebody's coming."

"Which direction?"

"The grass."

"Send somebody to look."

Abbasi nodded and ran down the hall.

Radan flipped on the light. He ignored Pari's "I told you so" look. "Get dressed."

She took a last drag on the cigarette, stubbed it out on the nightstand ash tray, and left the bed. Radan was already pulling on his pants.

Gunfire outside. Radan and Pari exchanged urgent looks and dressed faster.

A loud explosion rattled the window. Radan parted the curtains and cursed.

"What is it?" Pari said.

"The yacht blew up."

"Here!"

Radan turned, bringing up his hands, catching the AKM Pari tossed him. He yanked back the bolt handle to chamber a round. Now all he needed was a target.

RAVEN'S TRIGGER finger twitched before conscious thought commanded him to fire.

The M4 Commando spat a nearly-silent burst. The first gunman pitched back. He screamed as the 5.56mm slugs ripped through his chest and neck. Raven completed his right-to-left sweep, firing into the garage. He let a full-auto burst go, blasting the doorway gunner from belly to chest. The gunner dropped in the entryway. Raven changed mags on the run, grabbing a third grenade and pitching it through the door. He dodged to the side, back against the wall, as the deadly thump-and-boom filled the house.

Raven ran into the house, stepping over the dead body before him, the M4 Commando tight to his shoulder. A burst smashed into the wall beside him. He dropped, leaning around the corner, and fired back. A gunner hiding behind a couch decorated the wall behind him with red splatter as he fell.

Three down.

Two more.

Raven advanced, skirting around a dining table. He cut through a small kitchen to a dark hallway running left to right. Somebody fired two shots in his direction. Whoever fired couldn't see him. The rounds were probing shots.

Somebody was in the master bedroom. Maybe two people were in the master bedroom.

Raven leaned out and fired back. A small light lit the master bedroom, and he watched the silhouette of a man duck out of sight. He fired again and stepped into the kitchen. One last grenade. He pulled the pin and pitched it down the hall. The grenade bounced off the door frame and entered the bedroom at an angle. A woman screamed.

The grenade flew back through the doorway to bounce off the hallway wall and fly into the living room at the other end.

Raven dropped behind the kitchen counter. The wall took most of the blast, and it left his ears ringing more than before. Raven jumped up and started toward the bedroom with the M4 Commando ahead when Colonel Radan, minus his shirt, ran out with an AKM at his hip.

Radan tried to jam the muzzle in Raven's gut. Raven swung the stock of the M4 and clipped Radan on the chin, but the blow didn't stop the colonel. He collided with Raven's midsection and the pair tumbled into the wrecked living room. Raven lost his grip on the M4 Commando and the sling tangled around his left arm.

Radan aimed at Raven's face. The barrel was too long, and Raven batted it away. The M4 was pinned beneath him and his right arm still caught in the sling. He couldn't punch with his right. He wedged a knee between him and Radan and pushed hard, throwing the terrorist colonel off him. Rolling left, Raven shed the Colt and snatched the Nighthawk .45 from his hip.

Radan completed his roll on the other side of the dining table. He came up on one knee and raised the AKM. Raven fired once. The terrorist colonel's head snapped back, and he dropped like a puppet with cut strings.

Raven pivoted right. He fired twice through the doorway

as the woman emerged to take advantage of his distraction, and the .45 ACP slugs caught her in the chest and neck. She landed in the hallway face first, a pistol tumbling from her dead fingers.

Raven rose and holstered his pistol. Taking a Canon PowerShot from a pocket, he snapped pictures of their faces. A present for the CIA and Mossad.

Time to go.

Two minutes till extraction.

Raven grabbed the M4 Commando and left the house. He ran hard for the water. He'd arranged his own pickup, a mercenary he knew, who had a boat. He reached the shore and found a place to hide among a cluster of rocks and trees. The boat arrived. Its old engine chugged. The mercenary, an American named Hawthorne, flashed a light twice. Raven returned the flash with a light of his own. The boat approached the shore, and Raven ran out into the water to climb aboard.

As the boat's engine chugged, Raven sat up and watched the shore grew smaller with distance.

"All right?" Hawthorne said.

"Scratch five," Raven said.

"Good work."

Raven watched the departing shoreline with a grim set to his jaw.

Radan and his unit had spilled too much blood for Raven to feel true satisfaction. *Sure. Good work.* Deaths had been avenged. More had been prevented. Other threats now needed his attention, and he turned his mind to the future. His war without end wasn't finished. He feared it never would be. There were far too many Farzim Radans in the world. Worse, he couldn't stop them all.

But he'd die trying.

PART I

PART I

1

IT STARTED WITH A PHONE CALL.

Sam Raven answered his cell midway through the second blast of his ringtone. He undid his tie with his right hand as he said hello. Crisp air and the sound of trickling water filtered through the open windows.

"Mr. Raven?"

A woman's voice. Soft. Almost a whisper. German accent.

"Speaking."

"My name is Tanya."

"Okay."

"May I see you?"

"For what?" Raven pulled the tie from his shirt collar and tossed it on the bed.

"I want to defect to the United States."

Raven chuckled. "Unless I'm reading the calendar wrong, it's not 1985 anymore. You can leave Germany anytime you like with a proper visa."

"I'm serious, Mr. Raven. My name is Tanya Jafari and I'm a fighter with the Islamic Union. I was born in Germany and married into the jihad and now I want to come to the United States. I will trade information for a new identity."

"What information?"

"I know the White Widow."

"The who?"

The woman cursed. "Are you serious?"

"If you know enough to reach out to me," he said, "you know I'm out of the loop on *some* things."

He couldn't help his gap in information. He wasn't a CIA paramilitary officer any longer. He worked on his own now, his interests personal. Anything he needed to know—such as the details of the "White Widow"—he could learn through his network of informants.

The woman remained silent.

"Why don't you tell me who she is," Raven said.

"Call your friends at the CIA," she replied instead. "I will find you."

The line clicked.

Raven shook his head and hung up. *Dammit!*

He hadn't returned home to Stockholm to go back to work again. He had hoped to avoid work for a week or two. How did "Tanya Jafari" find him? He checked his Rolex. He'd stepped aboard his houseboat only ten minutes earlier. The open windows flushed out the stuffy air. *Can't a guy get a break?*

The "White Widow". He laughed at the name. Did she steal her moniker from a comic book? He blamed "the Jackal". Since the reign of Illich Ramirez Sanchez, every terrorist wanted a cool name to show off in the media.

Tanya Jafari, the CIA, and whoever picked her nickname from the Marvel Cinematic Universe, could wait. He wasn't lifting a finger until he had a shower and ate lunch at the marina club.

As the hot water sprayed over his body, he built a picture

of her in his mind. *I married into the jihad...* She was German. Blonde hair, blue eyes? He might cheat by looking up her name on the Internet. She sounded like one of the thousands of women from Western Europe who found their way to the Middle East. They either met jihadist boyfriends or found recruiters on internet forums or social media. Raven considered it an odd phenomenon. Perhaps her family had spoken to the media. Many others did the same when their daughters vanished from home to turn up in Syria or Jordan or Iraq or...

Nuts, he decided. Let her find him. He'd hand off Tanya Jafari to the CIA and let *them* deal with her.

Every soldier needed R&R. His was long overdue.

RAVEN STOOD at the rail of the King's Bridge in Stockholm, overlooking Klara Sjö ("Lake Klara"). It was a canal cutting through the city. Why the Swedes named a canal a "lake" was a question too amusing to ask. The waterways in the city didn't pool into anything the size of a lake.

But who cared? Raven enjoyed the view from the bridge. The evening was cool with pink sky above as the sun set. The water rippled below. Raven stared at the surface as if in a trance. He wore casual clothes for his night out and wasn't carrying his pistol. But the leather sap he also habitually carried rode in the right pocket of his slacks. He couldn't go out totally unarmed.

He ignored the other pedestrians passing behind him. The King's Bridge connected the Stockholm district of Norrmalm to Kungsholmen, an island in Lake Mälaren, also part of central Stockholm. Lake Mälaren was also not a lake.

The two one-way concrete sections of the King's Bridge arched over the Klara Sjö. Below, boats passed. A loud crowd on a party boat made Raven grin. He liked seeing people have fun. It reminded him of better times.

The canal didn't have the same effect on him as watching the ocean. The sight and sound of crashing waves did more to bring him peace than the rippling canal. He didn't have an ocean to look at, but the canal served his purpose. He wanted to get his mind off the constant state of war in which he found himself. He needed a respite from tangling with the worst the world had to offer.

A war without end wasn't the life he'd chosen. Fate had decided for him. He'd tried to resist, but the ghosts of his nightmares wouldn't leave him alone. They remained a constant as he battled the stream of predators who sought to destroy innocent lives. Raven often felt he made no difference. One fight ended; another began. His ghosts told him otherwise. He kept fighting in hopes of someday silencing the nightmares, but they persisted.

Enough melancholy. He cleared his throat, straightened, and adjusted his jacket. He crossed the top of the arch and walked down the other side. He was treating himself to a night of roulette at the Casino Cosmopol, and a dinner at the casino's Jackpot Bar & Grill.

He fully intended for the casino to pay for his dinner via his winnings. He had a system for roulette, and while he lost as much as he won, he could count on winning the price of dinner. Or at least breaking even. It all depended on how loud his stomach growled.

The casino required a cover charge; he paid at the door. Entering the restaurant, the hostess asked for his identification. Nobody under 20 allowed, and the staff checked all IDs. Older guests were no exception. Raven showed her his ID and made for the bar. It was still early, and the place wasn't full. He found a stool and signaled the bartender, a man named Sven. Raven had gotten to know Sven well over his frequent visits.

"Hello, Mr. Raven."

"Good evening."

"Your usual?"

"Please."

Raven's "usual" would make martini aficionados scream in agony. A shot of gin, shot of vodka, touch of vermouth, twist of lemon peel, *stirred*, because James Bond was an idiot. Nothing on the initial list would send the hobby drinkers to the roof. They also wouldn't admit such a concoction carried with it the scent of rubbing alcohol. Raven stumbled onto a solution one night, long ago, by accident. Two teaspoons of water after the pour. Cue the weeping and gnashing of teeth!

The extra water served a purpose. It muted the rubbing alcohol smell, *seemed* to bring out the flavor of both gin and vodka, and enabled one to enjoy a good martini. More than one actually. The unintended consequence was his martinis tasted like water. One could quickly polish off several and forget the natural result. Next-day hangovers were rough indeed.

Sven set a glass of ice water in front of Raven, with a teaspoon beside it, and proceeded to mix the martini. He poured the elixir into a glass, added the peel, and placed the glass in front of Raven with reverence.

"Your turn, sir."

Raven added the two teaspoons of water, stirred once, and set the teaspoon on a napkin. He swallowed a sip and smiled.

"Amazing as always."

Sven refused to add the water. It went against his conscience. He'd appealed to Raven not to do such a horrible thing the first time Raven made the suggestion, to no avail.

The bartender excused himself to serve other customers. Two young ladies dressed in their best night clothes took a lot of time ordering. They rejected several of Sven's suggestions. They looked as if they were finally legally allowed in the place. He smiled at them and raised his glass. They turned away and spoke close in hushed tones followed by giggles. Raven grinned. *Have fun, ladies. It's all downhill from here.*

Sven returned after finally serving them. "First timers," he said.

"I figured."

"Been out of town? Haven't seen you in a while."

Raven swallowed another sip. "Way out of town," he said. "I'm hoping to stay home for a few weeks."

Sven excused himself again. Raven reached behind the bar for a menu card. One could eat at the bar, but he didn't partake in such uncivilized behavior. He'd consumed meals in so many godawful places around the world he refused to eat anywhere but at a proper table when home.

But since the girls were ignoring him...

He laughed and took another drink. Tanya Jafari was long gone from his thoughts.

The chef's special of prime rib and fried potatoes caught his eye. He put the card back. He looked behind him. The tables in the restaurant were filling up fast.

He finished his drink, paid Sven and told him to keep the change. Then he said, "Your roulette table will pay for my prime rib."

"Good luck, Mr. Raven."

Raven nodded and turned to walk away. A chill went down his neck. Sven's good wishes carried with it a subtext he didn't want to acknowledge.

Very soon Raven would need much more than luck if he were going to keep on living.

2

THE WHEEL SPUN. THE DEALER COUNTER-SPUN THE WHEEL and the ivory ball raced along the track.

The interior of the casino always impressed Raven. Tiles with individual etchings lined a high arched ceiling. The ceiling was too high for patrons to appreciate the etchings, but they provided a nice detail.

Table games lined either wall with the roulette tables in two rows down the center.

Beyond the tables, a staircase led to the lower level where more games awaited.

A railed walkway, overlooking the game room, contained slot machines. Chairs and tables covered other spaces throughout the floors.

Raven paid attention only to the table in front of him. He stood close, near the dealer, a stack of chips in front of him and bets placed. His attention was on the wheel and the table. Other players crowded close. Their excited chatter might as well have been carried away in high wind. He was aware of everyone's position at the table and glanced around now and then to check his exposed back. But his focus was on the game.

He didn't feel in danger, but there were eyes on him.

Was Tanya Jafari here?

He focused on the game again.

Roulette was a game a lot of people played but nobody played well. It was easy to win if you spread out a lot of chips on the table, but one ran the risk of winning and losing at the same time. Raven had seen it often. Somebody would bet 125 krona across the table, won 50, but actually lost 75. The wider the spread, the more lost than won, and it only offered the illusion of success.

Betting on individual numbers was also a no-no for Raven, and the sign of an amateur too. Pinpoint accuracy in roulette wasn't attainable. In a game depending on randomness, he had to account for chance as much as possible.

The wheel slowed and the ball dropped. The dealer announced, "Red, 12, even."

Raven tapped the edge of the table as the dealer cleared chips and distributed winnings. Raven preferred the outside bets to the numbered rows. Much better chances of winning, as in this case. He'd placed 50 krona on the red square outside the rows. Any red result would have put winnings in his pocket.

Raven collected his 100 krona return and set the two chips aside. The winnings paid for dinner. Now for a little fun.

He continued to play, mixing the red and black boxes with corner bets, where one chip covered four numbers. He bet on corners close to the wheel covering squares one, two, four and five. The ball landed on black 24, at the far end of the table. A loss.

Raven shifted his next corner bet to cover 23, 24, 26 and

27. 50 krona. He also placed an additional 50 krona chip on the black square.

The wheel spun. The dealer counter-spun the ball. The sound of the ball running in the notch was mesmerizing. Raven reminded himself to breathe. Gambling was a form of combat. You couldn't take your eyes away from the target for a moment. One distraction and you're history.

The ball dropped with a sharp click.

"Red, 21, odd."

Groans around the table. Raven bowed his head and laughed. At this rate he'd get cleaned out. He'd started with 1000 krona and the losses were chipping away fast.

Then his stomach grumbled.

All right, he decided. *One more for the road.*

Fifty krona on the outside red square. Another 50 to cover the second 12 numbers on the board.

The dealer spun the wheel and flicked the ball into the slot. They rolled counter to each other and the ball snapped into a slot.

Raven shook his head.

"Red, 34, even."

He collected his 100 krona win.

But his bet on the column numbers had cost him 50. He won, and he lost. Such is roulette.

Raven cashed in, changed his chips for banknotes, and wandered back to the Jackpot Bar & Grill.

Raven stopped midway, moved to the wall to put his back behind something solid, and looked around.

Somebody *was* watching him.

But nothing around him suggested surveillance. Players filled every seat at the table games. On the walkway above, more players sat at slot machines. Some observed from the rail, but they were groups of people, caught up in their own conversations. Nobody was looking at him, per se. Nobody stood out and tripped his mental alarm.

He didn't think Tanya Jafari would be traveling with a friend. She'd be alone. There were no individuals, like him, floating around. If he was wrong, she was good enough to avoid his detection.

He left the wall, walking faster than normal.

Laughter greeted him as he passed through the archway of the Jackpot Bar & Grill. The two young women he'd seen at the bar earlier occupied a table with two gentleman and all four were having a good time. Raven smiled again. His 20s were further behind him than he wanted to admit. He had no wish to relive those days, but a quick visit wouldn't hurt. Long enough to correct a mistake or two; choose a different path.

But he'd made his choices. He had to live with them. The foursome at the table would have to live with theirs too. He wished them the best.

The hostess escorted him to a table in the center of the room. He asked for one in a corner. She took him there. He eased into the chair with his back to the wall, eyes on the front of the restaurant.

He didn't want his back exposed any longer.

3

RAVEN SCANNED THE MENU AGAIN BUT SAW NO REASON NOT to order the chef's special. Prime rib sounded fine indeed.

A shadow fell over the table. He looked up as Sven, the bartender, approached with a tray. He supported the tray on his right hand.

"Compliments of the house, sir," Sven said. He sat the martini, a glass of ice water, and a teaspoon on the table, along with a folded napkin. Raven thanked the bartender, who turned and fast-walked to the bar.

Raven unfolded the napkin. He smiled. Sven was a good man.

The woman at the bar is asking for you. Dark hair. Pink dress. German accent. I distracted her while you got your table.

Raven placed the napkin on the table and set the water glass on top. The condensation would smear the words.

He spooned water into his martini, stirred, and sipped. The waitress arrived and he ordered the special. No salad, no appetizers. The waitress departed. Raven sat back and watched the dark-haired woman in pink.

She sat alone, perched on the barstool with crossed legs.

Her left leg dangled. She wore black stilettos with red-tipped toenails. She moved the toes of her left foot with nervous tension.

When Sven passed her every few minutes, she asked him a question. He kept shrugging his shoulders. She looked toward the front of the restaurant, then glanced around. She looked over her left shoulder in Raven's direction and stopped short. Raven smiled at her and raised his glass.

She slid off the barstool, Cosmo in one hand, small pink purse in the other, and approached the table with purpose. She looked defiant. Almost angry. She was upset with him or had a nasty case of Resting Bitch Face.

Well, she is German...

"Mr. Raven." She stopped a few feet from the table.

"Miss Jafari."

"May I?"

"Sure."

She slid into the booth opposite him. She sat straight, her face stoic.

His guess at blonde hair and blue eyes had been off. Tanya Jafari's thick black mane washed over her freckled shoulders. She did have blue eyes though. Lines in her face showed she wasn't in her 20s anymore. Raven pegged her for mid-30s.

"You made a fool of me," she said.

"How?"

"I've been sitting here asking about you for fifteen minutes. I look like a stood-up schoolteacher who can't figure out she's been stiffed."

Raven laughed. "At least not in a good way."

"Enough."

Raven raised an eyebrow.

"Did you do what I asked?" she said.

"Why are you talking to me like you're a commanding

officer? I've done nothing since I returned home except lose a little money at roulette."

"Why are you being hostile?"

"I'm tired, Miss Jafari."

"People like us only rest when we are at war."

"And which war are *you* fighting, Miss Jafari?"

"I'm not fighting wars any longer. I want to stop fighting. I need to get out of the Islamic Union."

"They are a tough lot, yeah. I understand."

"Will you help me?"

Raven swallowed some of his martini. He studied her face. Plenty of lines indicated tough experience. Her eyes looked weary. Her bare arms were well-muscled, and her figure didn't appear affected by long-term sitting. She was, or had been, an operator. Western intelligence knew the Islamic Union was unique among jihadist organizations. They eschewed Muslim practices to get cells to blend into Western nations. Recruiting western personnel furthered their goal.

"I usually don't help people like you," Raven said.

She sucked in a breath. "But you—"

"Why do you think my reputation for assisting those in need extends to terrorists?"

She leaned close. "I told you I want *out*."

"How many people have you killed?"

"Only one and it was too many."

"How did you get involved?"

"A boyfriend recruited me."

"Your boyfriend in Germany?"

"It's a long story. Do you want to sit here all night?"

The server arrived with Raven's prime rib.

"No," he said, as the hot plate was set in front of him. "I want to enjoy my dinner."

The server said, "Will your guest be having anything?"

"A separate check," Raven snapped.

Tanya spoke an order in a voice tinged with anger. The server nodded and departed.

Raven's mood changed as he cut into the soft meat and speared a piece of fried potato on his fork. The prime rib was perfectly pink with not a lot of fat around the edges or the center. It was always a hit or miss meal with him. Too many places served prime rib with more fat than meat and you left 90% of it on the plate.

"Mmmm," he said, swallowing. "Very good."

"Are you mocking me?"

"You have a bit of a complex, don't you?"

"I need your help, Mr. Raven." Her face softened. "Please. I can't go back now."

"Marked for death, are you? Assassins in pursuit?"

"Exactly."

"Funny they haven't found you yet."

"I'm good at what I do, Mr. Raven."

"Do?"

"*Did.*"

"Uh-huh." He ate some of the mixed vegetables on the side of the plate. They crunched as he chewed. "Tell me what you have to trade."

She scooted closer, lowering her voice. "The identity of the White Widow."

"Never heard of her."

"She's in charge of the Islamic Union."

"They let a woman give the orders?"

"She's the wife of our late leader."

"Our?"

"Goddammit, Raven—" she stopped, lowered her voice. "It's a hard habit to break, okay?"

"No *mister* this time?"

"Are you going to listen to me?"

"I eat, you talk."

She swallowed a mouthful of her Cosmo. She set the glass down hard enough to swish Raven's martini.

"Don't spill my vitamins," Raven said.

"You're impossible."

"No, I'm hungry." Raven ate some more.

Tanya Jafari stared at him with hot eyes. Finally, she cleared her throat, shifted, and looked at the table.

"The White Widow is a woman named Francesca Sloan. She's British. Recruited the same way I was, through a boyfriend. The organization promoted him to leader after the death of their founder."

"Then what happened?"

"Francesca and her husband moved to a camp in Jordan to direct operations."

"What happened to Hunky Dude?"

"Killed in a US raid."

"In Jordan?"

"In the field."

"And his old lady took over?"

"She had to fight for it. The second- and third-in-command didn't want a woman. We were all surprised they finally said okay. The IU is trying to prevent the mistakes of ISIS and al-Qaeda."

Raven chewed a piece of meat. He had to admit the Islamic Union had done well in keeping a low profile. Their operations had been few and far between. They preferred to strike with precision rather than mass casualty attacks. A bomb here, a shooting there, a phone call to claim responsibility. Always high-profile military or civilian targets, the deaths of which made the news. Always.

"How does having the White Widow in charge avoid mistakes?" Raven said.

"She thinks like her husband. The leadership council wanted to maintain the command style."

"If she knows you're gone," Raven said, "she's not going to be where you say she is."

"But I know her face. I can identify her."

"The intelligence community can't?" Raven said. "If they know her name—"

"You don't understand. Her name is *not* known. You are the first person to ever hear it."

"Other than her family and presumably her husband."

"You *know* what I *mean*."

Raven sipped some water this time to wash down his last bite. He set the glass down. "All right. Suppose I do help. What do you want?"

"An escort into the CIA."

"I'll call and ask them to send a representative. If you're concerned about your safety, stay with me until they pick you up."

"But—"

"You don't need me to take you in. Let them come to us. Much easier."

"For you?"

"What did I tell you about being tired, Miss Jafari? You want my help; this is what I'm willing to do. What's the difference?"

"Well—"

"If you don't like the deal, you can always email them. The CIA has a link on the website. Might take a while for somebody to get back to you—"

"Can you at least take me to the embassy?"

Raven decided it was a fair compromise. He nodded. "Yes, I can take you to the embassy."

He looked up as the server brought her meal, roasted chicken with rice. The aroma was amazing.

"Anything more?" the server said.

"Go ahead and add this to my check," Raven told him. "Never mind what I said before."

"Very good, sir."

He turned to Tanya.

She said, "Thank you, Mr. Raven."

"Shut up and eat."

4

RAVEN SWALLOWED THE LAST OF THE FRIED POTATOES, DRANK some water, and pushed his plate away. He wiped his mouth.

"Can you sit tight a moment?"

"Sure," she said.

Raven left the table. At the bar, he asked Sven if he could slip into the back office to make a call. The bartender agreed and showed him to a room behind the bar. It was a storage room full of boxes containing liquor bottles. A bright overhead bulb shined.

Raven dialed a number on his cell and hoped the man on the other end picked up.

He did. "Wilson."

Clark Wilson, Senior Staff Operations Officer for the CIA's Special Activities Center, was one of Raven's contacts at the Agency, and an old friend. But Raven would be the first to admit he hadn't kept in touch as much as either would have liked.

"It's Sam."

"Howdy."

"I'm in Stockholm with a young lady."

"Congratulations?"

"No, it's work-related. Does the name Tanya Jafari mean anything to you?"

"Not at all."

"She's a German woman who joined the Islamic Union. She wants to defect."

"What is she trading?"

"The identity of the White Widow."

"Wow."

"Something you're looking for?"

"If she can give us a picture and a name, we'll give her whatever she asks for. You have no idea how long we've been trying to figure out who she is."

"All right. I've agreed to take her to the embassy. Can you make sure we can get in the door?"

"I'll arrange it right now," Wilson said. "Don't waste time. Go tonight. Ask for Russell Dillon at the gate. He'll be expecting you."

"Perfect."

He could drop Tanya at the gate and go home. Easy evening.

"Thanks for doing this, Sam."

"Be seeing you." Raven hung up and left the storage room.

Raven returned to the table. Tanya had a fresh Cosmo and the dinner plates had been removed.

"Where are you staying?"

"The Grand Hotel."

"We can go back for your things, and then we're going to the embassy."

"You work fast."

"As soon as I mentioned your White Widow friend, my contacts became *very* interested in what you have to share."

"I told you."

Raven downed what remained of his martini.

"Do you have a car?" he said.

"A rental, yeah."

"Good. I don't have one."

"No?"

"I refuse to pay the road tolls."

She laughed. Her laugh sounded like wind chimes. She looked normal when she laughed. He had to put her background out of his mind and get her where she needed to go. Then he could continue his much-needed R&R.

He told her to finish her drink and then they'd leave.

RAVEN HELD Tanya's left elbow as they went down the steps to the parking lot. Footsteps shuffled behind them. Tanya turned her head, and yelled, "Raven!"

Raven pulled his right hand from the pocket of his jacket. He gripped his leather sap, pivoted on the middle step. The man behind them had a gun halfway out, the snout of the pistol extended with a suppressor. Tanya screamed. Raven raised the sap and struck hard, once, twice. The gunman tumbled down the steps, landing on his belly. Raven scooped up the man's Glock 19X as a compact Mercedes screeched to a stop.

Tanya ran for the bushes along the wall. Raven remained in a crouch as two men piled out of the car.

Bystanders nearby screamed. Raven shouted for them to get down, get away. He lived by two rules. Rule One was no gun fights in public. The danger to innocents was too high. But he had no choice this time. The enemy had chosen the battle, and he had no time to lead them away.

All he could do was shoot fast and end the threat.

The driver remained behind the wheel, and he and Raven locked eyes. Dark hair, glasses, leather coat. The boss. Raven lifted the Glock and fired twice. The *phuts* from the suppressor made little noise over the commotion. One of the gunmen fell against the car and slid down, leaving a smear of red on the passenger side.

The second gunner, lifting a submachine gun, leaned into a firing position. Raven rolled right as the burst chewed into the concrete and ricocheted with a sharp whine. Raven fired again. The gunner's head snapped back. As he shifted to the driver, the man with the glasses put the car in reverse and backed away with a screech of rubber.

Raven fired again and again, tracing a line of shots across the windshield. The driver executed a screeching bootlegger turn and powered across the lot.

Tanya emerged from the bushes, dress and hair a mess, her mouth open in shock. She still clutched her purse.

He ran to her, grabbed her arm, and pulled hard. "Where's your car?"

She ditched her heels and took the lead, running hard across the blacktop, Raven staying back to cover her. No other threats showed themselves, but the man with the glasses hadn't departed either. He saw the car moving among the lot. A shark on the hunt.

Raven and Tanya dodged between vehicles, stopped at a silver Nissan. She popped the locks with a remote and dropped behind the wheel. As the lead killer powered his car down the aisle toward them, Raven ran around the back of the Nissan. He fired two more shots. The driver stuck a pistol out the window and returned fire, Raven staying low as the unaimed shots flew wide. He pulled the trigger again as the car passed, firing fast to try and hit the driver. No dice. The Glock's slide locked back over the empty magazines. Raven tossed the gun and ran to the passenger side.

Tanya peeled out of the parking space and took off in the opposite direction of the killer's car.

The tires screeched as the Nissan hit the street, Tanya making a sharp right turn into traffic. She sped through a changing light, crossing the intersection. Shifting lanes, she made the next left. The turn threw Raven against the door. He buckled his seat belt.

"Know them?"

"Not the shooters," she said. "The driver is Sila Kaymak. Turkish. Top killer."

"He missed tonight."

"He'll be back."

"Do you have a gun?"

"Little Beretta in my purse."

Raven grabbed the purse from the center console and flicked it open. He laughed. She'd given him an apt description. The "little Beretta" was a .25-caliber 950 BS. Hardly useful in the kind of fight they faced. It was a hideout gun. A last resort.

He closed the purse and put it back on the console.

"Straight to the embassy?" she said.

"Yes."

"Tell me where to go."

"Let's make sure we've lost our killer first." Raven told her to make the next right.

———

HE PUSHED the seat back for more legroom. The Nissan was too cramped for his height.

"How do you get around if you don't have a car?" she said.

"Stockholm has an amazing public transportation system."

She laughed. "You'd rather pay bus fare than road tolls? What's the difference?"

"The truth is," he said, "I'm home so little having a car

doesn't make sense. It would sit parked most of the time and probably not start when I returned."

"I see. You want something to complain about."

"You mean about the tolls?"

"Yes."

"I'm an American abroad," Raven said. "Americans complain about free meals."

"Germans do too."

"Human nature, I guess."

Raven shifted in the seat. Tanya performed counter-surveillance maneuvers like a pro. She made several turns, Raven checking their backside for the Mercedes. Convinced they were clear, he told her how to get to the embassy.

She stopped for a red light. "It's not a good life, is it?"

He turned to her. The glow of the stop light tinted her face red.

"What isn't?"

"What we do."

"There's a big difference between what you and I do, Miss Jafari."

"We both fight for a cause."

"Right. You kill people for not following your religion and I try and stop you."

"No! We're *defending* our *religion* and our *land* from people like you who want to take it!"

Raven laughed. But it wasn't the time to point out she hadn't been born in the land she zealously defended. "Nobody wants your land, Tanya. Nobody cares about your religion, either. We want you to stop strapping bombs to your back and walking into airports."

"And you bomb us to stop us. You invade our land and kill our children."

"Tell me another way. Seriously, I'm open to suggestions. *Talking* sure as hell hasn't helped."

"My point is we've both dedicated ourselves to righting injustice."

"You expect me to buy what you're selling? Because I'm not. *We* didn't start the fight, Tanya."

"My question, if you can stop arguing with me for a moment, is what has the fighting taken from us?"

"That's your question after your epiphany, Tanya?"

"Why are you attacking me? I'm trying to come clean with you, so you understand—"

"My fight hasn't taken *anything* from me, Miss Jafari." *If you only knew...* "Sounds like you're talking about yourself."

"Maybe I am. It's why I'm here."

A moment of silence passed between them. Tanya stayed focused on driving.

"How long were you in the Middle East?" Raven said.

"Five years."

"Not very long."

"The first year and a half was training," she said. The light changed and she drove forward. "They broke us down and built us up again. We needed to get the poison of the West out of our systems."

"I understand the process."

"I've only been a field soldier for two years."

"They sent you out on a mission, you killed somebody, and decided the romance was gone?"

Her jaw tightened. Her slender fingers gripped the wheel hard. He didn't feel bad needling her. He was testing her reactions. If she were lying, she'd crack. If she wasn't, she'd reaffirm her resolve with increased vigor. And vitriol because he had to be making her mad.

"Why don't you believe me, Mr. Raven? Why send four men to kill me if I wasn't telling the truth?"

"Do you know how many jihadists have tried to penetrate the CIA by pretending to defect?"

"Since I have no CIA agents to talk to, no, I'm not aware."

"Enough. If I hand you over to my friends, I need to make sure you're telling me the truth."

"And if not?"

"I'll kill you myself, *Tanya*. I'll shove a knife into your belly and get a snack after." Raven glanced ahead. "Make a right, then the next left."

She complied.

5

TWO MARINES STEPPED OUT OF THE GUARD BUILDING AT THE embassy driveway. Both carried sidearms and appeared ready to use them.

Raven powered down his window. While one Marine stayed on Tanya's side, the other approached Raven with a flashlight. The beam landed on Raven's face.

"I'm a US citizen," Raven said. "This is an emergency. Russell Dillon is expecting us."

"Who?"

"Russell Dillon. Call it in. He's waiting for us."

The Marine glanced at his partner. The second Marine remained quiet.

Raven said, "Dillon works in the *basement*, get it?"

The Marine returned to the building. His partner remained on Tanya's side. She kept her hands on the wheel because the Marine kept his right hand near his gun.

Raven sat still. The Marine in the guard building spoke on a telephone. It was a short conversation. He returned to Raven's side.

"All right. Go through the gate and wait in the parking

lot. Dillon isn't here yet, but Eva Yoshino will be out to get you."

"Thank you, Sergeant."

Both Marines returned to the guard building. The gate in front of them lifted. Tanya drove through, made a right into the parking lot, and stopped the car. She didn't turn off the engine. Raven told her to wait.

After a few minutes, a woman in a skirt and blazer combo exited the building and stopped at the car. She leaned in Tanya's window.

"Are you Sam Raven?"

He passed her his identification. Tanya snapped on the overhead light.

"Okay." She passed back the ID. "I'm Eva Yoshino. I work with Russ. He is on his way. Park over there and let's go inside."

Tanya stopped the car where indicated. She and Raven exited. They looked at each other. Relief washed over Tanya's face. The tension of the last hour had faded. He smiled at her. "Right to the front door," he said.

They followed the Japanese woman into the embassy. In her heels she matched Raven's height. She had long black hair straight down her back and sharp features. Her dark eyes remained suspicious. Raven couldn't do anything about her attitude for the time being. He was still suspicious too.

In the lower level of the building, Eva Yoshino put them in a conference room and departed. They sat at one end of the long table and waited.

Russell Dillon arrived ten minutes later. He wore a sweater over a white shirt and jeans. Bald head, stubbled jaw. His wedding band looked scuffed. Taking a seat, he said to Raven, "I don't know who you are, but you must have some influence to have Langley get me out of bed."

"I'm sure it's been a long day," Raven said. "But this is important."

"I heard." He addressed Tanya. "Start talking."

Tanya repeated her story verbatim. Dillon didn't take any notes. Raven added the part about the killers at the casino. Dillon promised to investigate the incident. "We'll see about getting the police to stand down. Agency personnel can collect the bodies."

Raven nodded.

"Miss Jafari," Dillon said, "your story caught the attention of the top brass back at Langley. They want you on a plane to the US tomorrow. They will debrief you at our Blue Ridge black site." To Raven: "Know of it?"

"I'm familiar." It was a secret facility in the Blue Ridge Mountains of Virginia. There, the CIA housed high-value enemy combatants they didn't want held overseas. Disguised as a park ranger station, an elevator led to the underground lair. There was no other word for it in Raven's estimation.

"You'll stay here tonight," Dillon said, "and a chopper will pick you up on the roof in the morning. It will take you to a private airfield where you'll board a jet for home."

"She'll need clothes and things," Raven said.

"And you?"

"Nothing. I'm not going."

"Yes, you are," Dillon said. "They want to talk to you, too."

Raven scoffed. "I'm only the delivery man."

"Hey. A day or two in the US won't hurt."

Raven opened his mouth to protest but Dillon cut him off.

"Non-negotiable, Raven."

Raven let out a sigh.

"The CIA thanks you for your cooperation."

Raven grunted.

Dillon rose from his chair. "I'll show you to your rooms.

Eva will take care of your clothes in the morning, Miss Jafari."

"And shoes."

Dillon glanced at her bare feet. "Of course."

"Wait," Raven said.

"What is it?"

"Considering the attempt on Tanya's life, she should give you her information now. You know in case we don't make it."

Tanya blanched.

Dillon looked at her. "Well?"

She hesitated, but said, "I agree. I have pictures on my cell phone I can share." She opened her purse and took out her phone.

"Let's go to our ops center, then," Dillon said. "We can plug your phone into a computer there."

Raven walked behind the pair as they went down a hallway. He should have guessed the Agency would want his input. He didn't see why they couldn't ask him questions over the telephone while he lounged on his deck, though.

Say goodbye to R&R.

But with any luck, he'd be back in a day or two.

THE EMBASSY ACCOMMODATIONS weren't terrible.

Raven's room might as well have been a small hotel room elsewhere in the city. Bed, bath, window overlooking the embassy courtyard. He closed the drapes. The view was worthless in the dark.

He splashed water on his face and decided his teeth could go one night without Colgate. Wouldn't be the first time.

He took off his shirt. A locket dangled from around his neck, nestled in the center of his chest. The scuffed sterling silver piece was always with him. He leaned his palms against the dresser and looked at his face in the mirror.

All he'd wanted was a rest. Now he was mixed up in another caper. He hoped it indeed only took a day or two. He had not chosen his path in life, but it had been handed to him by a cruel mix of tragedy and fate. The only link to his past life was the locket. He never talked about what it contained, but it motivated his crusade.

With a deep exhale, he removed the locket and placed it on the dresser with his Rolex and wallet.

A knock at the door.

He opened the door a crack.

Tanya stood in the hallway. She looked nervous.

"You okay?" he said.

"Let me in, the guards are watching."

Raven stepped back. She slipped into the room. He shut the door.

"What is it?"

"I don't know if I can do this."

"You've already started. Too late to go back now."

She folded her arms and turned away. "I'm a traitor."

"Yeah."

She laughed and turned back. "But doesn't that make me—"

"What? Bad? You told me yourself one death was too many. The Islamic Union may have turned you into a fighter, but they couldn't erase the one thing, deep down, we all have."

"Which is what?"

"A sense of humanity. What's right, what's wrong."

She shook her head. "I thought I was doing the right thing. I saw people being oppressed and attacked and wanted to do something."

"Out of love for somebody else?"

"Right."

"You never told me what happened to your boyfriend. The one who recruited you."

"He's dead."

"I'm sorry."

"He died while I was at the training camp."

"What happened?"

She shook her head. "Never mind. It was a mission. He didn't come back."

"Uh-huh."

Her eyes became teary. "Once he was gone, there was no reason to stay. I thought I needed retaliation. Now I don't know what I need."

"A new start."

She wiped her eyes. "You asked for suggestions on how we can settle our differences. I don't have any. But I hope to figure out another way. War is not the answer. Both sides have done enough killing and we're nowhere closer to an understanding than when the shooting started." She wiped her eyes again. "Is it easy? Starting over?"

"Not at all."

She forced a laugh. "You're not very good at making me feel better."

"I'm not sugar-coating, either. You're going to have a hard time adjusting, but if you deliver what you promise, the Americans will help you make a new life."

She tried to smile but couldn't. "Ahmad and I talked about our new life. It didn't turn out very well."

"Second time's the charm?"

She moved her eyes up and down his chest.

He said, "We shouldn't—" and she grabbed him and kissed him long and hard. He pushed her away.

"Tanya."

She appeared shocked. She covered her mouth. "I'm sorry, Sam. I didn't—"

"It's all right."

"I was afraid you hated me," she whispered.

"You deserve a chance."

"I shouldn't have kissed you."

"It's not a weakness to need somebody."

She wrapped her arms around him and held tight. "Don't abandon me, Sam. I've lost too much already."

Raven let out a sigh as he squeezed her back. He knew what it was like to be frightened. To have nobody on your side. She'd come to him because she knew he'd have sympathy for her plight. She trusted him. He'd done his best to break her down, find the lie behind her story. She hadn't cracked. The assassination attempt clinched it for him. She meant what she said. He owed her his best effort at protection and getting her to the United States. Because of her the CIA would end the Islamic Union's wanton killing.

In a sense, he and Tanya finally *were* on the same side.

"I won't leave you," he said into her ear.

She squeezed him again, then let go. She reached for the locket chain around his neck. "What's this?"

Raven lifted the locket from under his shirt. "A reminder of why I fight."

"What's in it?"

"It's my secret," he said. "It wouldn't mean anything to you anyway."

"Try me."

He put the locket back. "Good night, Tanya." He held the door for her, and Tanya went out. She didn't look back.

6

THE PICTURE ON THE WALL-MOUNTED BIG-SCREEN SHOWED A woman in a full hijab. Her exposed face was turned toward the camera. The face stood out among the others on the screen because it was white, and the rest of the faces belonged to men.

Clark Wilson stood with his arms folded, his tie slightly askew. His watch showed a little after six p.m. Stockholm was six hours ahead of Langley, and the daytime Agency staff were clearing out, overnight staff arriving. It was going to be a long night.

He stood off to the side of a long conference table. He'd spent most of the day behind his desk and welcomed the chance to stretch his legs. Two other people, older than him, sat at the table and examined the screen with him.

Christopher Fisher, Deputy Director of Operations and Wilson's boss, frowned. "It's almost too good of a picture."

"You think it's staged?" Wilson said.

The other persona at the table, Layla McCarthy, Fisher's assistant, shook her head. "Why stage this? She's been unknown to us since we learned she took over. This doesn't help her at all."

Fisher let out a breath. "Something isn't right."

"Tell me," Wilson said.

"How did she not see the camera?" Fisher said. "She's almost looking straight at the lens."

"Maybe this Tanya person," Layla said, "caught her at the right moment."

Wilson watched Fisher. He was a veteran paramilitary officer who took the desk job at Langley when he hit his mid-40s. Ten years older now, the gray was starting to show in his thick black hair. He had a rough face, like the surface of a rock. Wilson didn't doubt the man's intelligence. He hadn't earned the job through political shenanigans. He'd earned the seat through hard work and field achievements still classified.

"I don't like information," he said, "handed to us on a silver platter."

"Take the win, Chris," Layla McCarthy said.

She was in her mid-40s with short blonde hair and bony fingers. Her red nail polish matched her lipstick. Like Fisher, she'd risen through the ranks after years in the field. A rumor around the office said she'd lost two toes after being injured in Iraq. Nobody had the guts to ask her to take off her shoes.

"This is too easy."

Layla turned to Wilson. "Did we run this through facial recognition?"

"The Francesca Sloan name Jafari gave us checks out," Wilson said. "British subject. Wealthy family. Met a Pakistani man in Berlin while visiting on a tourist visa. Took off with him to the Middle East."

"Did we analyze the background?"

"We did," Wilson said. "The green hills behind her and the partial lake over her shoulder are in the Sind Province of

Pakistan. It matches information we have on an IU training camp in the region."

"Date on the photo?"

"It's almost twenty-four hours old."

"Late husband's name?"

"Tamal Alvi," Wilson said. "One of our paramilitary teams took him out two years ago. She took over command six months later."

Tamal Alvi, the founding commander of the Islamic Union, made the Most Wanted list of western intelligence after an attack in London's underground, killing 150 commuters, and a bombing at a mall in Nairobi, which left over 200 dead.

Wilson added, "Everything checks out, Chris. Jafari is on the level."

"I wish we had a little more," Fisher said.

"She'll give us more," Wilson said. "This is only to prove she has *something* to show us. She's not a low-level gofer. If this is a hint of what she has, we can stop guessing about the IU and put facts on paper."

"If nothing else," Layla said, "we have a picture for the file. We can add her to the terror deck."

The "terror deck" playing cards became a novelty for coalition forces during the 2003 invasion of Iraq. The cards allowed troops to identify wanted members of the Hussein regime. The cards continued, updated frequently with new "most wanted" targets as old ones were captured or killed.

"Where are Jafari and Raven now?" Fisher said.

"They'll leave at eight a.m. their time," Wilson said. "They'll land here about two a.m."

"You'll be there to meet them?"

Wilson let out a breath. "Yeah."

Fisher continued to examine the picture. He shrugged. "Okay. I guess we'll know more in a few hours."

"Chris," Wilson said, earning a look from the DDO. "What are you thinking?"

"I think this might be a penetration attempt."

"They're giving up a lot if it is. I'm with Layla. It doesn't make sense for them to sacrifice this much to try and get somebody on the inside."

"And once she's at Blue Ridge," Layla said, "what can she do?"

"Too much," Fisher said. "We have six other prisoners there. She can catalog every face. She can note our security. If they find a weak spot, they can stage a rescue attempt."

"You're reaching so far you're going to pull a muscle, Chris," Layla said. "Better see your doctor."

Wilson said, "We only have one other IU prisoner, and they know he's in our custody already."

"Right," Fisher said.

"The murder attempt Raven described," Layla said, "and the killer she named, prove they're not sending cannon fodder to bring her back."

"Jafari would be dead," Wilson said, "if Raven hadn't been there."

"I'm aware, thank you," Fisher said, "of Sam Raven's abilities."

"You're outvoted two-to-one," Layla said. "I say we go forward with the debrief and see what else she can tell us. She'll for sure tell us more than what's-his-name."

"Omar Talman," Wilson said.

Capturing Talman, a junior commander in the Islamic Union, had been a recent CIA success story. To learn more about the Islamic Union and its activities, including the identity of the White Widow, the Agency had placed a high priority on capturing any member of the command staff. Talman was the obvious target. He moved throughout Europe coordinating with field units.

The CIA team tasked with bringing in Talman had caught the man in Madrid, along with a two-man IU cell. The cell members had been killed in the fight while trying to cover Talman's escape. Their effort failed. Talman was brought, in chains, to the Blue Ridge facility and currently sat in a small cell with only a toilet for company.

"Not even advanced interrogation has cracked Talman," Layla pointed out. "If Jafari is volunteering, she'll be a wealth of information. We've never determined how the Islamic Union gets its funding. Maybe Tanya can tell us, and we can close them down top to bottom."

"It's a nice idea," Fisher said.

"If you don't like this," Wilson said, "let's keep the picture and throw Jafari to the wolves."

Fisher shook his head. "Stay the course for now," he said. He picked up a remote control from the table and aimed at the TV. He pressed a button. The screen blinked out.

"What if," Wilson offered, "Raven can get more out of her?"

"Go home and get some rest, but I want you back here as soon as they're in the air," Fisher said. "Call Raven on the plane." He and Layla stood up. "Ask him to start the debrief. Maybe then my gut will tell a different story."

"Okay," Wilson said.

The glamorous life of a spy.

Wilson shook his head. At least he didn't have a boring job. He hoped extra coffee kept him going when the time came to meet Raven. He wasn't getting any younger, and his body didn't like late nights or early mornings any longer.

The CIA was on the verge of taking a major terrorist leader off the board, and he wanted to see the operation to completion. As he followed his superiors out of the room, a surge of excitement pumped up his attitude.

Rest? Who could rest at a time like this?

7

THE SLEEK CESSNA CITATION LATITUDE SOARED OVER THE
Atlantic.

The insulated cabin blocked out most of the engine noise.
The low drone of the jets existed only in the background.
Tanya Jafari found herself tuning out the noise as she and
Raven played gin.

With leather seats on either side of the cabin, and a high
ceiling, the cabin was narrow. The high ceiling allowed
Raven to walk without hunching, which he appreciated.
Tanya, shorter than him, had no such worries.

They sat facing each other with a folding table of polished
wood between them. Plates of snacks provided by the flight
crew sat off to the side while they focused on the cards.

The crew contained two pilots and three security personnel. A stern-faced flight attendant saw to their needs with a
pistol on her hip. Two paramilitary security officers, also
armed with handguns, were there for emergencies. Near the
cockpit, in a closet, hung three Colt M4 automatic carbines.
Tanya felt very secure with the personnel and hardware
aboard.

Prior to leaving the embassy in Stockholm, Raven had accompanied Eva Yoshino, the other CIA rep, on a short shopping trip. They purchased clothes and needed items for Tanya and made a brief stop at Raven's houseboat for what he needed. He'd collected clothes and his Nighthawk Custom Talon .45 auto pistol. The flight attendant confiscated the gun as they boarded. Tanya asked him how he liked being defanged. He wasn't worried. The pistol waited in the closet with the M4s. He'd know where it was if he needed the weapon.

And Tanya expected there wouldn't be any trouble now. They were halfway to their destination. Short of a missile strike, the Cessna wasn't falling out of the sky. And the Islamic Union had no air force. Tanya put the thought out of her mind. Engine failure or another malady might occur, but she knew the possibility was remote.

Tanya slapped her cards down. "Gin!" She laughed.

Raven smiled. "Now I'm sure you're cheating."

She sat back and sipped a bottle of water. She glanced at the oval window beside her. Blue sky above, blue ocean below. Not a cloud in sight. The sun shined bright above.

Raven collected the cards and began to reshuffle. "Let's do it again," he said.

"In front of all these people?" She grinned.

Raven didn't avoid her eyes. The ice had thawed between them since his reassurances at the embassy, and he wondered if the CIA crew noticed.

"*Down*, girl," he said.

During the chopper ride from the embassy, she'd held his hand tightly.

Her tension finally faded once the Cessna took off. Relief filled her now. She was safe. The CIA had accepted her morsel of information and knew she was for real.

Raven shuffled the cards and Tanya cut.

Up front, a phone rang.

Tanya watched Raven's eyes flash over her shoulder. The flight attendant said, "Call for you, Mr. Raven."

Raven set the cards down. "Be right back."

She watched him rise from the chair.

Raven side-stepped between the chairs on his way to the front. The two paramilitary officers looked like linebackers. Their hard eyes watched him. The flight attendant, her face stoic, handed him the phone. It hung from a wall near the cockpit door.

Raven leaned against the wall as he spoke.

"Raven talking."

"It's Clark."

"Good morning."

"Or something," Wilson said, with a laugh. "I'm running on a cat nap and very strong coffee."

"What's on your mind?"

"Fisher has cold feet."

"I'm not sure I like where this is going."

Wilson recounted the meeting he'd had with Fisher and McCarthy. Raven listened without comment.

"Do you think you can get more out of her?" Wilson asked when he finished.

"Like what?"

"We'd love Francesca Sloan's current location."

"You want eyes on her."

"Yes."

"All right. She's cleaning my clock in gin, but I'll ask."

"Nuts, you're letting her win."

"No, seriously, the cards are against me."

"Sure they are. Get back with me when you can."

"As soon as possible."

Raven hung up. He returned to his seat.

Tanya said, "Is everything okay?"

"We're fine." Raven began shuffled the cards again. "They'd like to know where Sloan is right now."

"The picture wasn't enough?"

"We have a fellow at headquarters who's skeptical."

"I don't want to say more until we have a deal."

"You don't have the room to negotiate, Tanya," Raven said. "You'll get a deal, but you need to cooperate. If you refuse this, they'll have an excuse to shove you out onto the street."

"Then the IU will find me."

"Yes, they will."

She took a deep breath and drank another mouthful of water. "When I took the picture, Francesca was departing Pakistan for Syria."

"What's in Syria?"

"We have people in Damascus she needs to see. Then she's going to our base of operations in Sukkariyeh."

Raven raised an eyebrow. "Could be huge."

"It is huge. It's the Union's nerve center for Syrian operations."

"How long will she be in Damascus?"

"Three days. We use an apartment for meetings there." She gave him the building's address. "The Sukkariyeh conference is the important part of the trip."

"Why?"

"I'm saving some details for later."

Raven nodded. Syria was currently a four-letter word with US policy makers. The weapons and money provided to rebels fighting the Assad regime wound up in the hands of al-Qaeda and ISIS instead. The Russians, in their backing of Assad, increased tensions, and the possibility of a clash with the US. The current administration had ended US involvement in the region, and now it was a free-for-all. Various factions, from within and without, vied for control. The

Assad government, with Russian help, tried to beat back the tide. The battle had reached a stalemate. Another quagmire from which there was no easy victory.

Raven knew he was skipping over several details, but the problem was typical of any action in the Middle East. It was like walking through thick brush while dealing with a mass of barbed wire. There were so many distracting rabbit trails the original intent of the intervention faded. Even those who had ordered the mission couldn't explain why the US was there.

And now the White Widow had made Syria her hiding spot. At their nerve center to boot.

The problem now, as Raven saw it, would be getting the government to act. He knew the CIA still maintained a presence in Damascus and the region in general but didn't know the exact number.

Raven set the cards down again. "Excuse me." He rose from the chair. "Don't doctor the cards." He smiled.

"I have all the luck today," she said.

He winked and went forward again.

He caught Wilson right away.

"She's in Syria," Raven said, and told him what Tanya had explained.

"Excellent," Wilson said. His enthusiasm carried over the line.

"Do we have people in-country?"

"Small team, yeah," Wilson said. "They're in Damascus. If she's there, they will find her."

"Good luck. Give Fisher my best."

Wilson laughed. "Sure. He loves you."

"See you soon, Clark."

Raven hung up and returned to his seat. He dealt the cards, and they played another hand. This time, Raven won.

8

SYRIA WAS TOO NICE A PLACE TO HAVE A WAR.

But "Tiger" Joe Hayden, CIA officer, knew it was wishful thinking. Hell, Syria was in the Middle East. When hadn't there been a war?

He sat at a small table, back to the wall, in a Damascus café. He'd have preferred to smoke one of his beloved Cuban cigars, but when in Rome, do as the Romans do. He instead puffed on a hookah, enjoying the flavor of the tobacco. He rolled it around his mouth and blew a stream of smoke. The cloud joined the haze hovering beneath the ceiling.

Along with the hookah, he sipped hot cardamom coffee. The spice went well with the tobacco.

He wasn't alone in the café. Had he left the table to use the restroom, he'd have to step around dozens of other patrons at small tables to get there. And for a good reason. This morning, the café welcomed The Storyteller.

The Storyteller, dressed in a white robe and red fez, sat on a throne across the room. He read aloud from a book of Syrian history, dramatizing events of the past in a booming voice. He required no microphone. The patrons sat as if in a trance, taking in every word.

It beat the heck out of television. The workday hadn't yet begun, so the patrons had time to listen. Syrians wanted to know their history. He wished Americans shared the same passion.

Storytellers had once been ubiquitous in Syrian restaurants and cafes. As the years went on, they became less and less of a fixture. Only a few cafes in the city, and country, still featured storytellers, and only on certain nights of the week.

It was one of the joys of his assignment in Damascus. He was working under the cover of a United Nations humanitarian aid administrator, with a Canadian passport. While he did go deeper into the country to oversee such operations, he had two jobs. He kept one eye on the aid packages and the other open to observe terrorist and rebel activity.

The United States may have pulled out of Syria, abandoning the flawed policy of trying to topple the Assad regime, but officers like Hayden remained. There was work still to be done, albeit covertly. He didn't mind. It was a beautiful city, with wonderful people. If he could help end the current crisis and send the bad actors elsewhere, he'd consider his work a success.

He wasn't self-conscious of being the only white man in the café. Nobody cared. He was familiar enough to the owner to always have a table available. What bothered him was the circuitous route he'd have to take back to home base. He had to make sure nobody tried to kill him on the way.

His cell phone vibrated in his pocket. Once, twice.

He'd turned off the ringer before entering. He didn't want to disturb the listening. Setting down his coffee cup, he inspected the screen. A text message from home base. Two words.

Dad Called.

It meant he had to get back for a video conference with Langley. Something was happening.

He downed the rest of his coffee. Nobody in his right mind let cardamom coffee go cold. He left the rest of the tobacco in the hookah unsmoked. Such was life. He purchased a bag of fresh-ground cardamom coffee and said goodbye to the owner. The old man took Hayden's money and returned his rapt attention on The Storyteller. Tiger Joe left the café and stepped out onto the street.

He carried the bag of coffee in his left hand and kept his right hand in the pocket of his jeans. He didn't bother with a jacket despite the coolness of the morning. Hayden dodged other pedestrians on the crowded walkways and noted the heavy traffic. He carried no firearms, but he wasn't without defense. His right hand gripped the T handle of a sharp push dagger.

He wasn't any taller than the average Syrian, a hair over five-foot-six. He ran marathons to stay in shape, and his condition showed in his walk. An army veteran, he moved with fluidity and confidence. His Everyman face helped him blend into any crowd. There was nothing noticeable about him. He was perfect CIA material.

He cut through side streets and ducked into alleys, hiding in alcoves for several minutes at a time. Within an hour he returned to the building where the humanitarian mission kept its offices. Hayden and his CIA team occupied space in the basement.

The outside temperature's crisp 68-degrees and the clear blue sky almost too nice to leave behind. But duty called. There were plenty of days like this one to enjoy. Hayden showed his pass to the outer guard and entered the building. When he stepped out of the elevator to the basement office, his crew was waiting for him.

He had a staff of two. Colleen Andreev, a Russian expert,

had been attached to his unit because of the Russian activity in the country. Freddy Lymann, a former member of the Ground Branch unit of the Special Activities Center, had worked throughout the Middle East as a shooter. He now helped Hayden and Colleen sort incoming intelligence. He was no good in the field anymore, having lost part of his left leg to a bomb. Unless he wore shorts, they never saw his prosthetic.

"What did you bring?" Colleen asked.

Hayden tossed her the coffee. "Sounds like it will be a long day."

She opened the bag on the way to the coffee machine in a corner.

Hayden sat down beside Lymann. "What does Langley want?"

"In five minutes, we'll find out."

Colleen brewed the coffee, and the scent of the spicy roast filled the room. Calling it an office was an understatement. There were tables and chairs clustered in one corner of the bare room. The floors were uncarpeted concrete, the walls cold gray concrete, and there was an ever-present chill. Fluorescent bulbs shined above. Lymann sat in front of a big screen monitor connected to a variety of computing devices and blinking servers stacked in a metal rack. Wires ran everywhere.

No windows. Strategically placed circulating fans blew the stuffy air around.

Colleen returned with a mug of steaming coffee. Hayden didn't want any. Lymann grumbled. "How come you didn't bring me one?"

"I'm not your mother," she said.

Lymann cursed under his breath and left the chair for his own mug. Colleen smiled. Hayden shook his head. They argued like brother and sister.

When Lymann returned, the screen came to life. Clark Wilson looked at them through a camera on the other side of the world.

9

"WE HAVE TO CONFIRM THE PRESENCE OF AND TAKE OUT A major player in the Islamic Union," Wilson said.

"Hell of a hello, Clark," Hayden said.

"We have to move fast. She'll only be in Damascus for three days."

Colleen said, "She? You mean the White Widow?"

"Yes. We have an informant on the way to tell us more, but she gave us a picture and a location in case she didn't make it."

"This I have to see," Lymann said.

Wilson vanished from the screen. In his place was the photo of Francesca Sloan. Wilson gave Hayden and his team the rundown, leaving out Fisher's concerns.

Hayden grabbed a notepad of flash paper and a pen. "Where's the apartment?"

Wilson returned to the screen. "Corner of Ibn Battuta Street and Rawdat Al Midan."

Lymann rolled his chair to a neighboring computer and tapped two keys. A laser printer hummed and spat out a picture of Francesca Sloan.

Hayden, at another terminal, looked up the building's location. "Got it. Building under construction across the street, and on the opposite corner the produce souk."

"Good surveillance points?" Wilson said.

"We'll make it happen. You want confirmation, and then what?"

"Drone strike."

"Not in Damascus," Hayden said.

"Of course not. She's leaving for Sukkariyeh and an IU base. We need eyes on her because we don't know the timetable. We want to track her and make the drone strike when she gets to the base."

"Understood."

"How big is your tactical team?"

"Not big enough. It would be nice if we had a deal with the locals."

"Now's not the time to debate policy, but I get it. I'll send more people to you."

"Right."

"Joe?" Wilson said.

"Yeah, boss?"

"Don't lose her."

Wilson disconnected and Hayden turned to his crew. Colleen brought her coffee halfway to her lips.

"Make it to go," he said. "Both of you."

"Why?" Lymann said.

"We're checking out this apartment building. I have a feeling the Union may own the entire building." To Lymann, "Did you gas up the Rover this afternoon?"

"She's got a full tank, Skipper."

"All right, get the com units, and let's move."

Hayden and his crew left their chairs.

HAYDEN SAT on a park bench with a partial view of the apartment building. Behind him, green trees and the city's ubiquitous jasmine flowers. The flower grew everywhere in the city. Between him and the apartment building was a busy construction site. The crew was beginning their day and took no notice of him.

Lymann and Colleen remained in the Rover, parked a short sprint down the road at the busy produce souk.

Without binoculars, which would have given him away, Hayden had no close look of the building. He couldn't identify faces. But his general observation revealed details telling him Wilson had been correct. There were sentries on the roof.

"How many?" Colleen said over the wireless com unit in his right ear.

"At least four, all armed," Hayden reported. "They wander back and forth."

"A roof entry to bug the place is out," Lymann said.

"We wouldn't know where to put the gear anyway," Hayden said. "With our luck we'd put everything in the wrong room. Can you see movement in the windows?" he added. Colleen had binoculars.

"Negative. Most of the drapes on this side are closed."

"We can confirm the building is in use, and our mysterious informant is probably telling the truth."

"Can we go home now?" Lymann said.

Hayden paused for a moment, scanning the building levels once more. No decorations on any balcony. Satellite television dishes sprouted at the two roof corners facing him.

"I think we're done here, yeah," Hayden said.

Hayden told Colleen and Lymann to stand by with the motor running. He left the park and cut through the block behind him. From there Hayden made his way to the souk and the black Land Rover. The souk was packed with shoppers and vendors, and he blended easily with the crowd. He climbed into the back seat. Colleen drove off.

"How's the coffee?" Hayden said. He wiped sweat from his face. The 68-degrees of the early morning was climbing into the mid-70s.

"Still good," she said.

Lymann said, "We need to call in some help to keep the building covered."

"We'll handle it," Hayden said. "In the meantime, we need to do some shopping."

"Great," Colleen said. "Like we don't have enough tomatoes already."

Hayden laughed.

Colleen didn't think it was funny.

10

THE CESSNA CITATION DESCENDED. RAVEN AND TANYA, THEIR gin game long over, sat with their seatbelts strapped.

They watched the green forest flashing by below as the morning sun shined bright. Raven looked for the small airstrip in the distance but didn't see it. This wasn't his first landing at the secluded runway. It was a tricky landing. Pilots had to crest over trees and make a last-second dive to hit the runway correctly.

Tanya smiled at him. "This is getting exciting."

"Almost there."

He'd grown more confident in her story during the flight. She seemed more relaxed than she had been in Stockholm. He hoped Wilson and the Agency made her a proper deal.

The strip lay ahead. The jet banked to line up. The pilot climbed over the trees, then dropped the nose. The nose lifted once again before the back wheels smacked onto the runway with a screech of rubber.

The jet stopped at the end of the runway. The stern-faced flight attendant opened the door and lowered the steps. Raven and Tanya carried their luggage forward. The flight attendant returned Raven's gun and said goodbye. Two security men remained silent. Raven and Tanya stepped onto the tarmac.

Clark Wilson waited on the side of the runway. Behind him stood another security crew and two blacked out Suburbans.

"Sam!"

Raven and Wilson shook hands. Raven introduced Tanya. Wilson greeted her with a handshake and a "Welcome to the United States", then escorted both into one of the SUVs. A security officer with an M4 between his knees sat up front while they took the rear seats. The two rear seats faced each other, and Wilson sat across from Raven and Tanya.

The other members of the security team climbed into the second SUV. The engines rumbled to life and the vehicles began the slow crawl through forest pathways to a road.

"Nice flight?" Wilson said.

"She cheats at gin," Raven said.

Tanya let out another chime-tingling laugh. "He let me win." To Wilson she said, "Did my intel pan out?"

"So far," Wilson said.

"Good."

Wilson and Raven exchanged a look. It told Raven all he needed to know. The intel might be good, but there were problems at the office. Somebody had doubts. Probably Christopher Fisher. As always, the man needed more information.

Raven looked out a window. The SUVs moved at around 20 miles an hour through the rutted pathway, the lush forest passing slowly.

He'd dealt with bureaucracy at HQ same as all field officers. With contempt and creative solutions. He'd more than once gone around the backs of his superiors to accomplish a task. It was one of the reasons he'd left the agency, and the main reason he hadn't gone back. If he was going to take risks, he wanted the decision to be his alone.

Tanya said, "There's more you need to know about Francesca."

"I'm listening," Clark said.

"Operation Triangle."

"Which means what?"

"I don't know. She and the other commanders discussed it before leaving for Damascus. It's one of the reasons she's going there."

"We haven't heard any chatter about a new attack," Wilson said.

"You aren't aware of how we're communicating," Tanya said. "No more open communications. Now we have a different way."

"Explain."

"Gmail. Messages saved in draft folders. They don't send anything. Cell leaders have access to a single account and leave messages for others."

"You know the account?"

"They will have changed it by now."

"Changing accounts doesn't delete messages."

"Correct, but—"

"They can delete messages one-by-one," Raven cut in. "The account will be empty."

Wilson grinned. "Nothing is ever deleted in cyberspace."

The SUV made a turn and picked up speed. They were on the road now, a winding two-lane road taking them deeper into the mountains. And the CIA's secret facility within.

11

CHRISTOPHER FISHER'S DAY BEGAN EARLIER THAN NORMAL. With Wilson picking up Raven and Tanya Jafari, he scheduled a visit with Jack Rogers, chief legal counsel at the CIA. Layla McCarthy sat beside him in the big office.

They outlined the operation against Francesca Sloan. Fisher did most of the talking, with McCarthy adding a point now and then. They showed Rogers the picture of Sloan. "More information is forthcoming," Fisher added when he finished.

"When?"

"As soon as Tanya Jafari gets here."

They needed Rogers to sign off on a termination protocol. The drone strike had to be "legal", which meant following the rules of engagement the CIA had set in Syria.

Jack Rogers sat behind a clean desk with a picture of his family on one corner. In his 70s with gray hair, and a stern face, he'd been the CIA's chief legal counsel for over a decade.

"We can't have any collateral damage," Rogers said. He sat back in his chair.

"Are you saying no?" Fisher said.

"It's a no as far as a drone strike in Sukkariyeh is concerned, yeah."

"But we have a chance to knock out Sloan and her command council," Fisher said.

"I understand, but Sukkariyeh is a populated area. We don't know where she'll be in the city yet. I'm sure as hell not letting you fire a missile into an apartment building in Damascus either."

"What do you suggest, Jack?"

"Catch her on the way. Middle of the desert. Nobody but the bad guys will get hurt."

"And we let the rest of them get away?" Fisher said. "They'll clear everything out of Sukkariyeh as soon as news of her death reaches them."

"I can't authorize a missile strike in a civilian area," Rogers said. "You know the rules, Chris."

"Break them."

"The Senate Intelligence Committee will have my ass if I do. Never mind the DCI."

Fisher glanced at Layla McCarthy, who remained silent. Fisher knew he and Rogers would have to present the case to the senate committee too. If he couldn't get past Rogers, no way were they getting the approval of the committee.

The "rules" did more to hamper the CIA than help. After the debacle of US involvement to date, nobody wanted more trouble. Nobody wanted to admit Syria *existed* until the heat settled.

"Then we get her in the desert," Fisher said, "and play catch up with the rest later."

"It's the only way," Rogers said.

"When can we put this in front of the committee?"

Rogers checked his watch. "If we hurry, we can catch them in two hours."

"If she leaves Damascus before there's a decision," Fisher said, "we're screwed."

"Then you better hope she's a stickler for her schedule," the lawyer said.

"Ditto the committee," Layla added.

Fisher only frowned.

LAYLA MCCARTHY KEPT up with Fisher's quick pace as they walked down the hallway.

"Hayden and his crew," Layla said, "can follow Sloan. It will help if we have eyes on her."

"It puts them at risk of exposure, capture, or death."

"How important is this target?"

"This is why I like drones," Fisher said. "But put them on stand-by."

"I'll call when I get back to my desk."

"Damn rules of engagement," Fisher said. "All this 'mother may I' is letting the enemy get the upper hand."

"Don't forget we have Raven," she said. "He's always good for a cowboy act."

Fisher scoffed.

"What's your disagreement with him?" she said. They turned a corner and stopped at an elevator. Other Agency personnel passed by. Very few talked. It was too early for talking. Most CIA staffers were introverts anyway, more comfortable with their workstations than people.

Fisher took a deep breath, then let out a chuckle and shook his head.

"He beat me at poker once," Fisher said. "Took a few hundred bucks off me."

"Really?"

"He sat at the table with the smuggest smirk on his face. He made me so mad I blew every hand the rest of the night."

The elevator doors rumbled open. They stepped inside. Fisher pressed the button for their floor.

The elevator started upward.

"Raven was a good operative, and remains a friend of this Agency," Fisher said. "I appreciate his work, but he rubs me the wrong way."

"If we ask, he'll do whatever we want."

"He can't be in two places at once."

"But we have Tanya. If we miss Sloan in Syria, we'll pick her up again. She's on borrowed time no matter what happens."

"I hope you're right."

"And if the Intelligence Committee tells us no—"

"Raven doesn't have any rules of engagement," Fisher finished.

12

THE CONVERSATION STALLED IN THE SUBURBAN. RAVEN FELT content to look out the window at the passing forest. They were deep in the Blue Ridge Mountains and far from any civilian encroachment.

Tanya didn't seem to mind the silence either. Her gaze out the window went far beyond the immediate area. He wondered what she was thinking. He wondered what her life was like before she hitched her wagon to the Islamic Union. He hoped she could make something of her second chapter.

The road ended at a thick metal gate. An electronic card reader sat atop a steel post. The driver powered down his window to feed a card into the slot. A light on the box turned from red to green, flashed twice, turned back to red. The driver withdrew the card and the metal gate parted in the center, both sides swinging forward.

"Special card?" Raven asked Wilson.

"Can't tell you how it's made, but nobody can copy it."

"Rare metals?"

"Close."

The SUV passed through the gate. Raven looked back. The gate closed faster than it had opened.

Ahead, the front face of the mountain raised. Part of the mountain had been blasted out to make room for a rising steel door. The SUV passed under into darkness. But it wasn't dark for long. Rows of lights lit the area, and Raven noticed other vehicles parked nearby.

"Staging area," Wilson said. "All vehicles stay here. We'll take an elevator to the complex beneath the surface."

"You aren't kidding around with this place," Raven said. The SUV slowed to a stop.

"Nope. It's impregnable. Ain't nothing getting through, no matter what Fisher says."

"What is Fisher afraid of?"

Wilson waved Raven off. The security crew in the second SUV, behind them, opened the doors. Raven, Tanya, and Wilson exited into the cold cavern and stepped onto smooth concrete. Raven took Tanya by the elbow and they followed Wilson to an elevator. The double doors sat within a steel frame. This time Wilson used a key card, and the elevator doors opened. The three stepped inside, leaving the security team with the vehicles.

The elevator doors slid shut with a hiss.

"Hermetically sealed," Wilson said.

The cabin began its descent.

"How far down?" Raven said.

"Classified."

Raven laughed.

Tanya looked at both wide-eyed.

"Never seen anything like this?" Raven asked her.

"Once," she said. "In Germany. My father—" she stopped.

"What?"

She shook her head. "I left for more than one reason."

Wilson said, "We're going to the main entrance. You two

will be escorted into a side room for scanning. We need to make sure you don't have any tracking devices in your clothes, or under your skin. You'll have to hand over your weapons and cell phones."

"Okay," Raven said.

Tanya said, "Um—"

"There will be a woman taking care of you, Ms. Jafari."

She nodded.

Raven lost track of how long the elevator had been going down. At least a minute. The cabin finally stopped, and the doors slid open.

The chill of the white-walled wind bit into them right away. A uniformed duty officer behind bulletproof glass told Raven and Tanya to stop. Wilson used a retinal scanner and his pass card to go through a steel door.

A door to their right opened, and two more officers in uniform asked Raven and Tanya to follow them. The two men stayed with Raven while a woman took Tanya into a separate room. The men led Raven into an exam room. It was the size of a regular doctor's exam room, with a body scanner sitting against one wall.

"Gun and cell phone," one of the men said.

Raven handed over his pistol and phone. An officer deposited the items into a large plastic bag.

Raven kicked off his shoes and stripped. The officer gathered up his clothes and went out.

Raven stood, naked, in front of the other guard.

"Now what?"

"Step into the machine, please."

Raven placed his feet on yellow markings and put his arms up as directed. The officer went to a panel and pressed two buttons. Sounds came from the machine. A light shined on Raven's head. A circular wrap-around apparatus moved up and down the side, shining light on the rest of Raven's body.

The machine beeped.

"You're clear."

"Is this a nudist colony and nobody told me?"

The officer didn't smile. The door opened and the other guard returned with Raven's clothes. He pronounced them clean. Raven dressed again. The officers did not give back his phone or gun.

"They'll be kept at the desk," one explained. "No weapons or cell phones allowed in the facility."

"Now I really feel naked," Raven said.

The officers guided him out of the room, where he met Tanya and the female officer who had checked her.

"Are you clean?" he asked her.

"Squeaky," she said.

The two men stayed with them through the check-in process with the duty officer. Wilson assisted on the other side of the glass. The officer gave Raven and Tanya badges to pin to their shirts, which always had to remain visible. They were not allowed to roam without an escort. They leaned into the retina scanner one at a time so the computer could record their eye signature. Finally, the duty officer allowed them beyond the sealed door.

Wilson took the lead. They walked along a hallway, through a door accessed by Wilson's pass card, and into a conference room.

"Where are the other prisoners?" Raven said.

"Need to know," Wilson said. "You don't."

Raven laughed again. "Maybe I should rejoin," he said, "so I can learn all these wonderful secrets."

"Is that what it will take?"

Bottles of water and fruit waited on the table. They needed to start the debrief right away. Wilson picked up a handset from the middle of the table and asked for some-body named "Harmony". He put the phone down.

Raven handed Tanya a bottle of water. He took a long drink. A woman entered with a laptop and digital recorder. She set up on the table. Wilson introduced her as Harmony Moyer, their recorder. She wore a smart blue suit with her long hair tied back. Very little makeup gave her a girl-next-door appearance. Confident brown eyes. She didn't shy away from Raven or Tanya as she shook their hands.

She'd take notes, Wilson explained, and the conversation would be recorded as well. He asked Tanya to sit. Raven remained standing.

Wilson said, "We're going to start with basic questions, and work up to your involvement with the Islamic Union."

"I'm not saying a word," Tanya stated.

"What?"

"You get nothing until I get a deal," she said.

13

FISHER DIDN'T LIKE SITTING IN FRONT OF THE SENATE Intelligence Committee.

He understood the need for oversight of intelligence operations. No question there. But he didn't respect the people assigned as his overwatch. None of the 15 politicians on the panel had ever served in the CIA. Some had never worn a uniform. The Democrat from California, who chaired the committee, had recently walked away unscathed from a major scandal. The FBI outed her personal driver as a Chinese spy. He'd been her driver for over 20 years, yet the matter wasn't treated as a critical failure. It should have been. The Senator from California liked to run her mouth to show off her importance. She shouldn't be anywhere near the committee, and Fisher wasn't the only one who thought so.

But still she sat, asking questions in turn with the others, staring at him.

It was easy to compromise the panel despite their security measures. He had no faith in anything he and Jack Rogers said remaining secret for long.

Fisher and CIA General Counsel Jack Rogers made their pitch. They explained the defection of Tanya Jafari and her intelligence on Francesca Sloan. They presented their evidence connecting Sloan to the White Widow alias. Then the panel responded. They put up immediate barriers.

"She's a British subject," one senator said. "We should turn this over to MI6 and let them deal with her."

"Islamic Union bombings have killed Americans, too," Fisher retorted. "We've never deferred to another agency in cases like this."

"I don't approve of these drone strikes to begin with," said another. "The last administration was way too trigger happy. Can't we poison her food or something?"

"With all due respect, Senator, getting close to the White Widow isn't an option."

Fisher and Rogers, sat a table in front of the raised dais the senators sat behind, had to look up. As if the senators were gods on Mt. Olympus. Ridiculous.

"What do we know about this Operation Triangle?" another senator asked. "Are you sure it's real? Or is your informant making it up?"

"Tanya Jafari has no reason to lie to us, Senator."

"On the contrary, she has every reason to lie. She wants asylum. Or whatever she's asking for. She wants our protection."

"Her intel on Sloan has so far checked out."

"She gave you a picture," the jowly politician pressed. He was a Republican from Colorado, the newest member of the rotating panel. "She could have given you any picture. Are you sure it's this White Widow you're so scared of?"

Jack Rogers jumped in. "I've reviewed the information our informant gave us. Her background matches what we already know. What we've lacked is positive identification."

"I'm not asking you, Counselor."

Rogers pushed. "This target meets the qualifications for a termination protocol."

"It isn't for you to decide, Counselor."

"May we have a vote?" Rogers said.

"I'm not done—"

The chairwoman snapped, "Enough!"

Fisher's eyes settled on the senator from California. He took a deep breath. Apart from his dislike for her over the chauffeur fiasco, she usually supported the intelligence community 100%. For all her faults, she was at least a defense hawk, but not the type hip deep in the military industrial complex. She didn't vote for war to make money.

Unlike some of her colleagues.

"It's thin, Mr. Fisher," the senator said.

"We've confirmed as much as possible with the amount of information we have, ma'am," he told her. *Believe me, I wish we had more too.* "As I've said, all we've ever lacked is a picture of Sloan. And her name."

"You never knew she was British until now."

"No, we didn't."

The senator from California examined the pages in a folder in front of her. They all had received a copy of Francesca Sloan's picture, and a summary of Fisher and Rogers' testimony.

"All right. We can go in circles all day, but we have what we need. If our informant tells us there's an operation underway, we need to stop it. I'm not going to sit through more news coverage of another attack. All in favor?"

All but the jowly senator from Colorado voted to put Francesca Sloan on the kill list. Termination protocol approved. The document with a list of terrorist targets would now go to the president for the final decision. One more meeting. But Fisher knew the president well. He'd rubber-stamp the mission.

Too much mother-may-I, Fisher thought. *If we don't move fast, she'll get away.*

But those were the rules, and he had to work within them.

He wasn't Sam Raven.

The meeting adjourned, Fisher and Rogers left the chamber room.

"When can we see the president?" Fisher said.

He and Rogers sat in the back of a black limousine. The rear cabin was sealed so the driver heard nothing of their conversation.

"Let's talk to the DCI when we get back," Rogers said. "He can call POTUS direct. Sometime today, I'd suspect. The president has a light schedule."

"You checked?"

Rogers laughed. "For this case? You bet your ass I checked."

"The Sukkariyeh situation still bothers me."

"We need another solution than a drone strike, Chris."

"Tac team? Full crew, hit the building hard, grab intelligence and maybe a prisoner."

"Can your people pull it off?"

"Of course."

Rogers nodded. "Then we will propose it to the president as well."

"Good."

The vehicle moved through the stop-and-go traffic. Fisher stared through the tinted window beside him. He felt no sense of accomplishment. The grilling had been intense. But they'd met their objective. The White Widow would soon be no more. She wouldn't leave Syria alive.

———

TANYA JAFARI SAID, "Are you going to stare at me or hand me a piece of paper?"

As if on cue, the conference room door opened. A younger man in a suit, holding his tie in place, entered. He stayed long enough to pass Wilson a folder. Wilson thanked the man, who quickly departed. The door clicked shut once again.

Wilson slid the folder across the table to Tanya.

"There's your deal."

She opened the folder. A small stack of stapled sheets lay inside. Short block paragraphs filled each page.

"It's like a contract," Wilson explained. "It's a take it or leave it proposition. We already have what we need from you, so personally, I don't care what you do. If you want resettlement in the United States, I suggest you sign on the last page."

Tanya glared at him, then returned to the pages. She intended to read every word. If he wanted to play bad cop and pressure her, she could make him wait.

"I'll sum it up for you," Wilson said. "You stay here until we determine your usefulness is at an end. You get to pick where you go after. We'll give you money and set you up with a job. New name, new identity. After that, you're on your own. There will be periodic check-ins and an emergency number to call if you think you're in danger."

Tanya shook her head as she read each page. She grew more frustrated with every word Wilson spoke. With a scoff, she finally turned to the last, scribbled her signature, and passed the folder to Wilson.

"Fine."

Wilson moved the folder away from him.

"Now," he said, "first question. Tell us your background. Where you were born, all that."

Tanya folded her arms.

14

RAVEN LEANED AGAINST THE WALL AND LISTENED.

"I was born Tanya Distel in Berlin." She gave the year. "My father is Michael Distel. He's runs a janitorial company."

"Your mother?" Wilson said.

"She's dead."

"How?"

"Car accident when I was young."

"I'm sorry. Siblings?"

"None."

Raven drank down the last of his water bottle as she went into her education background. Kindergarten to high school to university. She met her late boyfriend through a friend while working for her father's company.

Raven crossed the room to a waste basket and set the empty water bottle inside.

The table phone rang, interrupting the conversation.

Wilson picked up. "Yes?"

He listened.

"Great news. Do you need me back at Langley?"

He listened some more.

"All right. No, we just started. See you in a few hours."

Wilson hung up.

Raven said, "Who called?"

"Fisher. They had a few challenges with the intelligence committee, but the panel voted in their favor. A termination protocol has officially been issued for Francesca Sloan. He'll meet with the president in two hours to get the final authorization."

"Excellent news," Raven said.

"Take good pictures," Tanya added. "I'll be able to identify the body."

"I bet this pleases you," Wilson said.

"You'll be taking a target off my back."

"Are you sure?" Wilson said. "Your former comrades will make the connection. We may have put a bigger target on your back."

"Do your part, and I'm sure I'll be fine."

Wilson smiled. "You can trust us. Now, let's get back on track. Did you know Francesca Sloan prior to joining the Islamic Union?"

"No. But we bonded at the training camp. Similar recruitment, motivation. They kept us separated from the men, so we didn't get to see our boyfriends much."

"Your boyfriend, her husband?"

"Right. They were already married when she arrived."

"What did she tell you about her history?"

"We didn't dwell on the past," Tanya said. "The only thing we thought about was the future."

"Uh-huh."

The probing carried on for another hour. Raven eventually sat away from the trio at the end of the table to continue observing.

He checked his Rolex, and realized he'd forgotten to adjust for US time. Six hours vanished from the clock. He didn't feel tired, but instead mentally fogged. Flying "back in time" caused the confusion. In a few hours, he expected it to pass.

Harmony Moyer, typing into her laptop as the conversation carried on, remained focused on her screen. She showed no reaction or emotion to the words said. Raven bet she'd heard a few doozies in her time.

Another hour ticked by, and they broke for lunch. Wilson led them into the break room, a sterile affair with Formica tables and hard plastic chairs. Wilson had ordered fast food burgers, fries, Cokes, nothing fancy, but hot and good.

They finished eating. Wilson called for a uniformed female officer and gave her instructions to show Tanya to her quarters. The women departed.

"It's not the Ritz," Wilson explained to Raven, "but the accommodations aren't terrible. She'll have a private bathroom too."

Wilson filled two cups at the coffee machine. One cup of black coffee for him, hot water to Raven. Raven tore open a bag of Bigelow Green Tea and dipped into the water.

"What do you think so far?" Raven said.

"It doesn't matter what I think," Wilson said, adjusting his chair closer to the table. "What matters is how her story checks out. We'll check her history backwards and forwards."

"Wasn't the deal a little premature?" Raven said.

"She didn't read the last page." Wilson grinned.

"What's on the last page?"

"The fine print. We can nullify the deal if she lies to us."

Raven nodded. "I think she'll check out fine."

"You would know."

Raven raised an eyebrow.

"She snuck into your room at the embassy, right?"

"I wouldn't say she *snuck* in."

"You let her in."

"Yeah. So?"

"Same old Raven." Wilson sipped his coffee.

"Nothing happened, Clark."

"Sure."

"She only wanted reassurance I wasn't going to skip out."

Wilson laughed. "Sure."

Raven gave up and changed the subject. "How's your family?"

Wilson blinked. He seemed surprised by the question, and Raven understood the reaction. He didn't normally ask. He had his reasons.

"They're good. Brenda is checking out colleges."

"Does she have her eye on any in particular?"

"California."

"Ouch."

"My wife isn't pleased."

"I have another question," Raven said.

"Sure."

"Tomorrow, next day, I'd like to take Tanya out. Show her the area, help her get settled. It might help to see what her new life might be like."

"We can arrange something. But not for long."

"Won't need long. Couple hours."

"It'll help for sure," Wilson said. "We're going to have her here a while. Cabin fever isn't something we want to deal with."

"Does the crew here rotate?"

"Two weeks in, two weeks out. Yeah."

Raven sipped his tea. The female officer and Tanya returned. Wilson and Raven stood.

"Shall we continue?" Wilson said.

Tanya didn't look enthusiastic. But she agreed.

15

HAYDEN HATED BEING STUCK IN THE BASEMENT.

He paced the floor behind Lymann's chair. The extra personnel Wilson had redirected to Damascus had come in handy. They'd had White Widow's apartment building under surveillance in shifts.

The extra men, with their various shades of skin tone, helped with security. The locals didn't always see the same three people hanging around the produce souk. Hayden, Lymann, and Colleen had exposed themselves too much over the last 24-hours.

But now the tactical team had point. And Hayden was stuck in the basement.

"Eyes on target," a voice crackled over the radio. "Two Toyota vans."

"I see the woman," said another. "Tiger-striped hijab. Face uncovered."

"Copy."

"Moving now."

"Alpha Team, stay ahead of her. Bravo, pick up the rear and look casual."

Hayden stopped and shook his head. He wanted to be there. But he couldn't risk ruining his cover as a humanitarian aid worker. He was too important to the CIA's needs to play cowboy.

He hadn't always been a behind-the-scenes chess master. Iraqi rebels fighting against the Hussein regime had given him the "Tiger" nickname during a battle. A special ops soldier lay wounded in need of rescue. Running into the middle of the battlefield, ignoring salvos of heavy fire, Hayden scooped up a fallen enemy's Kalashnikov. He fired bursts of covering fire as he dragged the wounded man to safety. The Iraqis exclaimed, "He fights like a tiger!" and the name stuck.

Now he paced a basement. A tiger in a cage.

Lymann said, "We got pictures."

The middle monitor showed overhead drone footage of the Toyota vehicles leaving Damascus. Another screen displayed Bravo Team's in-dash camera and their point-of-view progress.

"How long till they reach the desert?" Colleen said. She sipped yet another mug of cardamom coffee.

"They're on Route 90," Lymann said. "About a half hour if traffic isn't too bad."

"And then a seven-hour ride to Sukkariyeh," Hayden said. "Going to be a long wait."

"Too bad she's not going to get there," Lymann said.

The CIA wanted the drone strike to occur before the Route 53 connection. A long stretch of straight roadway between a cement mixing plant and a gas station made the perfect spot. After the gas station, they'd change to Route 53. They had a "53 Backup" in case of a miss, but Hayden didn't think it would be necessary.

He scoffed.

"You okay?" Colleen said.

"I wish I was there."

"Hey," Lymann said, "you and me both. I got this—" he smacked his fake leg. "What's your excuse?"

"I gotta babysit you two."

"You change diapers too?" Colleen said.

"You want to wear that coffee?"

She laughed.

Hayden went to another workstation. A tap of the keys pulled up secondary drone footage of the Sukkariyeh IU base. It was an L-shaped building near a stream outside the crowded city. The stream was part of the Euphrates. It was ridiculous the CIA lawyers refused a drone strike on the building. It was isolated enough for the missiles not to hurt civilians. It was also isolated enough for the tac team in the area to strike and get out before Syrian authorities arrived. A raid would better serve their purposes if there was information to be had within the building, but Hayden's frustration didn't subside. They were being micromanaged, as always, by old men who didn't know what it was like at ground zero and, worse, didn't care. They cared about optics and rules.

There could be no rules in war if you were going to win.

Which begged the question, were they supposed to win, or maintain a status quo to give the military industrial complex an excuse to build bombs and send young soldiers to fight? If victory wasn't the goal, why bother?

He didn't want to think about power brokers stoking war for the sake of profit, but also couldn't deny it seemed like it was the only reason he was sent around the world to do his job.

Hayden put the internal argument out of his mind. He examined the building further. Trees surrounded the structure. The trees looked tall, and more spread out on the empty lot adjacent to the building. A good shield to prevent helicopters from landing too close to the building. They'd created obstacles on the single roadway leading to the building. Wrecked cars sat on either side and in the center in a random pattern.

The footage rotated as the drone drifted overhead.

Hayden stared at the picture. A chill crawled up his back.

No sentries.

No sign of a welcoming committee for the Islamic Union commander.

No activity whatsoever.

The building appeared empty.

Hayden spotted Lymann in the chair while the latter took a break. He ignored the dashcam footage of Bravo Team and instead watched the drone footage. The drone's camera kept the two Toyotas dead-center.

Radio chatter filled the basement.

"Target approaching kill zone."

"Alpha Team breaking off."

"Copy, break. Bravo still behind."

A new voice, this one from the drone pilot somewhere outside Syria. "Missile lock. One away. Two away. Ten seconds to impact."

The "drone's eye view" didn't change. The two Toyotas continued traveling Route 90. They were long past the cement plant. Another three miles to the gas station and the Route 53 junction. No other traffic in the way. No last-minute abort order.

Ten seconds...

Five...

Three...

The first missile tore into the pavement in front of the lead Toyota. The black-and-white footage registered the explosion. The bright plume filled the scope despite the drone's high altitude.

The follow-up missile struck directly on the second

Toyota's roof. The explosion grew, flaring once more, before settling into a growing plume of smoke and fire.

"Targets destroyed," the drone pilot radioed. "Have a nice day."

The drone footage swung away as the pilot steered the Predator for home.

Hayden switched to the dashcam of Bravo Team.

"Get the firefighting rigs and get in there! We need bodies or teeth!"

"I don't think we'll get bodies, Chief."

"We need something to identify this woman. Move!"

The Bravo vehicle stopped. The camera showed the wreckage ahead. The Alpha crew radioed their arrival and readiness to extinguish the flames.

They didn't have much time. The CIA crew had to confirm the dead, and get out, before Syrian authorities responded. The desolate area worked in their favor, but the employees at the cement plant would see the smoke. An emergency phone call would be all it took to ruin the party.

Hayden wiped his eyes. The glare from the monitors always gave him a headache.

Lymann returned. He dropped into the seat beside Hayden. "Did I miss the touchdown?"

"Touchdown and the extra point," Hayden said. "Both Toyotas obliterated."

"I feel bad for the cars," Lymann said. "They never hurt anybody."

A telephone on the table rang. Hayden pressed the speaker button.

"Go, boss," he said.

Clark Wilson's voice came over the line. "You watching?"

"Yup. Good shooting."

"Tell the team in Sukkariyeh to hit the building."

"Building's empty," Hayden said.

"What?"

"Look at the pictures, boss. Ain't nobody there."

"Wait one."

The line clicked. Hayden and Lymann watched the Alpha and Bravo teams attack the blaze with fire suppression tanks. The white foam covered the destroyed vehicles. The smoke was lessening by the minute.

Wilson came back. "Hit it anyway. The team can tell us what's there or what isn't."

"Waste of money."

"I have a feeling you're right, Joe," Wilson said. "I'll be damned if I can explain it."

"She wasn't going there."

"Our informant says—"

"They know she's in custody by now. They changed their plans."

"Puts us behind the eight-ball."

"Yup."

"I'll get back to you."

"Okay." Hayden ended the call.

Colleen leaned over his right shoulder. When she spoke, he smelled the cardamom coffee on her breath.

"I love hunky firemen," she said.

"Take your pick," Hayden told her.

"They're all gay," Lymann said.

"You wish," Colleen told him.

The trio remained glued to their screens.

A nagging doubt remained in the back of Hayden's mind.

If the Islamic Union had evacuated the Sukkariyeh location, why had Francesca Sloan kept her travel plans?

Had they killed a decoy?

16

RAVEN CHEWED A GRAPE FROM THE FRUIT PLATE.

He and Tanya sat in the conference room once again, a uniformed guard at the door. Wilson was on his way.

The CIA man had been correct. The accommodations weren't terrible. Raven's quarters were small but comfortable.

But he was getting antsy.

It wasn't in his nature to stay in one place for long. He wanted to stay because of Tanya. She needed a friend close by. He was willing to be such a friend, for now.

He'd spent the previous evening answering Wilson's questions about his involvement. The questions had been routine, and he explained how she'd contacted him and their meeting at the casino.

He took a deep breath. Another day or two and he could go home. In the meantime—

"What do you think he wants?" Tanya asked.

"No sense in speculating," Raven said. "I'm sure everything is fine. They probably need you to see pictures of the drone strike."

She remained silent. He watched her pick at a fingernail.

The door swung open. Wilson rushed in. He excused the guard, who closed the door behind her.

Wilson set a laptop in front of him and raised the lid. He pressed the power button.

"Good news and bad news," he said.

Raven sat up.

"Good news, we have two of Francesca Sloan's teeth, and it's her. Confirmed kill."

"The bad news?" Tanya said.

"The Sukkariyeh base was empty. Cleared out."

Color drained from her face.

"They changed the meeting," Raven said.

"We think so," Wilson said. He typed a short password.

"Why didn't Sloan change her route?" Raven said.

"We're asking the same thing, Sam."

Raven glanced at Tanya for an answer. She shrugged. Her wide eyes told him she had no answer either.

Wilson waved her over. "We need you to check the picture."

"If you already know—"

"We'd like the confirmation, Ms. Jafari." He stepped back as she came over. "Are those her remains?" he asked.

She leaned close to see the screen. "Body is charred."

"Part of her hijab survived the fire."

"I see it. She wore the tiger stripes because they matched our training uniforms."

"She wore it in the photo you gave us."

"Yes." Tanya stepped back. "You pulled two teeth out?"

"With pliers, yeah. Nasty work."

Wilson pressed a button. Tanya winced.

"Close up," Wilson told Raven. To Tanya, "Well?"

"It's her. There's enough of her face left. I can tell it's her."

"The CIA thanks you for your service, Ms. Jafari." Wilson closed the laptop.

Tanya appeared sullen as she dropped into a chair. Raven went over to her. He sat next to her and put an arm around her. She touched his hand.

It took a lot to betray friends. Whatever her disgust of the Islamic Union's actions, bonds had been forged.

"We're going to need more information," Wilson said, "about other active Union operatives."

She nodded. "The second- and third-in-command will take over now," she said. "You want their names?"

"It will help."

She named two men. Wilson scribbled their names on a pocket notebook.

"They'll scatter to safe houses," she said. "I don't know where."

"You know of at least one, right."

She nodded. "The one I would have used in an emergency, yes. It's in Damascus." She gave the address. Wilson made another note.

"What else?" she asked.

"No more tonight," he said. "Get some rest. Tomorrow, Sam, why don't you take her out and get some fresh air, and we'll resume when you get back."

Raven nodded.

"Tanya," Wilson said, "what will happen with Operation Triangle now?"

"They won't stop it," she said. "We always planned for these contingencies. Any cells in the field won't know about the command structure change until they need to."

"They work independently?"

"Yes."

"Okay. I gotta get back to Langley. You two take it easy."

Wilson scooped up the laptop and left the room. The uniformed guard returned.

Tanya rose. "I need to lay down."

"Good idea."

Raven followed her out of the room. The guard escorted both back to their quarters.

RAVEN STEERED the compact Chevrolet along a winding road. Wilson promised they'd hook up with Highway 29, which would take them to Arlington, the nearest city to the black site.

He gave them a six-hour pass. "I'd like it better if you're back in five hours," he'd added.

"What would you like to do?" he asked as he drove.

They hadn't said much since leaving the facility. After last night, Tanya didn't seem in the mood to talk.

"I want to go bowling," she said.

Raven frowned. "Really?"

"I haven't been in so long. I used to go once a week. It's one of the many things I gave up when I—you know."

"Check on your phone."

She pulled a new cell phone from her purse. Wilson had not let them have their own phones back, but instead issued what they carried. They were supposed to keep the phones on them. Tracking software would enable agents to locate them in an emergency. The phones had a one-touch feature to send an SOS should the need arise.

Wilson at least let Raven has his pistol. He wore it under his jacket.

The GPS in her phone directed them to Round 1 Bowling & Amusement on Cooper Street. Between the number of miles they had to cover and traffic, it took forever to arrive. The Chevy wasn't the most comfortable car in the world.

The seat was too hard, the suspension too tight. Every bump jolted through the floor. Why couldn't the US government spring for a BMW?

The bowling center greeted them with noise and flashing video screens. At midday, most lanes were empty, but a few players tossed balls along the polished lanes. The thunder of each strike echoed.

The café and sports bar caught Tanya's attention first. She told Raven she wanted to eat something greasy first. They sat at a high table and ate decent pizza with extra pepperoni. A large video screen dominated the back wall. The leather couches in front of the screen matched the black-and-tan wood floor but looked unpleasant for sitting. The seats and backrests were at perfect 90-degree angles. Raven supposed the point wasn't to let people sit for too long.

Raven found the most amusement in a karaoke booth adjacent to the bowling lanes. A sign on the clear glass said the max capacity of the booth was eleven. Raven didn't like the idea of "private" karaoke. What was the point of singing your heart out, off key, drunk, and making a fool of yourself, if you weren't in an open bar with dozens of strangers staring at you?

But the pizza was good, the pepperoni spicy and the cheese gooey. They put leftover slices in a takeaway box. Raven paid for a lane and grimaced while slipping on the ridiculous bowling shoes. They could spray all the Lysol in existence into the shoes, and Raven would still burn his socks after. Tanya relished the process. She ran to get a ball before Raven finished tying the shoelaces. Raven selected a heavy red ball and joined her at the lane.

She had their names typed in, taking first position, of course, as he dropped his ball on the carrier.

"I've won trophies before, you know," he advised.

She hefted her ball with confidence. "Really?"

"When I was ten years old. I didn't like other sports, so my mother dragged me to bowling lessons. I had three strikes during the 'Manic Monday' tournament."

"You must be proud."

He grinned. "I'm going to wipe the floor with you."

She smiled back. "We'll see."

She brushed past him to take her position. Raven watched with his hands on his hips. For the moment he wanted to forget the circumstances of their meeting, what made her who she was, what made him who *he* was, and enjoy their time together.

But he couldn't help glancing around, looking for danger.

He'd lived too long in the shadows not to.

17

SHE WAS GONE.

Halfway through the first game Tanya excused herself to use the restroom. Raven bowled his turn and sat to wait. Five minutes became ten. Ten became fifteen. Raven went to the desk. He asked the woman there to check on Tanya. "I'm afraid she might be sick." He followed the woman to the ladies' restroom, waited outside while she went in. The woman emerged shaking her head.

She held a cell phone in her hand.

"Where did you find that?" he asked.

"It was on the counter. I'll put it in lost and found."

It was Tanya's phone. The one Clark Wilson had handed her.

"It's my lady friend's phone."

She handed it to him.

"Any windows in the restroom?"

"No," she said.

Raven described Tanya. "Did you see anybody leave?"

"Our guests come and go all the time, I wasn't watching."

"This isn't good," Raven said. The woman appeared

concerned, but also powerless. She stared at Raven a moment.

"I need to check out," he said, "and find her."

Raven went back to the lane, grabbed her purse, which she'd also left behind, paid the bill, and put his shoes on. He paused a moment. Tanya was still wearing her bowling shoes.

He had no idea what he was going to tell Clark.

He had to find her.

Jumping into the Chevy, Raven drove up and down each side of the block. He extended the search pattern to cover the two blocks before and after the bowling center. Tanya had to be on foot. He didn't see any bus stops. He also didn't see Tanya. No sign of her whatsoever.

He drove around some more, driving slow to the annoyance of other drivers. No Tanya.

He drove back to the bowling center parking lot and dialed Wilson. He had no other choice.

"She got away from me," Raven told him.

"What?"

"Tanya's gone, Clark. She left her phone behind too."

"Wait. Start over. Tell me everything."

Raven explained their activity and her visit to the restroom.

"She *walked* away?"

"Vanished is more like it," Raven said. "I drove in circles looking for her but she's nowhere near here."

"This doesn't make sense."

"I have a feeling it might make perfect sense."

"How so?"

"Either she's rejecting your deal and going on her own, or she played us."

Wilson fell silent. Raven's hand shook as he held the cell phone.

"You better get back here."

"I'm on my way."

"I don't know how we're going to explain this."

"You and me both, pal."

"Drive around again. One more time. We can't let this go."

"I'm going now."

Raven ended the call and started the Chevy.

WHEN RAVEN CALLED BACK with the same news, Wilson directed him to Langley. Christopher Fisher wanted to see him.

A guest pass waited for Raven at the security gate of CIA headquarters. He drove to visitor parking, and Wilson reached him as he locked the car with the remote.

Wilson looked pale.

"You okay?" Raven said.

"No, Sam. We're in serious trouble."

Raven followed Wilson into the building, through lobby security, and into an elevator. Wilson pressed a button for their floor. The elevator climbed upward.

Neither spoke.

Raven's mind raced. He focused on his second theory. She had played them. A phony defection to plant misinformation. The CIA had redirected resources at fake targets. Meanwhile, the Islamic Union furthered their progress on Operation Triangle.

She hadn't mentioned the name by mistake. Not at all.

How had he not seen through her? Or had he? Had he let his need to protect the vulnerable get in the way of his judgement?

He wasn't alone in making the call, though. The CIA had believed her too.

But...

Assassins had targeted her.

The White Widow was certainly dead.

Why sacrifice operators for a ruse?

It left him with option one. She was rejecting the CIA's deal and taking her chances alone. She'd given them everything she had. Staying locked in the Blue Ridge black site wasn't what she wanted. Did she have a backup plan? A new identity waiting?

The elevator let them off on the seventh floor. Short walk down a quiet hallway. Through a door to Christopher Fisher's office.

The receptionist waved them to the inner office.

Fisher waited behind his desk. He stood. Seated in front of the desk was Layla McCarthy. She stood too.

"What's going on, Raven?" Fisher said.

"Hello, Christopher." He smiled at Layla. "Hello, Layla."

"Sam," she said. "I wish we were meeting again under better circumstances."

"Ditto," Raven said.

Fisher snapped, "Answer me."

Wilson pulled two more chairs over to the desk. He and Raven sat. Raven carefully went through his story again. He left out no detail. The others listened carefully. He placed Tanya's CIA phone and purse on Fisher's desk as proof she'd left it behind.

When he finished, Fisher and Layla stared at him. Wilson looked at the carpet.

Fisher sighed and tapped his desk blotter. "All right. What are our ideas?"

Raven explained his theories.

Layla added, "It wouldn't be the first time a defector got cold feet."

"But each of those times," Fisher said, "the defector had been lying to us. Raven's second idea fits too."

Wilson chimed in. "She left her purse and the phone. She has no ID or money. She's wearing bowling shoes."

"She has some sort of plan," Layla said. "This wasn't a spur of the moment decision. She was waiting for the opportunity."

"Have you checked out what she told you," Raven said, "about her background?"

"We're still investigating her statement," Fisher said. "Our efforts were focused on the White Widow."

"We have to assume the black site is now compromised," Wilson said.

"Did she see any of the other prisoners?" Fisher asked.

"No." Wilson shook his head. "But she knows the location. She knows the security layout."

"No way a commando force could get in there," Layla said.

"Do we want to take the chance?" Wilson said. "Who says they need commandos?"

"What do you suggest, Clark?" Fisher said.

"We move the prisoners to another location until we determine whether there's a threat to the facility."

"And if they're waiting for us to move them?" Layla said. "We only have the one other IU prisoner, Omar Talman. What if they're planning a rescue? They wouldn't need to attack the facility if they can blow up a convoy."

Fisher said, "We can increase the force at the black site. Roving patrols in the forest. They won't attack. It's a suicide mission. But we'll add the personnel anyway."

Wilson nodded.

Fisher let out another breath. "I'm going to have a lot of explaining to do on the Hill." He turned to Layla. "We need her background check expedited. I want it done in an hour."

Layla nodded.

Fisher leveled a finger at Raven. "You're not going anywhere until we figure this out."

"I'm here for the duration," Raven told him. "This is my responsibility as much as anybody's."

"Stick with Wilson till I say so," Fisher said. "I'll get you a green badge, so you'll be able to move about the building. I'm going to distribute pictures of Tanya and send out a search party. We'll cover Arlington like flies. She'll turn up."

"And if she doesn't?" Layla said.

"Then we'll know she was a fake. Anything else?"

Nobody had anything more to say.

"Let's get to work."

18

OMAR TALMAN WAS RUNNING OUT OF TIME.

The guards talked too much, and the Islamic Union field officer knew how to listen without being noticed. He knew when Tanya arrived, and he heard the buzz about her disappearance. Her vanishing act was his signal. If he didn't move fast, the plan wouldn't work, and he'd be stuck at the black site until he died.

His cell wasn't much bigger than a closet. No bed. Only a toilet and a bare mattress on the floor. They'd given up on him. The interrogations had stopped weeks ago. He gave them nothing, despite the near torture of their techniques. He knew policy forbade them from going too far. He'd won by frustrating them. They'd thought he'd be a fountain of information; not so. Now they were going to let him rot.

Omar Talman wasn't a big man. He was tall, but thin and wiry, and the cell provided enough room for regular exercise. Push-ups, sit-ups, knee bends—he performed them all several times a day. He needed to stay in shape when "the moment" arrived.

The door opened. A uniformed guard holding a tray of

food stepped through the doorway. He remained curled in a corner. He regarded the guard with blank eyes. It was an act. They thought he was broken and subdued. They'd stopped ordering him to stay in place at the point of a gun months ago.

The guard bent to put the tray on the floor. A second guard remained in the hallway. He wore a Taser on his hip.

Omar Talman struck like a coiled rattlesnake.

He tipped the food tray into the guard's chest. The second guard grabbed the Taser. Talman shoved the first guard into the second. Both continued backward to smash into the hallway wall behind them. Talman continued his attack. Two solid blows into the first man's stomach sent him to the floor. Talman blocked the rise of the Taser in the other man's hand and struck with two fingers at the man's throat. The guard gagged. Talman punched him in the balls, then the stomach, and he joined his partner on the floor.

Talman scooped up the fallen Taser and ran.

The hallway seemed longer than he remembered, but his legs pumped like pistons. He turned left at the corner. Elevator ahead. As soon as somebody activated the alarm, they'd lock the elevators. He didn't want to get stuck. He bypassed the elevator for the stairwell.

By his estimation at the time of his capture, he was three levels underground. Long way up. But he'd reach the surface or die on the way. Survival was the priority, though. Tanya was counting on him.

He crashed through the stairwell door and took the steps two at a time, rounding each landing without pause. His bare feet didn't slip on the cold concrete. By the time he reached the second landing, the alarm blared. It echoed in the stairwell, hurting his eardrums, but he ignored the pain and kept going.

The response force would meet him with automatic

weapons. They wouldn't hesitate to shoot. But they might hesitate if he used one of them as a shield.

He reached the first level and crashed into the door. It didn't budge. He pushed the locking bar. Nothing. He peeked through the square of glass in the door. Three men with M16A4 rifles converged on him. They wore body armor. He waited.

Stepping back, he raised the Taser as the first man opened the door and ordered him to get on his knees. The muzzle of the M16 didn't bother him. He'd had guns pointed at him many times. Talman let the Taser to the talking, and the electrodes hit the man in the neck. He screamed, recoiling. Talman let go of the Taser, shoving the barrel of the M16 away from his face as he pushed the guard through the doorway. His partners aimed their weapons, but Talman's human shield blocked him from view.

Snatching the man's pistol, turning it in his hand, he fired rapidly over the guard's shoulder. One of the two guards dropped from a head shot. The other dodged back to avoid the falling body. Talman turned his captive around and shoved with his right foot. The first guard's body flew away from him. As the third trooper tried to fire, the autoloader in Talman's fist barked again. Another head shot. Talman ran to the guard he'd grabbed, shot him as he tried to rise, and helped himself to two M16s. He held one rifle in each hand. He left the pistol behind.

He ran down the hall. Shouting behind him. Talman pivoted, shuffling backwards, and fired a burst from both rifles. The salvos drove his pursuers around the corner. Talman turned forward and took the next right turn. Another door ahead. He blasted the lock and pushed through.

The main entry hall. The duty officer, behind his bulletproof glass, yelled into a phone. Three more security officers converged from a side door. The M16s in Talman's fists crackled. He aimed for the legs, cutting the security team down. Their bodies dropped like chopped trees. He stepped over them, firing into their heads. He grabbed another rifle when the first two locked open over empty magazines. With his free hand, he grabbed a key card from a security guard's belt.

He ignored the duty officer as he shoved the card into the slot near the door. The lock clicked. He charged into the office and shot the duty officer in the chest. The man's body crashed into his console, smearing the controls with blood, but Talman didn't hesitate. He flipped the switches to unlock the elevator to the surface, then stepped back. With the M16 at his hip, he fired into the panel until the action locked open. Sparks flashed as the bullets ripped through the electronics.

Exiting, pulling the door shut so the electronic lock engaged once again, he swung his rifle back the way he'd come. The three guards in pursuit were in the open, racing his way. He squeezed the trigger. The M16 bucked in his hand. The guards dropped as their legs and kneecaps popped, spreading blood across the white floor as they fell. More head shots ended their struggle to return fire. They were sitting ducks. Too much faith in their body armor, and not enough practice against somebody shooting back.

Talman moved to the dead men on the floor. He ripped spare magazines from a guard's utility belt, and he entered the elevator. The ascent to the surface began.

He breathed hard as the cabin climbed. He assumed they had a secondary control in the facility to stop the elevators. Until they saw the duty officer was dead and his equipment destroyed, they wouldn't realize the need for the secondary. The minutes ticked by at an agonizing pace.

When the elevator stopped, he began to panic. He

stopped panicking when the doors slid open. The parking area at the mouth of the mountain greeted him. More security troops waited.

Talman charged ahead, M16 to his shoulder, firing as he moved. One guard dropped. The others scattered to take cover behind vehicles. Talman found an SUV to hide behind and fired over the hood. He squatted behind the front passenger fender and fired around the bumper. He reversed and moved to the rear bumper, emerging from behind the car, his muzzle tracking targets. One burst, another. Two men down. He dropped and rolled as return fire came his way. Rising, he fired again, found another SUV for cover, and changed magazines.

The mouth of the mountain lay ahead. Several security troops remained between him and freedom.

Return fire smacked into the SUV. Talman flinched with each hit. He fired over the hood, then dashed around the rear once again. Another security officer, running from one car to another, winged a shot at him and missed. Talman's single shot took him down mid-stride.

Talman broke into a sprint for the opening. He fired as he ran, driving the final security guard to cover. Bullets buzzed past him as he reached the mouth and turned left. His feet finally crunched on dirt. He wore no shoes, and terrain bit through the bottoms of his feet and made him wince. He kept running, gaining the hot tarmac of the paved road. He raced across the shoulder of the road into the forest.

He grunted in pain as his feet landed on the rough forest floor. He pushed away the discomfort. Talman tore through the foliage, leaping over logs and debris, curving left as the ground began a downward slope. His lungs burned and sweat coated his body. He didn't dare stop to wipe his face.

Dried leaves, rocks, and pieces of twigs ripped into his feet as he ran. He had far to go and no time to waste.

The CIA had thought their Blue Ridge facility was top secret, but the Islamic Union had known about the location for a long time. The information had been easy to acquire. Too many people who worked there talked in public, at bars, and restaurants. Steady surveillance had enabled the Union to gather intelligence over a period of two years prior to Talman's capture.

The commanders, including the White Widow, reviewed the information on a regular basis. They'd determined the best landing spot for a helicopter was a natural clearing 500 yards west of the facility. Standing orders for anybody captured, should they escape, were to head for the clearing and await pickup. If Tanya hadn't infiltrated, he'd never have known they'd be waiting for him.

He kept running. Any troops still standing at the facility would be organizing a search, but he was well ahead of them. And if he died before reaching the clearing, it was fine with him. They'd struck at the heart of the CIA and their illegal prisons. The escape and slaughter inside would give the Agency a black eye for years.

They'd made a huge mistake when they thought Omar Talman had been broken.

HE WAITED at the edge of the clearing. His breathing had finally slowed to normal. The effects of his escape were beginning to creep through his body. Everything hurt.

When he heard the rotor blades of the rescue chopper, his spirit brightened. He tossed the M16 and ran into the grassy field. He spun around as he looked. The chopper cleared the trees and dropped into the field. He ran for the craft. The side door opened. Tanya waited inside. She urged him on.

Talman jumped into the cabin, landing hard, and Tanya pushed the door shut. The chopper lifted off.

"Omar!" she yelled. He rose and embraced her, holding her body tight against his. He touched her soft black hair, let it tangle around his fingers. There were some nights where he wondered if he'd ever feel her close to him again.

He wanted to say something, but his dry mouth prevented the words from forming. No matter. They would have plenty of time to talk later. For now, he held her close, and she didn't pull away.

VICTORY FELT SWEET.

Victory meant crushing the man she loved against her once again. Tanya Jafari finally broke the embrace and waved at Sila Kaymak, who sat at the controls. The Turkish Islamic Union assassin sent to "kill" her in Stockholm steered the chopper away.

Tanya stared into her lover's face. Omar looked thin, worn out. The blue jumpsuit didn't fit him at all. But fire sparkled behind his eyes. The same fire she'd fallen in love with. His arms felt strong, his body still lean. He'd held out against the worst his captors had delivered and pulled through.

She kissed him. He responded slowly. When he pulled away, he smiled.

"Come on, sit."

As the chopper banked, she helped him into a chair, taking the seat next to him. She grabbed his hand. He asked for water, and she grabbed a bottle of water from a side pocket of the chair. He drank the bottle down and finally spoke.

"You made it," he said.

"And now they will pay dearly for what they've done to us," Tanya Jafari, the *real* White Widow, told him.

PART II

PART II

19

FIVE YEARS EARLIER — BERLIN, GERMANY

It started with a phone call.

Tanya Schrader took a frozen dinner from the freezer and read the instructions. The long day at the office left her in no mood to cook tonight. When her phone rang, she set the package down and grabbed her phone from the purse on the counter. The caller ID said Francesca. She answered. "Hey."

"Where are you?" Francesca Sloan, a British employee of her father's company, also worked in the accounting department.

"Home."

"Come to the bar."

"Why?"

"Speaker's rally tonight. Some local Muslims are going to talk about the truck crash last week."

"Fran, I'm beat."

"You should see the main speaker. I'm calling him 'Sheik Ahmad the Hunk'." Francesca laughed.

"That's not funny."

The British girl stopped laughing. "Get down here. I got a table on the aisle."

Francesca ended the call and Tanya scoffed and looked around her kitchen. Every surface was spotless. She had decorations and pictures, but the place always felt lifeless. The idea of a relaxing night out instead of a frozen dinner appealed after all. All right. She would join Fran at the bar.

She knew about the rally at the beer hall. Everybody in the immediate neighborhood knew. People elsewhere in the city knew if they were paying attention.

The week prior, a local man, a refugee from the Middle East, crashed a truck into an outdoor café. He killed fifteen people. Police shot him as he attempted to escape. Jihadists claimed responsibility for the incident.

There had already been one public protest against Muslims in Germany. The protest leaders used megaphones to address the gathered crowd. They claimed terrorists had come to take advantage of and kill the German people. There was only one way to deal with such scum. Nobody wanted to think about the consequences of such actions. Many didn't want to acknowledge the uttered words. But Tanya knew the instigators had struck a nerve.

After the protest, signs posted around Berlin proclaimed:

ISLAM IS NOT THE ENEMY.
WE ARE A TARGET TOO.
THIS IS WRONG. COME SEE WHY.

Each sign showed the date and time of the beer hall meeting.

Tensions were still high after the crash and initial protest. Muslims in the city reported incidents of harassment. Francesca feared the harassment would lead to something worse and told Tanya of her worries. She'd seen similar events and backlashes in Britain.

As Tanya grabbed her purse and car keys, she wondered what the night might have in store. Hopefully something more interesting than sitting on the couch until bedtime.

BODIES OCCUPIED every available bench space except for the seat Francesca had saved. Fran had also ordered a stein of Tanya's preferred light beer. She took an appreciative sip as she looked around.

Usual mix of young and old faces. The older men dressed like college professors and leaned heavily toward tweed jackets. Their female companions also kept their attire conservative.

The younger people were an equal mix of free spirits and young professionals fresh from the office.

Tanya and Francesca fit somewhere in the middle.

Francesca still wore her work clothes. Tanya had changed to jeans and a Tee-shirt as soon as she returned home.

The hall represented the long history of public gatherings in Germany. Attached to a smaller bar, anybody who could afford the nightly rate was welcome to rent the room.

It wasn't correct to call it a "hall". The room was minuscule compared to the 5,000 seat Mathäser (now a cinema) when it was a beer hall. Nor was it anything like the Bürgerbräukeller where Hitler spoke in the early days of the Nazis. But the goal was the same. Provide a place for the public to listen to ideas and discuss the ideas afterwards.

The public often needed a personal outlet of expression. Call-in talk shows served the purpose but were impersonal. The beer halls provided the personal touch required. Tanya had attended many such meetings, mostly at the behest of her father.

Two men of Middle Eastern descent stepped on stage. One carried a notebook. He looked nervous. Tanya saw his hands shaking. The second man stood quietly, hands behind his back, a confident thrust to his chin.

Francesca leaned close. "He's the one I told you about."

"You met?"

"Before everybody got here, yeah."

"Sheik Ahmad the Hunk" she had said. He certainly fit the part. Every inch of his body appeared lean and well-muscled.

The man at the podium looked at his friend for encouragement and faced the audience again.

He introduced himself as Tamal and his friend as Ahmad. He spoke timidly at first, but as he continued his voice grew in confidence and volume. He talked about growing up in Iraq and fleeing to Germany during the United States invasion. He talked about giving up his home and his friends and everything he knew to make a new life in a new land. He feared his new home would reject him because of the actions of a few. He wanted Berliners to know his people wanted peace as much as they did.

When Ahmad finally took the microphone, he needed no notes. He spoke perfect English with a light accent. He told a similar story of escaping the Middle East. He added a touching account of his ailing grandfather. He hadn't wanted to leave Syria, but the war forced them out. And now Ahmad feared for the vulnerable in his family.

The audience listened with quiet respect and applauded when the speeches concluded. Some stood. Tanya stared at Ahmad as if in a trance. Francesca nudged her. "You didn't touch your beer."

Tanya put the stein to her mouth and rectified the error.

The two men stayed for questions after the meeting broke up.

Francesca and Tanya waited against a wall as the pair spoke to well-wishers. Some had more questions. By the time Francesca finally pushed Tanya to them, it was getting late.

But any thoughts of getting to bed early left Tanya's mind the second she met Ahmad's eyes. They were rich, dark eyes. She had to look up a little to meet his gaze, but she didn't mind at all.

"This is Tanya," Francesca said, "the co-worker I told you about."

Ahmad and Tanya shook hands and he asked what she thought of his speech. She appreciated his vulnerability and candor and offered to help spread the word.

They talked more about where they worked and their current lives. Tanya glanced behind Ahmad and noticed Francesca had cornered Tamal for herself.

As far as Tanya was concerned, it was a good night.

She departed after taking a selfie with both men, and an extra picture of only her and Ahmad. They exchanged cell numbers too. She wanted to see him again. He didn't object to the idea.

FRANCESCA LAUGHED WITH EXCITEMENT.

"I can't believe it!" she said. "Did you see how he was looking at me?"

"I saw how you were looking at *him*," Tanya said.

"He's better looking than Ahmad!"

"I wouldn't say that." Tanya laughed.

The two women stopped at Francesca's car and Fran unlocked the door. "Well, I guess I'll see you tomorrow."

"Try to get some sleep tonight."

"I'm too jazzed to sleep! Was this a *great* night or what?" With another laugh, Francesca slid behind the wheel and started the engine. Tanya crossed the parking lot to her car and sat behind the wheel a moment.

Yeah, Ahmad was a hunk, all right. And she had his phone number.

She started the car and drove home.

20

PRESENT DAY

RAVEN LOOKED ALONG THE TABLE AT GRIM FACES.

The conference room at CIA HQ looked identical the one at the Blue Ridge black site. Raven couldn't remember the last time he'd set foot in the headquarters building, but he'd had no time to look around.

Fisher sat at the head of the table. Behind him, hung on the wall, was a large screen television.

Clark Wilson sat next to Raven on one side, with Layla McCarthy, Fisher's number two, across from Raven.

Fisher opened the meeting. He looked tired. There were more lines on his face than Raven remembered from their last get-together; his hair was grayer. But the Deputy Director of Operations still held a commanding presence.

"Can anybody explain what the hell happened?"

Somebody tapped on the glass behind Raven. He turned to look as Wilson waved the man in. The man who entered was younger than everybody else. He was in his mid-20s, with a short haircut and sharp jaw, and wore the standard issue CIA suit-and-tie like a pro. He held a laptop and sat next to Wilson.

Wilson said, "This is Paul Heinrich, one of my top analysts."

"What do you have?"

Heinrich lifted the laptop lid and turned on the power. "A few pieces of the puzzle, sir."

"Short version?"

"Everything she told us was a lie. Sort of."

"What do you mean?"

"Tanya told enough of the truth to send us after Francesca Sloan," Heinrich said, "but made up her personal history."

Heinrich hit a few keys and asked Fisher to turn on the wall-mounted big screen. Fisher moved to the side to allow everybody to view the television.

A picture of a much younger Tanya Jafari appeared on the screen. It looked like a driver's license picture.

"She was born Tanya Schrader, in Berlin," Heinrich said.

"Not Tanya Distel?" Fisher said.

"Correct, sir. There are several Distel families in Germany, but none match with her. She lied about her father's business, too."

"In what way?"

"Her father is not a janitor. He is Hugo Schrader, and he runs one of the biggest venture capital firms in Germany. She worked for her father as an accountant. So did Francesca Sloan."

Raven frowned. "Wait. The Schrader name is familiar."

"It should be," Wilson said. "Hugo Schrader was a member of the Red Army Faction. Sat at the knee of Ulrike Meinhof. Wrote a book about the experience."

The Red Army Faction, aka the Baader-Meinhof Gang, active from 1970 to 1998, began as a group of student radicals pushing a left-wing agenda. They were also upset about former Nazis holding positions of power in Germany. When protests were ineffective, they turned to terrorism. The RAF killed a total of 34 people and lost 28 of their own over their most active years. Most of the original leaders died in battles with police or in prison. Others survived until the official disbanding in 1998. Raven wondered where Hugo Schrader fit in with the saga.

"He didn't get killed with the rest? Go to jail?" Raven said.

Wilson shook his head.

"I wonder how he managed to stay out," Raven said.

"He had dirt on somebody for sure," Wilson said. "Probably still does."

"Let's back up," Fisher said. "Tanya and Sloan met working for Tanya's father. How did they end up with Islamic Union?"

Heinrich said, "We can deduce that they both joined the Union the same way. Sloan ran off with her boyfriend, Tamal Alvi, whom we believed was the founding father of the group. She met him in Berlin. Her family spoke out in the UK press." He tapped another key, and a newspaper article appeared on the screen. "They say Alvi seduced her into joining the organization. She left everything behind to be with him. We know Alvi was active at a training camp in Pakistan. It's likely Sloan was there, too."

"And Tanya too?"

"Yes. According to Mr. Raven's statement, she trained at the camp in Pakistan."

"But there's something missing."

"Yes, sir," Heinrich said. "Tanya's family never spoke to the press."

"So, if she ran off with the boyfriend on her own—"

"They either didn't care," Heinrich said, "or supported her."

Layla McCarthy scoffed. "Insane."

"Like father, like daughter?" Raven said. "Did Hugo inspire his kid to fight the power like her old man?"

"Possible," Wilson said. "It would explain a few things."

"Like what?"

"Where the Islamic Union got its money from," Wilson said. "How they appeared out of nowhere so quickly."

Fisher said, "Schrader wrote checks?"

"We have no proof, but it's possible."

"Are you checking his financials?"

"We are."

"Where is Tamal Alvi from, and how did he turn radical?" Fisher said.

Wilson said, "Remember the guy who crashed a truck into a café?"

Everyone nodded.

"Alvi and his roommate, Ahmad, started holding public meetings after the attack. They wanted to show the German people not all Muslims were terrorists."

"What changed their minds?" Layla McCarthy said.

"Attacks on their families from a gang of thugs," Wilson said. "Ahmad's grandfather, who wasn't well at the time, was killed in one of the attacks."

Fisher turned to Raven. "Did she tell you anything about a boyfriend or a husband, Sam?"

"She did mention the name Ahmad on the flight over," Raven said.

Heinrich cleared his laptop screen and began typing. A thin man appeared on the screen. The picture showed him walking through an airport and carrying suitcases. He was dressed casually with a black leather jacket a size too large for his small frame.

"Ahmad Jafari," Heinrich said. "He shared an apartment with Tamal Alvi."

"There's your connection," Raven said.

"Status of Jafari?" Fisher asked.

"Quite dead, sir," Heinrich answered. "He died in the same raid where we killed Alvi."

"Was Tanya or Francesca the real White Widow?" Fisher said.

"Either both, or only Tanya," Wilson said.

"Why?"

"If she was lying about Francesca being the one to take command, it means *she* was in charge. Her father is the banker. Don't argue with the lady related to the man filling the bank accounts."

"Did we really kill Francesca Sloan?" Fisher said. "Or a double?"

"Can't answer at this time, sir," Wilson said.

"A double makes sense," Layla said. "Why sacrifice a key player?"

"All right, let's address the elephant in the room," Fisher said. "What was the point of her coming to us?"

Layla McCarthy said, "Getting Omar Talman out of the black site."

"Why?"

"Operation Triangle," Layla said. "She knows more about it than she admitted. She needs Talman to complete the mission."

"Talman escaped before we beefed up the facility," Fisher said. "Let's assume her arrival and disappearance was a signal to him. He acted when he did because he knew time was short. It lines up with the helicopter we spotted in the area."

Fisher paused a moment. Heinrich typed quietly.

"What we need to find out," Fisher continued, "is if they are still in the United States. We need to know how they plan to put Operation Triangle in motion and where they will strike, or if the plan is currently in motion. I'd also like to know why Omar Talman is so important she risked us discovering her ruse before they escaped."

Fisher turned to Wilson again.

"What are our people in Syria doing?" Fisher said.

"Hayden and his crew are in the process of rounding up suspects for questioning."

"There was nothing at the Sukkariyeh location?"

"Nothing, sir."

"Where are the suspects coming from? The crew from the apartment Sloan used in Damascus?"

"Yes, sir. Most of them scattered, but two remain in Damascus at a different hideout. Hayden and the tac team are going in shortly."

"Tell Hayden to proceed with caution," Fisher said. "This was a set-up, and we may get the short end of the stick no matter what we do."

"I'll tell him," Wilson said.

Fisher let out a heavy sigh. "This is a disaster. A lot of good men died at the black site. We were so caught up in taking down Sloan, we didn't properly vet Tanya to begin with. She played us, and we fell for it."

"She played *me*," Raven said.

All eyes turned to Raven. He said to Fisher, "You wouldn't have me in this meeting if you weren't going to ask me to stay aboard."

"You're here," Fisher said, "because one way or another, you're going after her, and we can't stop you. We might as well work together."

"And her father is my first stop. Where do I find him?"

21

"YOU'RE NOT A GOOD BOSS," COLLEEN ANDREEV SAID OVER the wireless.

"Tiger" Joe Hayden, seated in the passenger seat of an SUV, laughed. "Why is that?"

"You get to have all the fun while Freddy and I are stuck in the basement."

"For once," Freddy Lymann added, "Colleen is right."

"You two sit tight. I'll be back soon."

Hayden glanced at the driver. Carl Johnson, leader of the Alpha Team who had collected Francesca Sloan's teeth, raised an eyebrow. "They on your back all the time?"

"Always."

"They know everything is on them if you get whacked tonight, right?"

"They know," Hayden said, "but don't want to admit it. That was their way of showing concern."

Johnson looked like a linebacker. Thick chest, arms, neck. A formidable fighter. Scar tissue on his knuckles testified to how often he used his fists while working.

"If we have to get out of this car to do any shooting," Johnson said, "stick close to me and you'll go home tonight."

Hayden couldn't tell Johnson how much action he'd seen in his career. The operations remained classified. Johnson, a veteran CIA Ground Branch operator, had the idea Hayden spent his career behind a desk. It wouldn't hurt to let the big man think of him as a little brother for the night. "Will do," he said.

Hayden carried a pistol, and it was the first time in a long time he'd gone out armed. A Beretta Inox 92FS 9mm rode in shoulder leather under his left arm. Johnson had a pistol and automatic rifle.

The voice of another Alpha Team operator whispered through their wireless earbuds. "Targets confirmed inside."

"Copy," Johnson said. "What are they doing?"

"One's cooking. The other is adjusting the television."

Johnson turned to Hayden, "You ready?"

The two Islamic Union suspects were holed up in a house. The house sat in the middle of a field across the street from a school. Waiting to hit at night was a critical part of the plan. They didn't want to strike with school in session. The Americans weren't supposed to be in Syria. They had to stay under the radar and strike hard and fast and get away clean.

The hideout had all the markings of a trap, but the recon element of Alpha Team didn't report any other gunmen. Why the pair dubbed Suspect One and Suspect Two remained behind, Hayden didn't know. He hoped luck was on their side and the two men were part of continuing Islamic Union operations. Wilson's warning remained fixed in his mind. Anything was possible.

"Let's make some noise," Hayden said. "Remember I need at least one of them alive."

Johnson said, "Teams One and Two, initiate strike. We need one alive, but we'd like both without any holes."

"Team One copy."

"Team Two copy."

Johnson and Hayden exited the SUV and took cover on the driver's side. The warm night air touched Hayden's face. Taking out the Beretta, he held it in his right hand with the hammer down on a live round. Johnson, squatting by the front tire, kept his HK416 tucked to his shoulder.

Hayden wanted to be with the raiding party, but no dice. Strictly backup. To charge across the field behind the entry meant being mistaken for a hostile and shot by his own guys.

Not part of the plan, thanks.

Loose lights hung from wires on the wooden poles around the hideout. The driveway was a simple dirt path with a Toyota pick-up parked facing out. Hayden watched the truck for signs of movement.

The lights cut out. Hayden let his eyes adjust to the glow of the moon and the city lights behind them.

Flash-bang grenades kicked off the raid, the solid booms making Hayden jump. Automatic weapons fire crackled a second after the last boom. Hayden cringed at the shouts coming over his earbud. Gunfire punctuated the jumble of commands and signals from the raiding party.

"Sit tight, Joe," Johnson said.

Hayden grinned but kept his mouth shut. He wasn't nervous at all. He wanted to be in the fight.

And then he had his chance.

Movement near the garage. A body scaled the fence alongside the house and dropped next to the driveway.

Johnson said, "Move!" and took off running as if propelled by a rocket. Hayden ran behind him. Hayden didn't know if it was Suspect One or Suspect Two; who cared? The

Islamic Union terrorist ran for the Toyota, wrenching open the door. Johnson shouted, "Don't think so!" and kicked the door shut.

The terrorist swung a knife at Johnson's face. The big CIA man yelled as he fell, hitting the ground and rolling away to make room for Hayden. The terrorist lunged at Hayden, swinging the bloody knife. Hayden dodged back. As his opponent drew the knife back again, Hayden charged, swinging the barrel of the Beretta into his jaw.

The terrorist rushed and crashed into Hayden's midsection. Hayden's feet shuffled on the ground as momentum forced him backward. He twisted his body as the pair began to fall and landed on top the IU operative. He bashed him with the butt of the Beretta once, twice. Hayden tossed the knife from the man's loosening grip. He hauled the terrorist up halfway, swung the Beretta again, and landed a solid blow to the man's head. He let go. The terrorist fell unconscious.

Hayden secured the man's ankles and wrists with zip ties from his pockets. He ran to Johnson. Rolling the big man onto his back, he pulled Johnson's hand from his face. His palm came away streaked with blood.

"How bad?" the big man said.

"Got your cheek. You'll need stitches but you'll live."

"Feels like hell."

Hayden helped Johnson to his feet. The raiding party exited the property. They had Suspect One secured. He moved unsteadily on his feet, and two of Alpha Team held him up.

"Other's over here," Hayden said. Two black-clad shooters picked up the second terrorist.

Now they had to clear out. The raiders took the prisoners to other vehicles while Johnson and Hayden ran back to their SUV. Hayden took the wheel.

As the engine rumbled to life, Johnson said, "You've done this before."

Hayden put the SUV in gear. "Yup."

"You ain't no desk man."

"I wasn't always a desk man."

Johnson laughed, then groaned in pain. "Oh, man, this hurts."

Hayden accelerated from the hideout. "We'll get you patched up before the sun rises, don't worry." Hayden paused a moment, then: "Base, you copy?"

Lymann said, "We copy successful extraction of two assholes. Good job, boss."

"We're proceeding to the interrogation point," Hayden said. "See you in the morning. Keep the coffee on."

"You'll be lucky," Colleen chimed in, "if there's any left for you."

Hayden and the team traveled to a separate location outside the city. The cluster of tents provided privacy for the interrogation. A medic took care of the cut on Johnson's cheek while Hayden went to work on Suspect One and Suspect Two. He kept them separated so they couldn't communicate.

Hayden had ways to get them to talk. Within a few hours, he had information for Clark Wilson.

"YOU WORKING LATE?" Hayden said over the secure video connection.

Clark Wilson sat behind his desk in his office. The camera mounted on his flatscreen was pointed at his face like a pistol.

"I put a cot in the office," Wilson said.

Hayden laughed.

"Not kidding," Wilson said. "Tell me you have something."

"Not enough," Hayden said. He consulted a notepad. "We can confirm it was the real Francesca Sloan killed in the drone strike."

"They're sure?"

"Both confirmed."

"Why?"

"Nothing to live for now that her husband was dead."

Wilson frowned. It never ceased to amaze him how killers could feel empathy. They felt none for their victims, but they shared connections with each other same as everybody else. Another one of life's mysteries.

"Well how sad for her," Wilson said. "Pardon me if I don't weep."

"I asked about Operation Triangle," Hayden continued, "but they don't know anything."

"What were they left behind for?"

"Continuing operations in the region. They're supplying arms and information, cover identities, logistical stuff. Nobody told them about a major operation."

"Not in their position," Wilson agreed. "They'd know too much. All right, keep working on them. See who else they can lead to."

"Copy."

"Good job tonight, Joe."

"Thank you."

"Feel good to be out of your cage?" Wilson finally smiled.

"A little," Hayden said. "Still got a chain on my ankle, though."

"Won't be much longer at the rate we're going. We'll talk again in twenty-four hours."

Wilson ended the video connection and sighed as the screen returned to the desktop view.

He made notes on the conversation for his meeting with Fisher in the morning. He looked at the cot he'd put in the corner. It was an army cot with a canvas bed and steel frame. The hell with it. He was going home to sleep in his own bed. He grabbed his keys and jacket and left his office. He didn't bother to turn off the light.

22

Escaping the United States had not been hard.

Thanks to her father's connections, of course. Sila Kaymak landed the helicopter 500 miles from the Blue Ridge black site. They touched down at a small executive airport. Her father had arranged for one of his business jets to meet them at a private hangar. Tanya hustled her men aboard the Avro Business Jet, and they relaxed as the jet took off.

Destination: Paris.

The jet had all the comforts for a long trip. Tanya's father had gutted most of the seats out of the cabin to divide the plane into three sections. One for sitting, one for entertainment, and another for dining. The jet was also equipped with a lavatory and shower, which Omar made use of immediately.

All three had "go bags" prepared well in advance. Each bag contained clothes, personal items and pre-stamped passports in their cover identities. Each passport had proper US exit stamps so customs in Paris would ask no questions. They were traveling as executives with her father's company. There would be no questions asked but the routine ones.

Tanya had worked for her father long enough to know how to deal with airport routines. All Omar and Sila had to do was follow her lead and keep quiet unless spoken to.

Presently they touched down at Orly Airport in Paris and met no resistance. Sila Kaymak drove the rental to their hotel. Tanya Jafari didn't relax until she double locked the hotel room door. They were staying at the Mercure Paris Tour Eiffel Pont Mirabeau. A nice place with a long name but close to the Seine, which would be important for them later, and the Eiffel Tower should she get the urge to go look. Right now, the tower didn't interest her. Omar turned on the lights.

"I'm going to keep the drapes closed," he said.

"Perfect," she said, and began to undress. She kicked off her jeans and pulled off her Tee-shirt. Her pale white skin contrasted with his darker shade. Reaching back to unhook her bra, she frowned at Omar.

"Why are you standing there like a dope?"

"Tanya—"

She dropped her bra and let him have a look at her. Joy turned to disappointment.

"What is it, Omar?"

"I don't think I can."

She went to him and undid his belt buckle. "Of course, you can."

She felt his breath on her as she pushed his pants down, squatting in front of him. She told him to step out of the jeans. He did so reluctantly. She looked up at him. "Why are you behaving like a man about to be shot?"

"Tanya—"

She stood and leaned into his face. "Hey! We haven't been together—"

"In a long time, Tanya. I know."

"So, come on." She tugged at his shirt. "Throw me on the bed and ravage me."

He took hold of her wrists. Her eyes widened.

"Don't you want me?"

"Yes. But I need time."

"What did they do to you, honey?"

"Put me in a cage."

"You busted out! There's nothing wrong with you."

He moved past her to the bed, pulled down the covers, and finally removed his shirt. He dropped his boxers on top of her jeans. She smiled and came to him, wrapping her arms around his warm torso. His chest hair felt good against her bare skin.

"I still have something on," she said, nudging him. She felt his thumbs hook into the waistband of her panties and then they were on the floor too.

But he wasn't responding.

"Omar?"

"Let's get in bed," he said. "I can't remember the last time I slept in a real bed. We can hold each other. It's all I can do right now."

Her face softened. "All right." She slid onto the bed on her hands and knees, offering another view she assumed he examined with relish. Rolling onto her back, she gestured for him to join her.

He pulled the covers up, turned on his side, and pulled her close. She sighed and rested her head under his neck. She felt warm all over, partly from his body heat, the rest from desire now agonizingly frustrated.

"I'm sorry," he said.

"Just hold me," she said.

It didn't take long for him to doze off. He snored quietly. She didn't feel tired but fell asleep too. Their first time together since his capture hadn't gone the way she planned, but at least he was there, in her arms, and alive.

Twenty-four hours later, the pair lay half asleep in bed, entwined in each other, and Tanya glanced with lazy eyes at the nightstand clock.

"It's past noon," she said.

Omar mumbled into her neck. His body still felt hot against hers and she didn't want to let go. All the tension of the last few days had faded. She felt normal again.

"We missed breakfast."

He moved a hand along her bare leg, reaching between her thighs.

"Mmmmmm," she said.

"I can do one or two things," he said.

She didn't argue. Her body tingled as she let him probe inside her. She gasped as waves of pleasure rolled over her and squeezed him tight. She had gone without him for too long. She wasn't going to cut their time short unless she had to.

They didn't get out of bed until three in the afternoon. Showered and dressed, the drapes still closed, they ordered lunch from room service. Grilled chicken with rice and salad and a pitcher of ice water. Tanya checked in with Sila Kaymak, who was in his room two floors down. All was well. All on schedule.

Omar ate fast.

"Slow down," she told him.

"You wouldn't believe what they tried to make me live on," he said. "Maybe one meal every other day. The rest of the time they forced Ensure down my throat."

"A protein drink?"

"Their idea of torture."

"No wonder you lost so much weight."

He scoffed. "Don't remind me." He gestured at his plate. "I may need more after this. I'm almost useless."

"Not useless at all. Not the way you blasted out of there."

He shook his head. "Pure desperation."

"It comes in handy sometimes."

He nodded and went back to eating.

"What's next?" he said.

"The island," she said. "We'll stay there while Operation Triangle takes place."

He frowned. "Is it safe?"

"It will be. For a while." She looked sad. "Once the strike takes place, the Americans will scorch the earth to find us."

He stopped eating again. "Why did you come for me?"

"I need you."

"For what?"

"I need you *with* me, Omar. I don't want to be alone. I can't do this without you."

He nodded.

"Would you rather I left you there?"

"No." He ate some more.

"I admire how you held out," she said. "They didn't break you." She raised an eyebrow. "Did they?"

He shook his head. "I kept thinking of you. You helped me survive."

She smiled and ate some more.

Omar wiped his mouth and sipped ice water. He set down the glass. "How much did you tell the Americans about the new mission?"

Omar didn't know anything about Operation Triangle. Tanya and the IU leadership planned the mission while he was in custody.

She said, "Only the name."

"Are you sure—"

"We aren't using *our* people, Omar."

"Then who are we using?"

"It's brilliant," she said. "We've hired mercenaries, Omar. *White* men."

"Infidels?"

"Who are being well-paid to carry out a mission. We found cutthroats who have no loyalty to the United States whatsoever. They share more of our hated for the west than you realize."

"What purpose does this serve?"

"Think it over, Omar. The Americans will break their necks looking for leads. They'll harass our people, take prisoners, ask hundreds of questions. They won't find any answers."

"Because we're using white men."

"Exactly. The CIA will chase their tail, miss clues, and thousands will die. It's our crowning achievement."

"It's our death sentence."

She shrugged. "Our point will be made."

"And the point is?"

"They should never have killed my husband."

"Or Francesca's."

Pain flashed across Tanya's face. She put her fork down and sighed. "Yes. Or Francesca's."

"There's something you're not telling me."

"Francesca is gone, Omar. She died in a drone strike."

Omar blinked.

"She posed as me," Tanya said, and explained how she used Francesca's story to pass her off as the real leader of the Islamic Union.

"She *volunteered*?" Omar said.

"She never recovered from Tamal's death," Tanya said. "It was too much for her. She wanted to be with him again."

"A supreme sacrifice." He picked up his water glass. Tanya lifted hers and they toasted their fallen comrade.

"It was enough," she said, "to get me inside. To get you out."

"I'm not sure I'm worth the cost."

"You are to me," she said. "I've already lost Ahmad. I wasn't going to lose you too."

She pushed the remains of her plate to him. He set his empty plate aside and ate some more.

Tanya swallowed some water and watched Omar. He kept his eyes on his plate. She hadn't planned on falling in love again after Ahmad's death at the hands of the Americans. Her meeting him had been out of necessity as he carried out logistical operations in Europe. She'd immediately been smitten the confident operative with the hot brown eyes.

She struggled with the attraction at first. She felt like she was betraying Ahmad. But he'd have wanted her to be happy. She gave in, and Omar responded. They'd seen each other as much as possible until his capture.

The differences between Ahmad and Omar were huge. Omar was more careful. Ahmad had too much rage inside him, rage fueled by the murder of his grandfather. It made him reckless and ultimately cost him his life. Omar was focused, calculating, cold. Emotions did not affect him.

There was no going back now. The Americans knew who she was, and she'd embarrassed them. They'd rattle every cage to find her again. Her only course was to remain in hiding. She hoped the island headquarters provided long-term sanctuary. And if they ever tracked her down, the island provided many means of escape. She also considered altering her face. It might be the only way to avoid the CIA's kill squads and remain a thorn in their side.

But she could figure out those options later.

Right now, she had Omar back. Operation Triangle was underway. Nothing else mattered.

But Sam Raven wasn't far from her thoughts, either. She'd made a fool of him. He'd be looking for her too. And he might prove much more resourceful than the entire CIA.

23

HUGO SCHRADER ATE THE SAME SANDWICH FOR LUNCH every day.

Turkey, mustard, slice of cheddar cheese on wheat bread. Bottle of mineral water and an apple. Every day. He liked order and routine. Now and then proper business forced him to have lunch with clients or prospects. Those meetings might take place in fine restaurants, but the change in routine made the rest of his day difficult. Change threw him mentally off-balance.

Order and routine. Attention to detail. He'd avoided prison by sticking to rules. He'd become successful adhering to similar rules. At 75 years of age, Hugo Schrader saw no reason to change.

His hair hadn't fallen out, but most of the dark hair of his youth was gone, replaced by gray.

Schrader's vibrant eyes missed no detail. His close examination of even the smallest item added to his aura of power, his confident stride. He'd proven himself long ago. Now, he was the aged lion the young pups looked up to.

He sat at his desk in the corner office of a skyscraper

overlooking the Spree River. Schrader Venture Capital was the largest such firm in Germany. The previous year, they'd seen 2.3-billion euros in profit from start-up investments. There'd been a few losers, always were, but the winners made up the difference.

He watched the boats below while finishing his apple. There had been a time when his daughters leaned against the glass to watch the boats too. They'd mark the glass with their fingerprints and breath. Those days were over.

Tanya was across the world fighting the revolution.

His youngest, Hannah, barely spoke to him.

He tossed the apple core and sandwich bag in the wastebasket beside his desk. He then used a spritz of Windex and a microfiber towel to clean the top of his glass desk. He placed the Windex and towel in the bottom drawer. The intercom on his desk buzzed. He pressed the button. "Yes?"

"Mr. Dassler to see you, Mr. Schrader."

"He doesn't have an appointment."

"He says it's urgent."

Schrader frowned. "All right." He switched off the intercom and straightened his tie.

The door opened and Phillip Dassler entered the office. He was Schrader's IT specialist and managed the crew who made sure the company's computer systems functioned without hiccup.

He aided Schrader's side activities, too. Schrader had a sinking feeling his "urgent" visit meant bad news.

Dassler sat only when invited, and Schrader faced him across the clean glass top. "What is it?"

"We're being raided."

Schrader sighed. Dassler was thirty years younger, full of youthful arrogance, as he had been. The blond-haired IT chief looked thick in the middle. He tried to hide his gut with large shirts but with little success.

"Can you explain that in German?"

Dassler said, "Somebody is trying to infiltrate our computer systems."

Schrader shrugged. "Usual competitors looking for a weakness. What's the problem?"

"It's not usual at all, Mr. Schrader. I'm talking about government hackers. They're coming at us hard. They'll get through eventually."

"Move the sensitive data off our systems."

"In progress. I only hope we'll have it cleared off before they get through."

"It's a certainty?"

"Yes."

"Why is BND looking at my company?"

The BND. *Bundesnachrichtendienst.* German Federal Intelligence Service. The largest component of German intelligence.

Dassler's already pale skin lost a little more color. "I think it's the Americans, Mr. Schrader."

Hugo Schrader betrayed no reaction except to blink.

"Why?"

"I have no idea."

"Thank you for telling me, Phillip. Excuse me while I call Mr. Speidel."

Dassler nodded and left the office. He closed the door quietly behind him.

Schrader didn't pick up his desk phone. He now considered it tapped. He wasn't sure he should use his cell phone, but he knew how to make a call seem innocent while communicating critical information.

He selected a name from his contact list and plugged in a Bluetooth earpiece.

Two rings. Then: "Yes, Mr. Schrader?"

Sebastian Speidel was almost as efficient as Schrader.

Hugo also liked that his initials spelled out S.S. A novelty, but an appropriate one.

"See me at my office. Most important."

"Something wrong?"

"Get here as soon as possible." Schrader cut off the call before Speidel asked more questions. He might be efficient, but he had a habit of gathering all available information before taking action. Schrader was trying to break him of the habit.

While he waited, he told his secretary to cancel his afternoon meetings. He turned his chair to look out at the river. His mind raced while his face remained impassive.

What were the Americans up to?

What did the hacking attempt have to do with Tanya's visit to the United States?

Within thirty minutes Schrader's secretary announced Speidel's arrival. The office door swung open. Speidel wore a gray suit and black tie to match his black-framed glasses. Another blond, hair slicked back, straight jawline and prominent chin. "I'm here, Mr. Schrader."

"Somebody is trying to hack our computers, and Dassler thinks it's the Americans."

"I was afraid of such a thing."

"Sit down and tell me why."

Speidel took a chair and crossed his legs. "Francesca Sloan may have been killed."

"*May*?"

"I've yet to confirm. I'm only hearing chatter at this time."

"Once again you're waiting too long to give me information I need, Sebastian."

Speidel shrugged off the comment. "I'm not going to pass along gossip, sir."

Like Dassler, Sebastian Speidel did double-duty at Schrader Venture Capital. Dassler worked in cyberspace to keep Schrader's subversive activities from prying eyes. Speidel took the physical roll of enforcer, fixer, and intelligence chief.

"Tell me what you've learned," Schrader said.

"I'm hearing she was killed in a drone strike in Syria around the same time as Tanya was in the United States."

"What's the connection?"

"I'm not sure. The Americans are undercover in Syria looking for terrorists. They may have gotten lucky. Tanya is safe in Paris, after all."

Schrader nodded. He watched Speidel's face. The younger man's eyes and the shift in his sitting position suggested he had more to say. "What are you holding back?"

"I'm afraid Tanya didn't tell you the truth about her mission in the US. She may have compromised us."

Schrader's voice rose. "How?"

"There was a break-out in the detention center where Omar Talman was being held. A helicopter collected him. Who else but Tanya would attempt a rescue?"

"She might."

"Which means she wasn't only coordinating Operation Triangle. She may not have been coordinating at all. You'll remember, sir, I was against her visit to begin with. There was no reason for her to go."

"But my daughter is as stubborn as her mother," Schrader said.

"You need to talk to her before she reaches the island. Before the Americans unravel Operation Triangle and your activities along with it."

Schrader took a deep breath and let it out. "You're young, Sebastian. Back in the old days, we'd sweat out news like this, two or three times a week."

"I have told you everything I'm working on currently."

"Of course. Come back when you have more. I'm particularly interested in why our systems are being probed."

Speidel nodded sharply, rose from the chair, and exited the office.

Schrader turned to look out the window again, but the view didn't register.

When he was the age of Dassler and Speidel, he'd been in the Red Army Faction. Some called it the Baader-Meinhof Gang, but the group had never accepted the name as official. They weren't a gang. They were the vanguard of a new revolution to overthrow a corrupt system of government. His old comrades were dead. He was the only one left.

Schrader had decided to use capitalism in order to subvert capitalism. Revolutions weren't free. He used his wealth to fund what western intelligence might call "terrorist cells". He had no such derogatory view of them. They were freedom fighters. Young people eager for change.

Western ideology represented oppression of the poor and the promotion of the rich. He saw how much money his clients reaped. The successful ones paid back the investment and kept more for themselves while paying employees a pittance and expecting undying loyalty in return.

He imagined a world where everybody existed on a level field, with no more and no less than anybody else. But Schrader had learned long ago only the point of a gun brought about such a society. Far too many would resist a normal change of government, and the slow drip approach didn't appeal to him either. No matter which route he chose to implement the vision, the rich and powerful would fight back. But they didn't care who died in the process. They'd sacrifice as many pawns as necessary.

Society had to be broke before they could accomplish any significant rebuilding. Breaking down society required guns and bombs and a willing group to use them as designed. His activities may not bring about change, but they caused instability. From such instability leaders would emerge to lead the way to the promised land.

It was the young people who would carry out the change. The youth were ripe to come to power and make the world equal. They were currently living through the worst the old system had to offer. They knew the horror of inequality first-hand. In the old days, it had been a tough argument to make. Now? Not at all.

He might be dead by the time such changes occurred, but his crystal ball was clear. The revolution would happen. Sooner than the world realized.

Tanya, his oldest daughter, his protegee, was carrying out her end. The news of Francesca Sloan's reported death saddened him, as, he knew, it hurt Tanya more. Battle spared no soldier. Even the ones who walked away carried a permanent reminder of the fight. What made Schrader less sad was Francesca hadn't died a traitor. He'd seen his share of those, too.

He often feared his youngest daughter, Hannah, would betray him. As much as it pained him to do so, he knew he had to place her under surveillance. If the Americans were coming for him, they'd know she was a potential source of information.

If Tanya was his greatest success, Hannah was his failure.

24

RAVEN CLEARED CUSTOMS AT BERLIN'S TEGEL AIRPORT without fanfare. He traveled under one of his cover names. He'd have preferred a direct approach, but Clark Wilson convinced him otherwise.

"You can bet they'll be watching for you," Wilson said.

"They will disappoint me if they aren't. A head-on fight is better than sneaking around at this point."

"We don't want you getting whacked before you learn anything, Sam. You're on the payroll. Follow orders."

Raven laughed. "You know who you're talking to, right?"

Wilson had conceded the fact Raven was never very good at following orders.

But Raven also wasn't in the mood for a wrestling match with the CIA. Not this time. They were working toward a common goal. Cooperation mattered more than personal preference. This time.

Wilson had also advised Raven on a potential ally in the Hugo Schrader household.

"His daughter Hannah," Wilson said. "She's ten years younger than Tanya. We dug up a string of emails between her and Tanya. She begged Tanya not to go to the Middle East. She didn't want to be left alone with their father."

"He abused her or something?"

"They don't get along. He filled them with stories of the glorious Red Army Faction growing up. Tanya ate it up. Hannah thought it was disgusting."

"Sounds like Tanya was predisposed to turning subversive and found her excuse with Ahmad Jafari."

"A fair assessment."

"Where do I find Hannah?"

Wilson provided her current apartment address and told Raven to work his magic.

Except Raven had no ideas for how to approach the younger of the two Schrader daughters.

There wasn't time for the standard cultivation of an asset. No "meet cute" and conversation followed by a pitch to help the Americans catch her sister. Operation Triangle was in progress. The Islamic Union would strike sooner rather than later. Raven had no intention of playing games when innocent lives were at risk.

The CIA provided the location of a local safe house, but Raven wanted to save it for a backup. After navigating the busy terminal to baggage claim, he collected his two suitcases. Outside in the crisp summer afternoon, he found a cab. The driver took him to the Radisson Blu Hotel where he'd reserved a room.

"How is Paris?"

Hugo Schrader sat at his desk, his back to the window, holding the desk phone to his ear. A sweep of the telephone system revealed no tapped lines.

"I'm fine, Papa."

"Tell me what you did in America."

Silence.

"Tanya?"

"I did what I told you, Papa. I put elements in motion for the project."

"You're lying, Tanya."

"I am not."

"What happened to Francesca? What aren't you telling me, Tanya?"

"I did—"

"What?"

"Other things."

"You were there to get Omar, weren't you?"

"More or less. He got himself out. I only gave the signal."

"You've exposed us, Tanya. You've put the project in jeopardy."

"Nothing can stop what we are doing, Papa."

"They'll try."

"There's somebody you should watch for," Tanya said. "His name is Sam Raven."

"Why him?"

"He brought me to the Americans. I used him specifically because I knew he'd believe my story."

"What story, Tanya?"

"I told them—" She stopped. "Not on the phone, Papa."

"I'm getting the general idea."

"Francesca sacrificed herself for us, Papa. It was the only way to send the Americans off course."

"Tell me more about Sam Raven," Schrader said. "Tell me what he looks like. Better yet, send me a picture."

RAVEN DIDN'T BOTHER to unpack right away. He used his phone to plot directions to Hannah Schrader's apartment. She was fifteen minutes away if traffic wasn't terrible. A five-minute phone call arranged for a nearby Hertz office to bring him a rental car. They brought him a blue Audi A5.

Only after signing for the car did Raven unpack—sort of. He left his clothes in the suitcases but removed the X-ray proof bottom of one. Inside waited his Nighthawk Custom Talon .45 autoloader, shoulder harness, ammunition and spare 8-round magazines.

He drove to Hannah's apartment complex and parked curbside around the corner. His shoes tapped on the quiet lobby's tiled floor. A wall of mailboxes, elevators, rear exit to the courtyard. All very clean and Germanly spartan. There was no tenant directory. In the middle of the day, he expected she was still at work.

He drove to Schrader Venture Capital and found curbside parking space a block away. He returned on foot, pausing a moment to watch the boat traffic in the Spree. The busy locals on the sidewalk ignored it. Across the street, a pair of tourists snapped pictures of the waterway.

The lobby of the skyscraper buzzed with activity. Men and women in suits stood around talking or hurrying in and out of elevators. He spoke to the security guard at the front desk and asked to see a representative. When the guard inquired why, Raven told him he wanted to discuss an investment proposal. The guard made a call and told Raven to wait. He found a black leather seat in the corner and sat with his back to the wall.

A tall man in a dark suit and black-framed glasses found him there.

"Mr. Cooper?"

Raven had used his cover name of Isaac Cooper. He stood, smiling, extending a hand. "Yes. Who might you be?"

"I am Sebastian Speidel, special assistant to Mr. Schrader."

"I didn't realize I'd get the royal treatment."

"We will talk here. My job is to make sure you meet our qualifications. If you do not, we go no further."

Raven put his hands in his pockets. "Sure."

"You're American?"

"Yes."

"Why are you in Germany?"

"My business partner and I want to expand into the European market. We make custom musical instruments. High-end guitars."

"Uh-huh."

"We've picked up several endorsements already in the States, and we're negotiating with members of Ramstein to use our equipment."

"Who?"

"Ramstein. One of the biggest heavy metal bands in your country. I thought everybody in Germany knew of them."

"No."

Raven laughed. "Of course. My mistake."

"Mr. Cooper, we do not work with companies who generate less than one million dollars."

Raven blinked. "Oh. Well. No problem there. When I say high-end guitars, I mean equipment with a starting price of five thousand US."

"Surely you cannot generate one million a year selling guitars."

"I can prove it, of course."

"You have sales records with you?"

"At my hotel. If you'd like to schedule a formal meeting, I'd be happy to provide details."

"Very interesting. What sort of investment help would you be looking for?"

"I don't want to talk numbers here in your lobby, Mr.

Speidel. We have a modest proposal I'm sure your company will appreciate."

"Hmmm. Well, I will have to discuss this with Mr. Schrader. I have a feeling you will be too small for us, no matter your gross sales numbers."

Raven shrugged. "German musicians will like our products."

"Who did you say you represent again?"

"I didn't actually. Cooper Instruments. We have a web page. Cooper Instruments Dot Com."

"Of course." Speidel smiled. "We will research and get back with you."

Raven pulled out his wallet and made a show of looking inside. He sighed with a shake of his head. "I'm out of business cards."

Speidel only smiled.

"I'm staying at the Radisson Blu," Raven said. "I'm not hard to find."

The two men shook hands again and Raven left the lobby. He didn't look back to see if Speidel was watching him. Raven had no doubt he was.

SEBASTIAN SPEIDEL ENTERED the office of Schrader's secretary. He said nothing to the woman and knocked twice on Schrader's door before stepping inside.

Schrader did not look up from his paperwork. He held a gold fountain pen and scratched his signature on several sheets.

"What is it, Sebastian?"

"Sam Raven just paid us a visit, Mr. Schrader. The picture Tanya sent us was accurate."

Schrader scribbled his name on another sheet of paper, set it aside, and signed another. "And?"

"He's staying at the Radisson Blu."

"Good. Kill him."

"Yes, sir."

Speidel left the office.

25

RAVEN FIGURED ON ·A DIRECT APPROACH TO HANNAH Schrader but not in public.

Not with her under surveillance.

The two goons who followed her from work to a bar wore pressed gray suits. They fit well with the rest of the bar's happy hour clientele. Hannah didn't notice their presence. Or was she used to them being there?

She met two girlfriends at a small hotel bar. It sat off the lobby, tempting new arrivals as they headed for the elevators. The décor wasn't fancy. The mirrored walls made a futile attempt at making the place look bigger than it was. Muted televisions screens on two walls played either news programs or sports.

Raven took a seat in a back corner and read a newspaper. There weren't many patrons, so he had a decent view of Hannah, her friends, and the goons who watched her.

Hannah Schrader wore a typical skirt-and-blouse combo. She'd removed her heels after sitting down, and the shoes rested beside her chair. She sat with her elbows on the table, leaning toward her friends, her nyloned feet on the floor.

Hannah's bright blonde hair matched one of the other girls. The third member of their trio was a brunette who wore her hair very short.

The brunette apologized for insisting on the hotel instead of their usual bar. She didn't want to "see you-know-who tonight". Hannah and the other blonde didn't mind. Hannah exclaimed, "Alcohol is alcohol!" as the waiter brought their drinks. Hannah was a whiskey drinker. The waiter placed a double in front of her.

The brunette ordered fried mozzarella poppers before the waiter departed. Raven cringed. Fried cheese? It wasn't a worthwhile snack at any time of day.

Her two minders glanced at her from time to time but didn't make the effort obvious. They kept up an animated conversation with a running commentary on the sports program.

He sat with his paper and martini and waited.

He needed Hannah alone for his approach to work. Would the goons hang around?

HANNAH SCHRADER EASED her car through the automatic gate. She parked in a spot with her apartment number on a post. Raven lost sight of her as she crossed the parking lot to a connecting gate. She'd travel through the courtyard to her place in the complex.

The answer to the question about the goons came fast. They followed her home, taking the turn before the complex and driving off. No need to watch her when she was at home, Raven supposed.

He still didn't know if the surveillance was routine or new. Was Hugo having her followed in case the CIA came calling about her sister?

Raven left the rented Audi parked on the street and entered the complex through the lobby. Stepping out onto the courtyard, he found a bench. He sat with a view of Hannah's third-floor balcony. The light snapped on behind the glass balcony doors.

He leaned back on the bench with crossed legs and stretched his right arm along the back edge. The courtyard, shielded from the street by the buildings, was quiet. Nearby flowers filled the air with a pleasant scent. Raven waited with a mix of uncertainty and confidence.

He had to win Hannah over and fast.

He hoped his approach worked. And he hoped he could keep Hannah out of danger.

GETTING out of her suit and stockings was always the best part of Hannah Schrader's day. She traded her work clothes for jeans and a sweatshirt. In the kitchen, she filled a pitcher with water and proceeded to water the plants around the living room. Some hung from the ceiling, others supported on stands in corners. They were lush and green and added to the apartment's color explosion. She'd covered the walls with brightly colored Egyptian tapestries. Red and green furniture, loud throw rugs. She lived alone and had nobody else to impress.

She flipped the latch on the patio door and stepped onto the balcony. More plants lined the top of the wooden rail.

She hadn't minded meeting Jenny and Val at the hotel bar. Catching up with the pair was always a highlight of her week. They'd grown up together and had a tight bond. But their regular bar had dancing. She needed a few drinks and a couple of spins on the dance floor to rid her mind of the funk she fell into every day she worked for her father.

Hannah worked in the press office. She coordinated coverage for the company's business activities. She didn't interact with her father often. Their differences had become too great over the years. He kept trying to maintain contact, but she always pulled away. Especially since Tanya left.

Her father was not a good man. Deep down she knew he'd never see the error of his ways. He'd instigated too much violence already; several murders she was sure of.

She wanted to quit and leave Berlin. With her mother gone, and Tanya playing guns with terrorists, she was the only one who might be able to shed light on their activity. But she knew her father often had men watching her. Contacting German intelligence or visiting the US embassy was out of the question. She'd be intercepted and taken to her father and then what?

Hannah didn't have any interest in politics and didn't understand the appeal of setting off bombs and killing people over disagreements. Somehow her father had pulled Tanya into his point of view, but not her.

She filled two pots and returned to the kitchen for more water. Out on the balcony once again, she watered the third plant in the line, and paused. A man sat on a bench in the courtyard. She didn't recognize him as a regular resident. The community within the building was small and she knew most of the faces. His was different. What was also odd to her was that he wasn't fiddling with his phone. He was sitting still.

She continued moving down the plant line. Maybe he was more comfortable being alone than she. She didn't want to live alone, but decent guys were hard to find. Hannah filled the last pot with water. As she turned to go back inside, she stopped. The man at the bench had gone.

Then she heard a knock at the door.

RAVEN CLEARED his throat as he waited. He stood dead center to the apartment door's spy hole to give Hannah an unobstructed view of his face.

The peep hole darkened a moment before he heard her say, "Who is there?"

"My name is Sam Raven. I need to talk to you about Tanya."

A sharp intake of breath; a latch rattled. The door opened but stopped when the chain above the locks pulled taut. Part of Hannah's face appeared in the gap.

"What about Tanya?"

"I'm an American agent," he said, keeping his voice low in the hallway. "Tanya is planning to kill thousands of people and I need your help to stop her."

Hannah's eyes widened.

"If you let me in, we can talk about it," he added, "and if you say no, I'll leave."

The door slammed. The chain rattled. The door opened again, and she moved back. "Hurry."

Raven stepped inside.

26

"WHY WERE YOU WAITING ON THE BENCH?" SHE SAID.

"Making sure your minders weren't watching you."

"The two men at the bar?"

"I saw them," Raven said. "They went their own way when they saw you come home. I thought they might have backup waiting."

Hannah Schrader dropped her head and ran both hands over her face. "He *always* has people watching me."

They stood in the entry way. Hannah turned and went into the kitchen. Raven stayed a few steps away as she filled a glass of wine. She didn't offer him one. Hannah leaned against the counter and said, "Okay, talk."

Raven told her the story from the beginning to his arrival in Germany. Hannah didn't touch her wine the entire time. She set the glass down.

"I think I'm going to be sick."

She brushed past him on her way down the hall. The bathroom door shut. Raven wandered into the living room. He blinked in surprise at the colorful decorations. He sat on the couch.

The toilet flushed and a few moments later Hannah emerged. She grabbed her wine from the kitchen and sat across from him.

"This has been their plan all along."

"What has?"

Hannah said, "Creating a new terrorist group. I know everything! I suspect a whole lot more."

"Sounds like it's your turn to tell a story."

"My father's a nut. When Tanya started going out with Ahmad, he didn't like it at first. Then he started getting ideas."

"What kind of ideas?"

"After that truck attack, there was this wave of anti-Muslim sentiment through Berlin," she said. "It didn't last long. Couple weeks. But there were roving gangs going around attacking Muslims and I think my father was paying them."

"Why?"

"Ahmad and Tamal were paranoid about being targeted," she said. "They were doing their speaking events, right? Visiting the beer halls, trying to get people to understand not all Muslims are terrorists."

"I think I know where this is going," Raven said.

"Take a guess?"

"Ahmad and Tamal's families were attacked," he said. "Somebody killed Tamal's grandfather, right?"

"No, it was *Ahmad's* grandfather. Tamal lost two members of his family, I forget who, but after it happened, those roving gangs vanished."

"And your father changed his approach?"

"He kept having Tanya, Francesca, and their boyfriends over for dinner. He kept telling the men that they needed to strike back. They needed an organization and manpower and money. He *offered* to supply what they needed."

"How did they react?" Raven said.

"They were angry. And my father can be very persuasive. It took a few meetings, but they agreed."

"And your sister and Francesca Sloan went along?"

"Especially Tanya. She wanted to help Ahmad avenge his grandfather."

"Did Tanya know your father had the grandfather killed?"

"Absolutely not. She and my father were always talking about the old days of the Red Army Faction. With Ahmad she saw her chance to further the cause, or some crap like that. I tried to tell her, but she wouldn't listen."

"You have proof?"

Hannah shook her head. "I think I know where to get proof. All I had at the time was suspicions. It clicked for me when two men were arrested for beating a Muslim in the street. One of them was a man I'd seen at my father's office."

"Uh-huh."

"You sound like you don't believe me."

"No, unfortunately, I do. It's a lot to take in. The CIA figured it was Ahmad and Tamal's idea to form the Islamic Union. We suspected your father might be funding them, but the idea of him manipulating the group into existence never occurred to us."

"He calls the Islamic Union his proxy army. Can you believe that?"

"He gets to finish what Meinhof started and, more or less, keep his hands clean."

"So he thinks," she said.

"Tanya took over when Ahmad and Tamal died, right?"

"She faced resistance, but my father threatened to cut off the money if she wasn't installed. She's his eyes and ears. She reports regularly."

"Where is she now?" Raven said.

"I don't know. But now Tanya has become this monster

my father can't stop. And he doesn't want to! He thinks it's some sort of achievement." Her face softened. "But poor Fran. Tanya worked hard to convince her to go. Fran wanted to stay behind and find other ways to help, but she also didn't want to leave Tamal."

"Where is this proof you mentioned?"

"My father's safe. At least there will be something there for you to work with. There's an investor party tomorrow."

"Can you get me inside?"

"As press officer I have to be there to talk to the media, and nobody will look twice if I'm giving a reporter a tour."

"Good idea."

Her eyes dropped to her wine. She still hadn't touched it. Finally, she took a long drink.

Raven could only imagine the stress she felt working with a man she knew was a monster. He admired her fortitude. It took a strong spirit to put up with the surveillance and the knowledge in her head. Never mind the suspicions. She didn't need to dwell on suspicions when she had hard facts of her father's wrongdoing.

Raven said, "Who else has your father financed? I'm assuming his venture capital firm is a front for funding more than the Islamic Union."

She shrugged. "I don't know for sure. You'd have to grill either Sebastian Speidel or Phillip Dassler."

"I've met Speidel," Raven said. "Who is Dassler?"

"He handles the computers. If my father is keeping any records hidden, Dassler would be the one to hide them among the company servers. There's talk around the office that somebody is trying to hack the servers, and Dassler is working overtime to keep it from happening."

Raven nodded. "My friends in the US," he said. He smiled. "Sounds like they're keeping him busy."

"Tomorrow at the party," she said, "I can get you into my father's office."

"I don't want to put you in danger, Hannah."

"I've *been* in danger since this started!" she said. "I won't be *out* of danger until my father is arrested."

"Hannah," he said, "we aren't interested in *arresting* anybody."

She swallowed more wine. She emptied the glass. "Well," she said, "I suppose he deserves whatever he gets."

Raven bit off his response to her comment. He shook his head instead. The damage Hugo Schrader had inflicted was too deep to repair. The man had two beautiful daughters, the world at his fingertips. He let it all go because of leftover dreams of "the revolution". He had no idea how lucky he was simply to have his daughters beside him. Raven knew a lot of guys who didn't know how lucky they were yet lived with the fact that he wouldn't be counted among them.

Because of people like Hugo Schrader.

"I'll take you up on your offer," Raven said, "but then I need to get you out of here. You won't be able to stay."

"I don't care if I never see Berlin again after this."

"You might," he said. "We'll take it a step at a time."

They discussed the party and how to contact each other during the festivities. She saw Raven out and he walked down the hall with a heavy weight on his shoulders.

He lived by two rules. The first was no gun fights in public where innocent people might be hurt. He wasn't in the business of creating more victims. His arrangement with Hannah set the stage for at least *one* innocent person being harmed. He wasn't sure he could keep her shielded from the worst. Her father was a fanatic who had killed people to manipulate others into carrying out his personal agenda. Raven had come across more evil characters in his time than he cared to admit, but Hugo Schrader took the cake.

Back in the rented Audi, Raven returned to his hotel. He had a long report to make to Clark Wilson.

If the CIA supplied some backup, Raven decided, it might help their odds.

He needed all the help he could get on this mission.

27

HANNAH REMAINED ON THE COUCH WITH A BLANK STARE.

Her mind was a jumble of thoughts and emotions. She felt numb. There was no way to recapture the ugly truths she'd spoken. What had remained internal for so long, subject to endless debate, now took on a life of its own.

The thought of her father not surviving didn't bother her. The coldness of such a realization added more shock to her system. Was this a temporary feeling? He was her father; how could she not care?

Too much damage over the years, she realized. Too much "rah-rah revolution" between him and Tanya while her objections went ignored. He'd never taken a moment to understand why she didn't agree. He thought she was wrong; he'd tell her how wrong she was until she finally said, "Yes, Papa," and accepted her proper place.

No.

What about the innocent people he'd killed? What about taking advantage of other people's pain to make *them* kill for *him*? All in the name of an insane "cause" with no end in sight. Only more death and destruction.

More thoughts crashed through her mind.

How would she live after he was gone?

Why had she *really* stayed?

Fear of being alone?

Hoping he would turn around?

Hannah had no answers. And now it was too late.

Her father and her sister had to be stopped.

RAVEN DROVE down the underground parking ramp beneath the Radisson Blu. He parked the Audi and exited. A chill crawled up his neck. He opened his jacket for easy access to the Nighthawk Custom Talon under his left arm. The snout of the attached suppressor extended through the end of the holster.

He squatted between the Audi and the car next to his and listened.

Fluorescent lights buzzed. A hum of HVAC units rumbled above. Feet shuffled. A whisper.

An ambush.

Raven took out his gun and clicked off the safety. He didn't want a fight here. The garage was a death trap and anybody leaving the hotel might get caught in the crossfire. He had to get to the surface. Lead his ambushers away from bystanders. He glanced over the trunk of the Audi. The ramp to the street looked about 50 yards away.

The red dot of a laser sight flashed on his chest.

Raven fired once. With no clear target, he aimed the gun at an upward angle. The snap of the suppressed .45 echoed in the concrete confines. The slug whined off a pillar. The red dot vanished. Somebody yelled. Raven broke into a run for the ramp.

Suppressed gunfire cracked behind him. The rapid *phuts*

filled the space. Raven's pulse raced and he ran faster. The salvo smacked the ground, nipped at his heels, and punched through cars.

Raven cut right, another salvo behind him. He reached the ramp and turned left, covered by walls on either side. The chilly night greeted him as he gained the sidewalk. He held the Nighthawk close to his leg to keep it hidden.

Traffic was light on Karl-Liebknecht-Strasse in front of the hotel. He didn't cross the street. He jammed the gun back in its holster and ran along the sidewalk. The hotel bordered the Spree River. KLS crossed over the river. As he neared the edge where the road ended at the waterway, he saw no access under the overpass.

A glance back. Three men emerged from the underground garage. Their heads moved back and forth as they looked for him. At a break in traffic, he ran across the street. A construction zone hidden behind a cluster of trees waited. Raven reached the other side when he heard a shout.

The building under construction consisted of a wooden frame. Building materials and heavy vehicles filled the area. Raven ducked within the trees. Shadows enveloped him. The three men dodged cars and ignored horns as they followed.

The construction area would have to do. At least there was nobody present with the workday over.

And now the kill team was coming to him. If he could keep the advantage, the fight wouldn't last long.

Raven's shoes scratched on gravel as he ran for a forklift. A stack of two-by-fours sat on the blades of the lift. He dropped behind the wood.

The killers fanned out through the trees. They carried CZ Scorpion EVO 3 submachine guns with the stocks folded. Each weapon equipped with a suppressor.

Raven took out his gun and stretched out on the ground. The gap between the ground and the two-by-fours gave him a small view. He saw the legs of the killers as they closed the distance.

He stayed still, breathing deep.

One of the killers edged closer to the tree line. His next step would expose him as he entered the construction area. The killer stayed by the tree trunk as he scanned with his EVO 3 tucked close to his body.

The killer put a hand to his ear. The team was communicating via wireless ear buds. He lowered his hand and put it back on the Scorpion. But he didn't move from his position. Raven had no way of seeing where the other two were. He needed to take out the first killer, grab his weapon, and search for the other pair.

Then the killer moved.

He rose, bent at the waist, and stepped into the open. Raven fired. The .45 thumped in his hand. The killer dropped face first onto the gravel. Raven fired again. He eased back from the forklift, stood, and glanced around. The other pair wasn't in sight. But it didn't mean they wouldn't see him when he broke cover too.

Raven took the chance. He raced around the forklift, extended the Nighthawk to his right. No shots came his way. He reached the dead killer, grabbed the back of his shirt and dragged the man into the cover of the trees.

Raven put away his gun. He took the Scorpion and searched the killer's pockets for more magazines. He found two spares in the man's jacket. They held 20 rounds and had clear plastic on each side to show the number of rounds. Raven put the magazines in his own jacket pockets.

Raven stayed in the trees as he moved left. Street noise covered his approach. He neared the partially constructed building.

The two remaining gunmen weren't together. Raven

watched one of the shooters looking around the scattered construction material. Where was the other?

He stayed low and left the trees, entering the partial building through a gap. His foot scraped on the dusty concrete floor. The gunmen ahead whirled around. He brought up his gun as Raven pulled the EVO 3's trigger. The SMG chattered a short burst. The round stitched the gunman stomach to chest, and he fell against a wheelbarrow.

The crash echoed. Raven ran to the fallen gunman and scooped up his Scorpion. An SMG in each hand, he pivoted left. The third gunman fired over the top of a wall. Raven rolled right as the suppressed rounds smacked the ground.

Raven fired both Scorpions, missing as the gunman moved from the wall. Raven scrambled to his feet and charged for a gap as the gunman appeared in the opening. Raven fired. The EVO 3 in his right hand spat a burst and locked open on empty. The EVO 3 in his left fired longer before the mag emptied, and most of the rounds hit the third gunner.

The man's right leg and part of his gut took the blow of the salvo. Raven kicked the man's Scorpion away as he hit the ground. His wail bounced around the partial building. Raven needed to hurry. He dropped the two SMGs and drew his .45 and shot the gunner in the head. The man lay still.

Raven put his gun away and ran. He needed distance and time to work his way back to the hotel. Hugo Schrader had made his first move. Now Raven had to return the favor.

28

SEBASTIAN SPEIDEL DROVE THROUGH THE ARCHWAY AS THE automatic iron gate swung open.

Schrader's home sat on the shore of Lake Tegel. With its own private beach, the home overlooked Reiswerder Island, which sat in the center of the lake.

At night, only the lights inside the house marked the property. The forest in the area was so massive it almost choked the patch of open land on which Schrader had built his home. Speidel followed the paved road. In the darkness on either side, he knew cameras followed the car. The security team inside knew of his arrival.

Two armed men met the car at the front of the house. Speidel parked in the circular driveway and exited the car. The guards didn't acknowledge his arrival, but instead escorted him inside. Up a spiral staircase to the second floor, the guards brought him to Schrader's study. The old man stood by a pair of open French windows looking out into the dark. A chill filled the room.

"Not much to see this time of night," Speidel said. The guards departed. One shut the study door behind him.

"No," Schrader agreed. "But I like to imagine my own view when the sun goes down."

Speidel had sat and talked with the boss on the balcony many times. On the wall adjacent to the balcony, Schrader had his crew construct a set of steps embedded down the length of the wall. A support rail alongside the steps helped steady anybody descending the emergency escape route to the patio. From there, the plan called for heading for the lake and Schrader's boat there or gaining alternate access to the garage.

"What do you imagine?" Speidel asked.

Schrader looked over his shoulder with a grin. "I'm keeping that to myself."

The study was as spartan as everything else Hugo Schrader touched. Bare walls except for various paintings Speidel had no interest in. No book cases. Small corner bar. Conference table in another corner. Clean desk with computer and printer.

Schrader moved to his desk. Speidel stood in front of the desk. There were no chairs for him.

"Raven is dead?" Schrader said.

"No."

Schrader raised an eyebrow. "What happened?"

Speidel described the confrontation between Raven and the three killers as he knew it. Having not been there, he was relying on their lack of contact and police reports after the discovery of the bodies.

"Unfortunate."

"Yes, sir."

"What is also unfortunate," Schrader said, "is that the CIA managed to penetrate our servers."

"What did they download?"

Schrader chuckled. "Nothing. We booted them out. The hack was very brief."

"They might have found something."

"From a small scrap of data that may be incomplete? I think you overestimate them."

"We need to—"

"Wipe the servers. Yes. In progress. If they try again, they will find nothing but legitimate business information."

"And the rest of our files?"

"Secured on the backup servers on the island, Sebastian."

"What about Raven?" Speidel said.

"Will he be at the party tomorrow, or leave the country?"

"He knows you know who he is. I can't imagine he'd be stupid enough to show up."

"What do you think he'll do?"

"He was seen near your daughter, sir. If he thinks Hannah has any information the CIA can use, he'll grab her and go."

Another eyebrow. "Explain."

"Hannah met friends at a hotel bar. The men I had following her spotted Raven watching her. They trailed him as he followed Hannah to her apartment."

"Did he visit her?"

"They think so. He parked his car halfway down the block. My men turned off to go around the block and see what he did. They didn't have orders to enter the apartment."

Schrader nodded.

"What do we do with Hannah, sir?"

Schrader let out a sigh. "It's regretful, but she must die."

"Are you positive?"

He nodded as a hint of sadness washed over his face. "She left me a long time ago. Tanya is my triumph, Sebastian. Hannah is my failure. Tanya will finish what I started.

"If Raven shows up," Schrader continued, "let him take her. Follow them to their destination, which will probably be a CIA safe house. Then, wipe them out. We'll send a message with the corpses."

Speidel said he would issue the new orders. Schrader dismissed him.

RAVEN SLIPPED BACK into the hotel through another exit. He made his way to his room and shut the door.

He opened the drapes. The windows didn't overlook the street. They instead overlooked the inside of the hotel and the tall blue aquarium in the center of the lobby.

The aquarium was a tall cylinder of water on a platform supported by steel legs. Bright lights inside highlighted the blue water and the fish swimming within.

Sitting on the edge of the bed, he called Clark Wilson in the US.

"I need some CCTV cameras scrubbed," Raven said.

"What happened?"

"Schrader made a move. Sent three killers after me. I left the bodies at a construction site across the street from the hotel."

"Which hotel?"

Raven gave him the name and the nearby streets.

"We'll cover the cameras," Wilson said. "It's good you didn't wait to call."

"Not my first rodeo."

"What else is happening?"

Raven filled him in on his meeting with Hannah Schrader and the party the following night.

"It is no longer safe to attend, Sam," Wilson said.

"Meaning what?"

"Our hacking team managed to break through Schrader's firewalls for exactly thirty seconds," Wilson said. "We grabbed a little data, but who knows if it's worth anything."

"So far this doesn't mean anything to me."

"Now they're erasing the servers."

"Destroying evidence?"

"They'll have a backup somewhere, but Schrader is covering his tracks. We won't get anything from his computers. Which means he'll have another surprise waiting for you at the party."

"Which means," Raven completed, "Hannah is in danger."

"Do you think she has any information we can use; maybe details she hasn't thought of?"

"We'll have to ask."

"Get her to a safe house. I have two other guys in the area who can back you up."

"Who?"

"Macedo and Storey. You don't know them but they're good."

Raven checked his watch. "We need to move fast. Have them meet me at Hannah's address. I'm going there now."

"Take it easy, Sam."

"You get those CCTV cameras scrubbed and I'll get Hannah to the safe house. The clock is ticking on Operation Triangle and if we don't find a lead—"

"You don't have to tell me, Sam. I'm well aware of the stakes."

"Keep them in mind. Talk soon."

Raven ended the call.

29

RAVEN CALLED HANNAH ON HIS CELL AS HE DROVE.

No answer. The call went to voicemail.

Raven dropped his phone into a cup holder and tried not to think the worst.

The point of his personal crusade against the world's predators was not to create more victims. But sometimes, no matter his effort, the worst indeed happened, and he found himself standing above the bodies of those he tried to save.

The only course of action after each tragedy was scorching vengeance. Make the enemy pay. He didn't want to add Hannah's name to his list of failures.

Raven weaved through traffic and drove faster.

THE ELEVATOR RIDE didn't take long but felt like an eternity.

Raven stepped off on Hannah's floor and listened. Only the muffled sounds behind locked doors greeted him.

Holding the Nighthawk .45 under his jacket, he advanced along the hall. Stopped at her door. No sign of forced entry.

The outward appearance meant nothing. If she knew the crew her father sent, if he had sent anybody, they wouldn't have to force their way inside.

He knocked hard. "Hannah, it's Sam."

He counted the passing seconds by the thumping of his pulse.

The lock clicked and the door opened, stopped by a chain. Hannah's worried face filled the gap.

"What?"

Raven stepped closer. "We gotta get you out of here *tonight*."

"But—"

"Your father is sending people, they're on their way."

Hannah shut the door, unhooked the chain, and let Raven inside.

Any relief he felt as she shut and locked the door didn't last long. All it meant was he'd arrived first. Unless he was overreacting. Would the old man really send a kill team after his daughter?

Raven explained the attempt on his life as she packed, and the more he spoke, the faster she moved. Hannah filled a small suitcase with clothes and essentials. Wiping sweat from her brow, she said, "Where are we going?"

"CIA safe house. Then we get you out of the country."

"For how—"

Raven's phone rang. He held up a finger and answered.

"This is Greg Macedo," the caller said. "Wilson sent me."

"There's supposed to be two of you."

"Mitch Storey is in the car with me. Where are you?"

"Asset's apartment. What's your 20?"

"Parked outside."

Raven described his car. "We'll be out in two minutes."

"We're in a silver BMW."

"I'll stay on your six all the way."

"Copy."

Raven hung up. He said to Hannah, "I don't know how long."

Her excited eyes examined his face. But her expression also showed resolve.

"We better go," she said, "and stop my father and sister from doing something terrible."

Raven took her suitcase in his left hand. They exited the apartment.

RAVEN PUSHED a Bluetooth bud into his ear and dialed Macedo. The elevator descended quietly.

"Macedo."

"It's Raven, on our way down."

"We have at least one carload of opposition. Four shooters. Just arrived."

"Where?"

"West side of the building. They have a partially obstructed view of the main entrance."

"Can you see the back of the building?"

"Storey is on foot checking it out, stand by."

Raven mouthed, "It's okay," in response to Hannah's concerned face. But he did ask her to hold the suitcase.

"Mitch is back," Macedo reported in Raven's ear. "Another car, two men, clear view of the back steps."

"Get him back there. I'd rather face two than four."

"He's on the move."

The elevator doors slid open. Raven and Hannah stepped into the lobby.

"Do we go together?" she said.

Raven grabbed her arm and led her across the lobby.

They stepped near the rear doors leading to the courtyard. They had to cross the open space to reach the rear exit.

Two gunners waited on the other side.

Four in front.

Did any wait in between?

Raven paused to re-evaluate his choices. He faced a situation violating Rule One. No gunfights in public. He didn't see a way to avoid a fight and it put people at risk.

Unless there was a way to use the public to his advantage.

He motioned Hannah into a corner.

"Macedo?"

"Yeah."

"Backside is out. How can we distract the first car?"

"How about an accident and an argument?"

"Do it."

"Stand by."

"Have Storey meet us in the lobby."

"Copy."

"He'll ride with us."

"Copy all."

Raven shielded Hannah's body as he watched the front doors. A chatty couple entered, too involved in their conversation to notice them.

The rear lobby doors opened and a stocky man with a goatee and wearing dark clothes entered.

"Storey?"

"Raven?"

"Name one of Clark's kids." Raven's hand inched to the holstered .45.

"Daughter. Brenda. Looking at colleges."

"In Wisconsin?"

"California."

"All right."

A blast of horns from the street stopped Raven's next remark.

"Our cue," Storey said.

"Out the front, turn left. Follow the sidewalk. Audi at the curb."

Storey took the lead. He stepped outside first and looked around. He waved Raven forward. Raven and Hannah exited, and the trio turned left. They walked fast. Raven clicked the Audi's remote key to flash the lights and unlocked the doors.

More indignant horn blasts. Cars jammed both sides of the street. Raven didn't look back but heard yelling. Macedo's voice with other voices yelling back.

Raven stowed Hannah's suitcase in the trunk and the three of them slid into the quiet confines of the Audi. Storey took the back seat.

Raven started the car and said, "Macedo, fall back."

More horns, traffic unmoving in the street beside them.

"How do we get out?" Hannah said. "We're stuck."

"We'll slip out as traffic improves."

"But we're sitting ducks."

"Yes and no," Raven said. "Your father's men are after you. Collateral civilian damage isn't on the menu."

"You're sure?"

"I'm betting your life on it, Hannah, yeah. I'm sure. They won't risk a fight here."

"But later?"

Raven shifted in his seat. He knew of two enemy cars they had to shake. Were there more?

A fight was inevitable, but if he had a chance at controlling the time and place, the odds might shift in their favor.

"That's why we have Mitch," Raven said. He glanced at the stocky man in the rearview mirror. "What are you packing?"

"Stainless Beretta 92," Storey answered. "Twenty-shot extension mags."

"Artillery may not be our biggest problem," Raven said. The horns finally stopped. Traffic began to move.

30

MACEDO CHECKED IN.

"I'm hanging back a few car lengths."

"How's it looking?" Raven said.

Berlin at night was almost as busy as daytime. Headlights glared in the side and rear-view mirrors. Oncoming traffic contributed more visual chaff. It made watching for a tail tough. He had to watch for familiar headlamp shapes behind him.

"I think we have one," Macedo said. "Can't confirm but he's staying with you."

"Despite my evasive turns?"

"They're good."

"All right, stand by."

Raven glanced at Storey, who turned to look out the back, then faced forward. He shook his head.

Hannah offered nothing but a nervous glance.

There might not be a way to follow Rule One.

He disconnected from Macedo and called Clark Wilson.

"What's up?" Wilson answered.

"We're hot. Safe out not an option. We need immediate extraction."

Wilson cursed. "Hang on."

Raven drove on. Using the center touch screen, he examined the GPS map for any open spaces where he could lead Schrader's kill team. He wanted to try and control where the fight happened.

"I know a spot," Storey said. "It's an office park," he added. "It will be empty this time of night."

"Tell me how to get there," Raven said, then held up a finger as Wilson returned.

"Sam, I can re-direct a plane from Switzerland, but the cabin will be full, and you can't talk to anybody."

"How long?"

"Two hours to Templehof. Hangar 3-A on the east edge."

"Get them here as fast as possible. We'll deal with our situation here." Raven hung up and pressed the accelerator as he followed Storey's directions.

He updated Macedo, who already knew of the office park location, and broke off to get there first.

"When we arrive," Raven told Hannah, "I want you to get on the floor and make yourself small."

She stuttered getting her reply out, but said, "Okay. I trust you."

The sentiment did not brighten Raven's outlook.

RAVEN MADE a sharp turn into the business park. Most of the buildings still had light shining through windows. Some were dark. Streetlamps spilled light across the pavement.

"What's Macedo packing?" Raven said to Storey.

"Pistol same as me and an HK UMP."

Macedo said in Raven's ear, "They're turning in behind you."

Raven wrenched the Audi left and bumped the edge of a curb as he entered a parking lot. The lampposts didn't help concealment. Their brightness made the Audi an easy target. Raven pressed the accelerator again. The Audi took off across the open space for a cluster of trees on the far edge. The light didn't shine there.

"I'm on foot," Macedo advised, "closing on your position."

"Light 'em up!" Raven shouted. He braked hard and threw the car into park.

Storey opened his door and rolled onto the pavement. Hannah crawled under the dash. Raven jumped out with the Nighthawk .45 in his right fist.

The lone enemy car closed the distance. Storey broke left, in a semi-circle, firing his Beretta. The nine-millimeter pistol snapped and flashed fire. The enemy car swung perpendicular to Raven, and Raven added the buck and roar of his .45. Windows shattered. The car peeled off. The staccato chant of Macedo's Heckler & Koch submachine gun joined the chorus. Tires popped. The enemy car halted. Gunners piled out, four of them, each man swinging submachine guns to bear.

Raven charged; his eyes locked on the gunner who emerged from the rear passenger door. The gunner lifted the snout of his SMG into Raven's face. Raven slammed the man into the car, pushing the SMG's barrel from his face. The gunner's strength became evident as he pushed back, slamming a knee into Raven's gut. Raven ignored the flash of pain. The .45 barked twice. The gunner crumpled at Raven's feet, leaving a smear of red on the side of the car. Dropping to a squat, Raven stowed the .45 and grabbed the gunman's SIG Sauer MPX. The selector switch was set at full auto.

Raven stayed low as he moved to the front of the enemy car.

Storey, engaged in a ground fight with one gunner, looked to be holding his own. Macedo blasted one gunner while a second lined up a shot. Raven fired. The short burst ripped open the gunman's back and sent him sprawling.

Macedo crouched to reload. Raven ran to Storey. The gunner rolled the stocky CIA man onto his back and drew a knife. Storey slammed the Beretta against the man's head to no effect. As the killer plunged the knife toward Storey's neck, Raven tagged him. The SIG MPX stuttered, the killer's face imploding under the impact of the nine-mil stingers.

Storey threw the man's body off him.

Raven held out a hand and helped the CIA man to his feet.

"Any holes you weren't born with?" Raven said.

"I'm fine."

Macedo ran over. He was thinner than his compatriot, wearing a North Face jacket. "We gotta scoot."

"Let's take my car," Raven said. "I'd rather keep together."

Raven ran to the Audi with Macedo and Storey behind him. When he opened the door, Hannah peeked up from the passenger footwell. The panic on her face faded when she saw Raven. The three men climbed into the car and she retook the passenger seat.

"Is it safe?" she said.

Raven laughed and sped out of the parking lot.

THEY WAITED in the Audi near Hangar 3-A where Wilson had arranged the pick-up.

Nobody spoke, and Raven's thoughts raced with what he needed to do next.

He had to see Hannah safely away but wasn't getting on the plane. He could not leave Berlin with Hugo Schrader still alive.

Raven needed to send a message to Tanya. Her father's death by his hand would communicate everything he wanted to tell her.

She touched his leg.

"You're not coming with us, are you?" she said.

He turned to her. She blinked as she watched him.

"No," he said.

"I understand what you have to do."

"I'm sorry."

"It's okay."

Was it? Raven didn't want to press her further.

Presently the bright lights of a small jet shined on them, the idling engines filling the night. Raven and his crew exited the Audi. Macedo said, "Do you need the HK?"

"All my gear is back at the hotel," Raven said. "Keep it."

The CIA men grabbed their weapons and Hannah and escorted her to the jet. The side door opened, steps lowered, and the two operatives hustled her into the plane. Hannah looked back. Raven wanted to wave, but it didn't seem appropriate. The steps rose, the door shut. The jet began to taxi away.

Raven stood watching as the plane traveled to the runway. He didn't let out a breath until he finally saw it take off into the night sky.

31

SPEIDEL ENDED A CALL ON HIS CELL. HE LOOKED INTO THE smoldering gaze of Hugo Schrader.

Speidel opened his mouth but nothing came out.

"What?" Schrader snapped. "Tell me."

"Raven had help," Speidel managed.

Schrader locked his hands behind his back and straightened. "Explain."

Speidel told him what happened outside Hannah's apartment. Police reports about a gunfight at a business park told the rest of the story.

"No idea where they are now?" Schrader said.

"I imagine either a plane or a CIA safe house. Or a safe house Raven arranged for."

Schrader nodded and moved to the French windows looking out on the balcony. They were on the second story of the house, and below the balcony lay the back patio.

Schrader looked out into the night, in the direction of the lake. Behind him, Speidel's nervous heartbeat settled. Perhaps he wouldn't be shot over the failure.

Schrader lifted his face to the ceiling and let out a sigh.

"Sir?"

"In a way, I'm glad," Schrader said. He turned to face Speidel. "I know I gave the order, but knowing Hannah is still alive—" He stopped.

"I don't understand," Speidel said.

"Because you're not a father."

Speidel let a moment pass. Schrader added nothing further. "What do you want to do now?"

"The Americans may have failed to breach our servers, but Hannah won't help them either. She left with Raven to get away from me. Meanwhile, Operation Triangle moves ahead."

"Yes, sir," Speidel said.

"But they may try to grab me," Schrader added. "I want the guards ready for anything."

"I'll see to it now, sir."

Schrader nodded. Speidel hurried out.

RAVEN DROVE the Audi back to his hotel. His cell rang several times along the way, but he ignored the call. It was Wilson calling to find out why he wasn't on the jet. If he had found the answer with Macedo, Storey, or Hannah, he was calling to talk Raven out of his plan.

Raven was in no mood to listen.

He wanted to hurt Tanya. There was only one way to do such damage. Hugo Schrader had it coming. He'd spent decades financing death and destruction from the shadows. By proxy. Prison was too good for him.

In the hotel room, he ordered a small meal from room service while he prepped his gear. As he ate, he cleaned and oiled the Nighthawk Custom and reloaded the partially spent magazines. Next, he oiled and assembled the separate parts of his Colt M4 Commando. The automatic carbine had been hidden in the same X-ray proof suitcase compartment as his pistol.

There were four other tools of the trade in the compartment. Four high explosive frag grenades. He hooked them to a combat belt and set the gear on the floor. He needed a nap before the night's action. Raven turned out the lights and reviewed his plan as he dozed off.

THE SUPPRESSED M4 Commando kicked against Raven's shoulder. The first of two perimeter guards dropped. His body landed with a thud, crunching dry overgrowth on the ground.

The second guard didn't return fire. His back to Raven, he bolted, Raven's follow-up double-tap missing. The guard dropped and rolled behind a tree. His panicked voice filled the night. Raven started running. The gunman was talking into a radio. Raven leaped over the fallen body. Pivoting as he landed, he raised the M4. The gunman's message stopped short. His wide eyes took in the black-clad wraith standing over him.

Raven fired twice. The earpiece fell out of the guard's ear and a muffled voice on the small speaker asked him to continue. Raven ripped the radio unit from the dead man and held the earpiece to his own ear. Whoever was on the other end kept asking for an update.

Raven dropped to a squat. He tried to penetrate the darkness surrounding him with a left-to-right scan. Coming upon the pair he'd killed was an accident. He hadn't seen them in the dark forest surrounding Schrader's property. The thick canopy of treetops above blocked out the moonlight. Shadows blended with tree trunks; various forest shapes filled his eyes. The ground held the danger of tripping over unseen obstacles.

He knew he should abort since the dead man had alerted his fellow troops.

But he had to proceed with the mission.

Raven left the body and jogged a few yards to another position, sliding onto his belly. He had to get through the section of forest before reaching Schrader's home. Now the opposition knew they had a breach. His attack-plan was flying out the window and he wasn't anywhere near the main objective.

He listened as the boss—the voice sounded like Sebastian Speidel—called for the gunner Raven killed. When he continued to not get a reply, he directed the force to search in pairs. He didn't know where the two dead men had been.

It gave Raven the chance he needed.

He listened to more radio chatter from other gunmen as the force began their search.

He backed away from the tree he lay beside and squatted a moment. He heard boots crunching the forest floor as the search teams stalked him. Raven moved forward, a few steps at a time, using concealment as he advanced. He didn't want another engagement so far from the house.

He scanned as he moved. He didn't stare at any single space, but kept his head moving. He wanted to catch any movement not consistent with the environment. The forest shadows might confuse him in the heat of battle, but there were ways to overcome the handicap.

Raven neared the end of the tree line where it met the property's lawn. Raven looked around. The house was huge, many lights on within, with silhouetted figures near the front porch. Speidel, probably, directing the search.

A trio of luxury sedans sat in a line in the circular driveway. Raven stayed low as he followed the edge of the lawn.

Most of the troop sounds were behind him, but then two shadows split and moved between tree trunks. Raven dropped flat. The two gunmen passed without noticing him. He remained in place until they had gone, but there were others, close by. He heard them whispering.

Then the radio burst with more chatter. Somebody had discovered the two bodies.

Raven hustled. Speidel shouted for his crew not to rush the area but to spread out in search of the intruder. Raven grimaced. *Intruder. Singular.* He thought Raven was alone. Raven wished he wasn't.

Maybe he was making a mistake.

But there was no turning back now.

He kept moving.

32

THE FOREST WRAPPED AROUND THE FRONT AND SIDES OF THE Schrader house. As Raven reached one side, he once again stretched out on his belly. The search party hadn't branched out to this portion of the grounds. Speidel continued to direct from the porch. Raven shook his head. Naughty, naughty.

The wall sat about 20 yards away. Covered windows, trimmed bushes at the base. Raven broke cover and ran to the wall, stopping under one of the windows. He smashed the glass with the buttstock of the M4 Commando and lobbed a grenade inside. The blast lit the room and shook the house. A fire started. He bolted from the window and ran around the corner to the front. The trio at the porch, reacting to the blast, didn't see him. He opened fire, the M4 spitting quietly. One gunner dropped. He shifted his aim to Sebastian Speidel, but the boss crashed through the front door. Raven's burst missed. He tagged the second gunner in the chest. The man tumbled down the porch steps.

Raven rolled a second grenade under one of the cars, a Maserati coupe. He ducked around the corner. The explosion sent a wave of searching heat flashing by. The fireball lit the grounds. Two secondary blasts, the other two cars, joined the fray.

Raven reversed course. He ran around the back of the house, steering wide of the back patio stretching along the length of the rear. Thick smoke from the burning cars drifted across the compound.

The radio chatter in Raven's ear was a stream of shouting and incoherence. Sporadic shots cracked. The troops were firing at each other, or at shadows, in desperation.

Raven reached the opposite tree line and took cover. He slapped a fresh magazine into the M4 Commando. The front of the house was ablaze now, the fire from the cars spreading to the structure. Raven used a tree trunk to block the glare of the flames. His eyes itched from the drifting smoke.

The side of the house Raven now faced contained the garage. Concrete curved from the garage door to the circular driveway in front. Raven faced too many troops for a frontal assault, but he could smoke out his quarry. When Schrader made his getaway, Raven would have him.

He tucked the carbine to his shoulder.

He waited. Anxious minutes passed.

HUGO SCHRADER'S body shook as he hid under his desk.

The study door crashed open.

"Mr. Schrader! Where are you?"

Speidel!

Schrader scrambled from his hiding spot and leaned both hands on the desktop.

"What's happening?"

"It's Raven! The front of the house is on fire, and one of the first-floor bedrooms is burning too."

"The cars!"

"I know! We have to use the boat now."

"It will only get us across the lake. What then?"

"We improvise."

Schrader nodded. He wasn't shaking anymore. He had a plan, a structure, a sense of order in the chaos.

"The easiest way out," he told Speidel, "is down the wall."

Speidel ran to the French doors. He pulled them open. Smoke drifted inside, enough to make him cough and step back. He issued orders over the radio to keep the troops looking for Raven.

Schrader joined Speidel on the balcony. Speidel climbed over the rail. He stood on the outer ledge a moment and stretched out a foot onto one of the stone steps running bottom to top on the wall. The steps led to the patio. From there, they would run to the lake and Schrader's motorboat. It wasn't a fast craft. Schrader used it for fishing. But with the cars destroyed, he had no other means of escape.

Schrader waited until Speidel reached the halfway point. He took a deep breath and climbed over the rail. His stomach lurched. He was two stories up. It wasn't as if he was descending the side of his skyscraper office building. He'd practiced the escape many times, but never attempted the effort under stress.

Raven was out there with high-powered weapons.

Schrader would be a fly on a wall as he made the trip down.

Raven could swat him without breaking a sweat.

"Hurry!"

Schrader blinked. Speidel had reached the patio. He was still standing in the open. He was trying to show Schrader it was safe. He was being stupid. He should have taken cover.

"Sir, come on!"

If I slip, I'll break a leg or worse...

Schrader inhaled deeply and reached a leg out for the nearest step. Then his other leg. Holding onto the adjoining bar installed beside the steps for stability, he started down.

Nobody fired at his back. His confidence surged. Resolve replaced doubt. Drifting smoke stung his eyes, but he ignored the discomfort. Another step. Another. Almost...

His right foot slipped. Schrader let out a cry as he shuffled for a hold, but gravity took over. He plunged to the concrete below and screamed.

SEBASTIAN SPEIDEL KNEW a broken ankle when he saw one.

The boss landed on his right foot, the ankle snapping. Rolling onto his side, Schrader tried to stifle another yell. He batted Speidel's assistance away.

Speidel ignored his boss and grabbed him under each arm, hauling the older man upright.

"Lean on me!"

Schrader put his weight on Speidel's left side, holding his right foot off the ground. He used his left as best as he could as the pair crossed the patio to the grass. The lake seemed so far away...

Speidel almost stopped as something buzzed over his head. Another buzz behind him. Suppressed gunfire! Speidel surged forward. Schrader yelled in protest.

And then Schrader's body jerked and the older man fell from his grasp. A hammer-blow struck Speidel in the shoulder and he fell too.

NOBODY EXITED THE GARAGE.

Raven looked up from the IR optic mounted on top of his carbine.

Where was Schrader?

A scream from the patio caught his attention.

Raven peered through the sight and swung the M4 Commando to the right. He laughed. There was Schrader on the ground, Speidel helping him up. Raven didn't take the time to figure out how they reached the patio.

His finger tightened on the trigger.

A twig snapped behind him.

Raven rolled left. He stopped on his back and brought up his weapon in search of targets.

In the dark, his mind racing, he felt disoriented. But moving shadows presented themselves. He fired. The carbine stuttered. A gunner's clipped yell signaled a hit. Raven shifted and fired again, another gunner dropping. Still on his back, he buttoned out the empty magazine and slammed home a loaded stick. He looked left, right, twisted his body in another direction. No further threats.

Rising, he re-acquired Schrader and Speidel. They were halfway across the patio. Heading for the lake? Raven didn't care. He braced against a tree and fired single shots. Two missed. The third scored. Schrader dropped. The fourth took down Speidel.

Men shouted nearby. Gunners closing fast. Raven bolted across the field to the patio. He had to be sure. Even if he caught a bullet, he had to know he'd killed Hugo Schrader.

33

SEBASTIAN SPEIDEL ROSE TO HANDS AND KNEES. PAIN FILLED his body. His eyed watered from the smoke and strain. Blood drenched the side of his suit.

Raven let him get no further. The M4 Commando spit twice. The 5.56mm tumblers ripped open the back of his head and he remained a motionless heap.

Schrader lay on his side. Low moans escaped his mouth. Raven used a foot to push the older man onto his back. He stared into the man's pained face.

Schrader's eyes looked blankly at Raven.

"Guess you'll miss your party," Raven said. "Sucks, don't it?"

Raved fired once. Schrader's body spasmed, then lay still. The man's face relaxed. He'd met the end he'd caused for so many others.

Raven felt no remorse.

But now he had to escape.

Gunfire nicked at Raven's feet as he ran.

Men shouted as they pursued. From behind, and on his right.

Darkness was his friend, the smoke from the burning house hanging thick in the air an ally. Raven was exiting the way he'd arrived. He needed to shake the gunners and get back to the hidden Audi.

Raven dived into the tree line. He had one grenade left and tossed it at the nearest gunners, those converging from the right. The other set was at the patio now, and both units would soon form one.

The grenade blast flashed brightly. Men screamed. Gunfire snapped. Raven ran. He had two enemies, the gunners and now the terrain. A fall like the one Schrader took would doom him same as it had the terror master.

Branches reached out like bony fingers. The uneven ground made balance critical, Raven sucking breath in surprise at the rise and fall of his sprint. He leapt over a fallen log only to land on slanted ground. He fell hard. The ear bud from the stolen radio popped out of his ear. Rushing boot steps and shooting told him all he needed. As shots nicked foliage around him, he knew they'd zeroed on his position.

He braced on the fallen log and fired into the shadows, shifting the muzzle, shooting on instinct. He couldn't see any better than the enemy. No yells indicated hits.

Somebody yelled to cease fire. Raven reloaded. The new boss kept shouting instructions. Raven had an idea. The boss didn't want his guys shooting at themselves. Fair enough. But if Raven could *trick* them into shoot each other...

Raven unscrewed the suppressor from the end of his weapon and slipped it into a pocket.

He stayed low. The searchers were not being quiet. Raven scooted back from the log, rose to a crouch, and squeezed the trigger.

He let one half burst go left. Swinging in the direction of the second unit, he fired a longer burst. Pivoting, he ran hard. Hell with the terrain. If he didn't get to the Audi he was finished.

He ran, dodging, jumping, listening. The gunners opened fire in response to his bursts. Each side had heard the shots hit near them and they responded in kind. The chatter of automatic weapons lasted at least three seconds until somebody yelled for another cease fire. He'd confused them and bought a little more time. They'd reorganize before continuing.

Raven now had a chance to get out of there alive.

He didn't look back.

HANNAH SCHRADER JERKED awake with a startled yelp.

Several faces turned her way.

The CIA plane was quiet and comfortable. Leather single seats and longer leather bench seats lined the interior. The cabin crew had herded her, Macedo, and Storey to the back upon their arrival. She had no complaints about the accommodations. But the grim faces of the well-armed and powerfully built CIA crew up front, the jet's primary passengers, were not friendly. She turned away from their investigative gaze.

Macedo, next to Hannah, touched her arm. "You okay?"

Hannah nodded. He left his hand where it was. The touch felt comforting. She let her heartrate settle and said, "My father is dead."

"How do you know?"

"I know." She closed her eyes. "I just know."

Hannah brushed Macedo's hand away and he withdrew. Storey, across the aisle, resumed reading a magazine he'd found on the jet.

She curled up in the chair and turned to face the fuselage

on her right. She'd closed the window shade when they left Berlin. Part of her didn't want to watch her home city fade into the distance.

She didn't know if she'd ever be back.

She'd didn't know what to make of her life now.

Hannah had information to share, but she didn't know if the details would help the Americans. They'd want to know how Tanya, as the first heir, now had control of the company. Her father was gone, but his money would still finance terrorism until they removed Tanya from the equation. Then Hannah would take over. She'd dismantle the monster piece by piece.

She knew all about the company, but where Raven might find Tanya wasn't a detail she could share. Tanya might be anywhere in the world. She may not have even left the United States.

Hannah hadn't only left her father's world. She'd abandoned what little life she carved for herself. What would her friends think?

But she didn't dwell on her friends for long. Her thoughts circled back to four words bouncing between the spaces of her mind like a stray tennis ball.

Her father was gone.

He'd funded terrorism. He'd tried to have her killed. Despite everything, he was still her father. And as she started to quietly sob, she decided there was no sense in pretending otherwise.

PART III

PART III.

34

"WHERE ARE YOU?" CLARK WILSON ASKED.

"My own safe house," Raven told him. "I'm still in Berlin."

"Do you understand the shit show you unleashed?"

"I have plenty of popcorn."

"I'm serious, Sam. The German police are going nuts. Those men you killed at Schrader's place? They all have connections to terrorism or neo-Nazi factions. His body lying in the middle of the mess is a PR nightmare."

"I'm not interested in what the Germans think," Raven said. "We fought two world wars so we don't have to care what Germany thinks."

"Fisher wants to know why."

"Tell the Deputy Director I wanted to send a message to Tanya."

"What kind of message?"

"You got to us, we can get to you."

"You're acting like this was personal."

"It *is* personal, Clark. She used *me*. I *brought* her to you. Her man killed a lot of good people at the black site. Did you forget that?"

"We haven't forgotten anything, Sam."

Raven said nothing. Wilson paused too. The silence carried on a moment. Raven was happy for the break. He and Clark needed a second to calm down. If the CIA wanted an apology, Raven wasn't going to oblige them. He had nothing to apologize for.

Wilson said, "They think we took Hannah out of the country."

"She'll be a valuable source of information. Use it to your advantage."

"What do you mean?"

"Ask the German government if they'd like to know how one of their most prominent citizens built his own terrorist army."

Wilson paused a moment. "Explain."

"If I have to explain, you haven't talked to Hannah."

"Dammit, Sam, help me out! I can't be everywhere at once."

Raven ran through his first conversation with Hannah. "Her father took advantage of Ahmad and Tamal. They were in the public eye and had vulnerable family members. He paid his goons to harass Berlin Muslims in general and target the two families in particular. The goons killed Ahmad's grandfather and two members of Tamal's family. Schrader convinced both to turn their rage into action. Follow?"

"And he was the money man like we thought."

"Correct. Hannah says there is proof in her father's office safe. I wasn't able to get there."

Clicking computer keys sounded in the background. "I'm taking notes for Chris," Wilson said. "Anything else?"

"No, start there. I think the Germans will cool their jets once they realize the scope of the problem. There's more to it than a dead CEO surrounded by neo-Nazis."

"Right."

More typing.

"Okay, I sent an email to Fisher and I'll go see him after we hang up. We'll deal with Berlin. You do your thing."

"Do you have anything useful for me or am I officially on my own?"

Raven looked out the small window of the apartment "safe house" and watched the activity on the street. He was in a quiet neighborhood in Berlin. The ground floor of the building across the street had a line of shops and restaurants. Raven wanted to go out and eat but didn't think it was smart to move around during the day. If Schrader or Speidel had any contacts on the local police force, they might have given them his picture.

Wilson sighed. "We have scraps, Sam. Crumbs."

"With enough crumbs you can make bread. Did you get anything useful from the server hack?"

"The hack so short it almost doesn't matter?"

"Yes."

"We found a name. Well, part of a name, and we've had to do some digging because of the missing pieces."

"Tell me."

"Ben Doyle."

"Arms dealer," Raven said. "He hangs out in Madrid, last I heard."

"Right. The British have an interest in him so there's always eyes on him."

"Will they help us bring him in?"

"We haven't asked."

"Are we going to ask?"

"Depends on you."

"What do you want me to do?"

"We'd like to question him, Sam. *Question*. Not mutilate. No more of your cowboy crap. We want to know if he's supplied the weapons for Operation Triangle, or if he's done any work for Schrader in the past."

"Doyle keeps his mouth shut. He works with the type of efficiency Schrader would appreciate."

"Find out."

"And if the answer is yes?"

"Bring him in and we'll do the rest."

"Operation Triangle may happen tomorrow, Clark. We don't have time to play question and answer."

"And we're wasting time talking about it," Wilson said. "Get to Madrid."

"All right."

Raven ended the call without saying goodbye. He yanked out his Bluetooth earpiece and tossed it and the cell phone on the sofa to his left. Leaning against the window frame, he stifled a curse. He didn't blame the CIA for being upset, but also didn't appreciate the lack of urgency. If they didn't stop Tanya, they'd have a bigger disaster to deal with than an angry German government.

MADRID WAS A BEAUTIFUL CITY, but Ben Doyle knew there were drawbacks making life less than ideal.

He sat in a gaudy café with pea-green walls and warped brown-and-white checkered tile floor. The owner's idea of decorations was every piece of junk he could find. The odds and ends hung from the ceiling on wires, collecting dust, or were glued to the walls. Sloppy glue residue was visible around the edge of every item. Doyle thought all Spaniards were lazy. "Manana" the chant of the country. The café confirmed his prejudice; the bored attitude of the wait staff didn't help.

But the café served excellent espresso which he sipped while eating a strawberry Danish.

Other "not so good" elements sat within the café too.

First, the American tourists. Loud. Mostly obese. They occupied several tables, none familiar with the other, and talked loudly about sightseeing plans for the day. They looked around the café in wonder, as if it were a cute piece of Madrid culture. It was, but for the wrong reasons.

There were other patrons, quiet ones, natives, who watched the Americans with careful eyes. They were the pick pockets who roamed Madrid, preying on tourists with no fear of the police. The cops didn't care what they did. They'd follow the tourists and wait for the opportunity to lift a wallet or two.

In a sense, Ben Doyle was in the same class. But his protection payments didn't extend to various western intelligence agencies who kept an eye on him from time to time. He had instead made a deal with one of them. Protection in exchange for information when they asked. Only when they asked.

The observations didn't get in the way of his business.

Ben Doyle sold guns.

Lots and lots of guns.

He didn't move heavy ordnance. If you wanted missiles, tanks, or fighter planes, he wasn't the guy. If your shopping list required assorted small arms, ammunition, and explosives, he could beat the big guys.

His career started by helping the "New" IRA in Northern Ireland move drugs. The profits from the venture financed the purchase of the Hotel Sensanna, where he lived, and start the gun business. The hotel was the perfect front to cover his illegitimate career and launder his gun money.

A few days ago, he'd completed a major deal for such

items for a client in Berlin. The client was happy. Doyle's bank account was happy too.

He had another deal coming up at three in the morning, this one much smaller, only two cases of submachine guns. But a deal is a deal. Sitting in the cafe with his espresso and Danish gave him time to think. He decided the exchange would be his last.

All he had to do was tell his associate.

When she entered the café, he stood and smiled. He knew other eyes were locked on Amira Raferi but he didn't care and she pretended not to notice. Amira was half Egyptian, half French, and all gorgeous, packing her slender figure into tight jeans and a Tee-shirt a size too large tied above her belly.

"Hello, Ben," she said quietly as they embraced. She spoke English well, but her heavy French accent overpowered every word. They sat. He waved at a passing waiter and was ignored. He shook his head.

"Never mind," she told him.

"You don't want coffee?"

"We have a problem," she said. "About tonight."

Ben Doyle shook his head and broke off a piece of his Danish. "Go ahead," he said, chewing. "Give me the bad news."

For sure, the coming deal would be his final one.

He was growing weary of "problems". Always problems. Never ending problems.

Amira leaned close and began to talk.

35

"THERE'S A RUMOR," AMIRA SAID, "FRANCO IS GOING TO HIJACK the guns."

Doyle sighed and closed his eyes, pinching the top of his nose. Franco. The hot-headed leader of an upstart ETA cell who thought he was Genghis Khan. The world belonged to him; he simply hadn't conquered any land yet.

He'd bid for the guns same as Doyle's paying client. He didn't have the budget to beat the client's final offer.

Doyle opened his eyes and watched one of the pick pockets follow out an American couple. How he envied the pick pocket at the moment.

"I'm too old for this," he said.

Amira frowned. "I didn't expect you to answer that way."

Doyle wasn't "old". Almost 40. He looked trim and healthy with close-cropped hair and matching beard. Without the beard he had a perpetual "babyface" as his mother used to say.

He didn't answer her. His gaze wandered over her shoulder to the front window. People walked. Traffic moved at a slow pace in the congested street. What he saw were people free of the kind of problems he faced on a daily basis. It was time to join them.

"Ben?"

"What?"

"How do we handle Franco?"

"Change the location of the meet. Tell nobody."

"I know where he is right now."

"I'm short of assassins, Amira. Change the meet. I want an extra crew of gunners too."

"I'll arrange it."

She scooted back her chair and exited the café. Doyle downed the last of his now-cold espresso and followed her after a few minutes. He left the last bits of his Danish behind. He didn't leave a tip.

THE EXCHANGE TOOK place without interruption. Doyle, Amira, and two vans filled with four-man gun crews met the client on the bottom level of a mall parking structure. Money and guns changed hands. Nobody went home with any bullets in them.

Doyle returned to his penthouse apartment at the top of Hotel Sensanna. He felt worn out mentally and physically and tried sleeping. He couldn't. Sitting in the dimly lighted living room, his smoldering gaze stared at nothing in particular.

In the time it took to finish a half-glass of Glenlivet he'd made up his mind. He'd turn over the gun business to Amira and run the hotel. His intelligence buddies wouldn't like the news. He figured he'd still have to answer questions when they approached him. There was still enough criminal activity in his past to hang him. He would if he could. He didn't want to sit in dark parking lots waiting for somebody to maybe kill him any longer.

He was young enough, and rich enough, to enjoy the rest of his life.

Doyle climbed back into bed with a feeling of calm about him. He'd made the right decision. He dozed off.

RAVEN ENJOYED his visits to Madrid. He'd toured the city three times in the last five years. The architecture was the main draw for him. He appreciated the mix of modern with historic buildings. Raven was fond of old things, buildings or other useful objects. It told him not everything faced obsolescence. He often felt like a dinosaur, out of place in a narcissistic world. The resilience of "old things" gave him hope he was wrong.

But he wasn't in the city to admire the history this time.

He had a target, questions needing answers, and a ticking clock. Operation Triangle never left his thoughts for long.

Raven checked in at the Hotel Sensanna and quickly unpacked the basics. There wasn't time for elaborate surveillance. Raven needed to move fast, which meant picking up Doyle's trail and squeezing him hard. He hoped the British agents Clark Wilson had mentioned weren't in the city for one of their "now and then" visits.

He knew Doyle occupied the penthouse. All Raven needed was a way up there or wait for Doyle to come down.

AMIRA WOULD ARRIVE in ten minutes.

Ben Doyle decided not to dress up. His conversation with her wouldn't be long and they wouldn't leave the hotel. Well, *she* would when they finished. Doyle intended to lock himself in the penthouse and get to work on his exit paperwork. Amira needed all the details of the business. Client lists, supplier information, and knowledge of Doyle's secret "inventory" locations.

The information he'd give her, should it fall into the wrong hands, might put him away for life. And jeopardize governments and individuals who bought large quantities of black-market weapons. Especially the governments looking to get around UN regulations.

He found her in the downstairs bar. She had a Manhattan in front of her and a martini waiting for him.

"Gin?" he said, taking the stool next to her.

"Of course." She smiled. "What's going on? I thought I wouldn't hear from you until the next deal."

Doyle sipped his drink. The elixir was ice cold and hit his stomach hard. He nodded hello to the bartender. The bar was doing its usual brisk business with both guests and street clientele filling seats.

"I'm getting out," he told her. "I'm giving you control of the gun business."

She set her drink down. In the low light of the bar, she looked striking. Tan skin and dark eyes, the high cheekbones, and intense expression she wore when she wasn't smiling. She looked at him with a mix of curiosity and surprise.

"What?"

"Everything is yours now."

"You can't do this."

"I *need* to do this," he said. "This Franco situation clinched it for me. It's not fun anymore."

"Well, okay." She swallowed more of her drink. "How do we do this transition?"

"I'll provide you with documentation. Everything you need to know. You'll be able to take over without a hitch."

"I'm truly surprised, Ben. I didn't expect to be your heir."

"Who else but my second-in-command should take over?" He lifted his glass. "A toast. To your new future, and mine."

She smiled. Her eyes lit up. They clinked glasses.

RAVEN DIDN'T KNOW who the woman was and didn't care. Girlfriend, associate, whore, it didn't matter. What mattered was he had Doyle in sight. He waited at a table, with his own martini, as they completed their conversation.

To his surprise, the woman left after finishing her Manhattan. He didn't watch her go. Instead, he signaled to the bartender for another drink.

Raven left the table and started across the bar.

A man stepped in front of him. About as tall as him, with blond hair. He shook his head.

Raven said, "Excuse me," and started to pass, but the man put out a heavy arm and blocked him.

The man opened his sport jacket enough to show Raven the butt of an autoloader under his arm.

A voice behind him said, "Not another step, Mr. Raven."

A woman. He turned. Then he smiled.

"Well, Miss Watson. Is the game afoot?"

"*Don't* start."

Misty Watson folded her arms and locked an angry gaze on Raven's face. She was shorter than him, with long red hair, and pale white skin.

Raven laughed. Misty Watson worked for MI6.

British Intelligence.

Typical.

"My dear Watson," Raven said, "what a pleasure to see you. Shall we talk somewhere?"

"Keep up the 'Watson' crap and we'll be talking in a cemetery."

Raven's smile vanished. From the look on her face, she appeared to mean every word.

36

MISTY WATSON WALKED AHEAD OF RAVEN WITH THE BRUTE behind him. They exited the hotel to the parking lot. Misty clicked the key fob to a black Mercedes Sprinter Passenger Van.

Raven whistled as Misty opened the rear doors and gestured for him to enter. He stepped into a plush cabin. Space was narrow. Plush bench seats waited on either side of the cabin with a small table in the center. The table was folded upright, creating a partial barrier.

"Sit down."

Raven cleared his throat and sat. Misty climbed in and sat opposite. She folded the table into its flat position and pulled a laptop from a cargo bin below her seat. She placed the computer on the table.

The brute shut the rear doors and assumed his position behind the wheel. A half barrier on Misty's side blocked part of Raven's view of the man.

Misty typed commands into the laptop and used the mouse pad to make a selection. She tapped the pad twice.

Raven watched her. The glow of the screen lit up her face.

With the glare, some of her freckles showed through the light layer of makeup. Her white blouse and black slacks fit tight over her petite frame. Raven reflected she always felt fragile despite the hard muscle under her skin. Their past intimate moments had always been short but memorable.

"It's nice to see you, Misty," Raven said.

"I'm Misty now?"

"You hate it when I call you Watson, my dear Watson."

She glared at him over the top of the screen.

"Hey," Raven said, "you know who you're talking to, right?"

"I'm talking to an embarrassment."

"Really?"

"We know about Berlin," she said. "We know about Operation Triangle and the boondoggle the CIA is in the middle of."

"Is there a leak?"

"No," she said. "Christopher Fisher called my boss and they had a long talk. Seems Fisher is touchy about you going off the reservation in Berlin. He doesn't want similar bloodshed in Madrid. Ben Doyle is an MI6 asset. I'm here to make sure you don't murder him."

"I have no intention of murdering dear old Ben."

She scoffed.

"What do you want, Misty?"

"Fisher and my boss decided on something. If Operation Triangle is an attack with three separate targets, the UK might be one of the targets."

"We were assuming three targets within the United States. The US is the country that killed Tanya's husband, after all."

"The matter has been decided, Raven."

"So, we're working together now?"

"Does that bother you?"

"Why should it, considering we've worked so well together in the past."

This time she laughed.

"Or are you my watchdog?"

She raised an eyebrow.

"Going to handcuff yourself to me, Misty?"

She tried to fight the grin, but her lips pulled back into a smile anyway. "Behave, Sam."

Raven grinned. Misty rotated the laptop to allow Raven to see the screen. A photo of Ben Doyle sat on the left side of the screen. A column of text information filled the right side.

"Ben Doyle has been an informant for about six years," she said. "Every now and then he passes along useful information we've been able to act on."

"You know what he's doing right?"

"Using us for protection."

"You aren't bothered?"

"No. Not when we get to round up bad guys now and then based on his information."

"He's throwing you crumbs."

"Can you read?"

"I'm not illiterate, no."

"You're acting like it. See this list? These are the terrorist attacks Doyle helped us foil thanks to his information."

"He sold out his own clients?"

"In a few cases, yes. Other time he heard information through the grapevine and passed it along. These aren't crumbs, Sam."

"I don't work for the CIA," Raven said. "I don't work for you, either."

"I have my orders, Sam. If you want to question Doyle, we are going to be there. If you refuse, we are taking you off the playing field. The CIA is ready to pick up where you left off."

"Fisher really is upset about Berlin, isn't he?"

"You have no idea."

Raven exhaled. There was no use in getting angry. He could have a talk with Christopher Fisher later. Clark Wilson had kept a lot from him during their last chat. He supposed it wouldn't have mattered either way. Raven's commitment to the mission wouldn't waver. With or without official sanction, he'd shut down Tanya Jafari and Operation Triangle.

"How can you help me, Misty?"

"It's to your benefit I'm here. You won't have to break into Doyle's penthouse or grab him off the street. All I have to do is snap my fingers." She held up her right hand and snapped for emphasis. "He'll do what we tell him. He may be scamming us, but he knows he needs to cooperate too."

"All right. When do you propose to snap your fingers and make him cooperate?"

"Why not tonight?"

"I don't want a full crew."

"It will be you, me, and Sean."

"Who's Sean?"

The brute behind the wheel called back, "I'm Sean, mate," in a Cockney accent. "Sean Mason."

"A pleasure," Raven said. "I trust you know how to use the handgun under your jacket?"

"I'm former SAS."

"Of course, you are." Raven faced Misty again. "Okay, no more argument from me. We're in this together."

"I'm glad you see it my way."

"Oh, my dear Watson," Raven said, "you know if I refused, there wouldn't be anything you could do about it."

"I wouldn't," she said. "Sean, however—"

Raven laughed. He glanced at the former SAS man, who watched him in the rearview mirror. Sean was laughing too. But the doubt in his eye gave Raven the upper hand. The Brit might be tough, but he knew Raven's reputation. He didn't want to find out if he was up to the task of taming the outlaw.

Raven felt the same way. He wasn't in the business of beating on allied forces.

Cooperation was the best course of action.

"Is there anything else to talk about?" Raven said to Misty.

"No." She closed the laptop and returned the unit to the storage compartment.

"I suggest we go back inside," Raven said, "and let you do some snapping."

37

SEAN MASON, THE FORMER SAS MAN, SHOVED.

Ben Doyle staggered from the doorway, his arms flailing as he protested. He stopped before tripping over a chair.

"What the hell?"

"I should be saying that to you, Ben," Misty Watson said. She stepped around Mason and approached Doyle.

Raven shut the door.

Misty folded her arms. "Take a seat."

Ben Doyle's furtive glance shot between Misty and Sean and settled on Raven. "Who is he?"

"He's a rookie in training," Misty said. "Don't worry about him."

Raven stayed by the door with his arms at either side. *She'll pay for that later.*

"I need a drink."

Doyle moved away from Misty to a corner bar and filled a glass. Raven glanced around. Doyle liked dark colors. None of the furniture, drapes, or paintings contained any brightness.

Misty said, "Sit over there," and gestured to a corner

dining table. Doyle glared at her but obeyed. She joined him on the opposite side. Raven and Sean moved closer.

Raven didn't plan to interject unless Misty went sideways with her questions. Misty insisted—on the elevator ride up— she take the lead because Doyle was used to her. Raven didn't see a reason to argue.

"What do you want now?" Doyle said. "This isn't how we usually do business."

"It's an emergency, Ben." Misty rested her arms on the table and folded her hands.

Doyle swallowed a gulp of his Scotch. "Okay."

"You've been holding out on us, Ben."

"No, I haven't."

"Why the silence about the man in Berlin?"

"Who?"

"You know who, Ben."

"I haven't done any business with anybody in Berlin."

"Hugo Schrader? The name means nothing to you?"

Ben Doyle's face blanched.

"You are holding out."

"I've done business with Schrader in the past but not lately."

"Your reaction says otherwise, Ben. Come clean or we take this elsewhere."

Doyle said nothing.

"I'll plug you into a chemical cocktail," Misty said, "and you'll tell me everything I want to know. Then, our deal is over. I'll throw you in a van and we will transport you to the UK where you'll never see the sun again."

Doyle laughed. "How long have you been waiting to give me that speech?"

"I'm not fooling, Ben."

Doyle sighed and set down his glass. "Yeah, I did a deal with Schrader."

"How long ago?"

"Couple weeks."

"You didn't think we needed to know?"

"I didn't have anything to tell you!" Doyle insisted. "It was a straight deal for small arms. Bunch of guns, ammo, and explosives. I had no idea what their intentions were."

"You could have said something anyway, Ben. Makes me wonder what else you haven't told us."

Doyle left the table. Sean turned his body to track Doyle to the bar where he refilled his glass. Doyle leaned against the bar.

"It's in my files," he said. "Schrader contacted me through his usual representative, a man named Speidel. I didn't send the guns to Berlin. I sent them to Greece instead."

"Who was the contact in Greece?" Misty said.

"I have to look at my files."

"Something wrong with your brain, Ben?"

"No, Misty," Doyle said. "I write things down so I don't have to remember them. You should try it sometime."

"Get your files, Ben."

"This is rich," he said, laughing. "I'm getting out of this business. Turning everything over to one of my associates. I'm going to relax and run this hotel."

"We saw you in the bar."

"Then you saw the demise of my involvement in the gun business."

"Well," Misty Watson said, "you may be done with the gun business, but you aren't done with us. We'll still expect information from you on a regular basis."

"Going to be a bit difficult."

"You'll find a way. Files, Ben?"

Doyle set down his glass. He looked at Raven and Sean Mason. "You two want to come along?"

Raven and Mason followed Doyle down a short hallway.

Doyle provided a spiral notebook open to the appropriate pages. The names, dates, and shipping locations corresponded with the deliveries ordered by Sebastian Speidel.

Misty took the notebook, said, "Toodles, love," and led Raven and Mason out of the penthouse. As Raven pulled the door closed behind them, he looked back. Doyle stood fuming. The gun seller was getting off easier than had Raven questioned him alone. With MI6 hooks still in his hide, maybe he'd have preferred the rougher treatment.

The elevator car descended. Raven pulled the notebook from where Misty had it tucked under her arm. She said, "Hey," but he ignored her. He scanned the page.

"We can go over this in my room," he told her.

"You buying dinner?"

"The CIA is buying dinner."

Sean Mason cleared his throat.

"Sorry, mate," Raven said. "Go report to HQ or something."

"I see how it is," Mason said.

"Mind your own business," Misty told him. To Raven: "If the CIA is buying, does that mean—"

"I will buy the most expensive bottle of champagne on the menu."

"You might annoy me, Sam, but you sure know how to make up for it."

Raven grinned and handed back the notebook.

It would have killed the mood to point out buying dinner from the hotel put money in Doyle's pocket. Raven decided not to mention it. He'd handed over the notebook, hadn't he?

Raven's room didn't have a dining table. Instead, he and Misty sat next to each other at the work desk jammed against the wall. The house special of the night was salmon, garlic mashed potatoes, and fresh vegetables with a lemon butter sauce. Misty thought there was too much lemon; Raven found it perfect.

Champagne with salmon might make most foodies cringe in terror. Misty didn't mind breaking such rules. Raven accommodated as promised with a 2006 bottle of Krug Brut costing $300 US.

Misty attacked both food and champagne. After downing her first glass in nearly two swallows, she took her time with glasses two and three as she ate.

Doyle's notes displayed minute details. Schrader's rep, Speidel, ordered eight assault weapons, and eight sets of C-4 explosives. Doyle had shipped the contraband to Greece two weeks earlier.

Doyle listed an import company called Stathoti Logistics as the receiver. He'd addressed the shipment to the attention of one Stavros Stathoti.

"His name ring any bells?" Raven said. He scooped up some mashed potato, added a piece of salmon, and ate.

Misty mumbled "no" through a full mouth.

Raven set his fork down and called Clark Wilson.

Wilson did not answer.

"This is Paul Heinrich, Clark's number two," the man on the other end of the line said. "Clark is out for the day."

"He deserves the rest," Raven said. "I need a check on a name."

"Okay."

"Check out Stavros Stathoti of Stathoti Logistics in Greece."

"Where in Greece?"

Raven consulted the notebook. "Piraeus. Port city five miles southwest of Athens."

"Stand by."

Raven glanced at Misty. She finished the last of her meal and emptied her third glass of Krug into her belly. She smiled at him with glassy eyes before her grin turned to terror. She covered her mouth as she burped. Then she laughed.

Raven rotated his chair away from her. She left the table laughing.

Paul Heinrich returned to the line. "Ready?"

"Listening."

"He's not a choir boy but we don't have much on him. Interpol suspects Stathoti is involved in drug and arms smuggling."

"No proof?"

"No. He's not on anybody's radar, either. He must work hard at not being noticed."

"His life is about to change. Thanks, Paul."

"Anytime."

Raven ended the call. Misty was still laughing. Raven turned. She was half on, half off the bed.

"Are you done letting the air out of your head?"

She sat up. "What did your contact say?"

"To Greece, Watson!"

"Oh my god!" She bounced off the bed and came at him. She leaned over and stabbed at his chest with alternating jabs of her index fingers. "Why. Do. You. Always. Call. Me. Watson!?"

He blocked most of the jabs, laughing when she scored, and grabbed both her wrists.

"Rookie in training?"

She laughed. "It was funny, and you couldn't say anything to stop me."

She struggled against his grasp. He didn't budge.

"Let go of me."

"No."

"Let *go* of me."

"Make me."

She pulled harder, her mouth open in a smile, her lips wet, eyes locked on his. He let her pull him out of the chair but held tight. He let go, spun her around, and gave her a swat on the behind before shoving her onto the bed. She bounced on the mattress, rolling out of the way before he landed on top of her. She laughed as she tackled him and forced him onto his back. She swung her legs over either side of his body, pinning his own wrists against the bedspread.

"How do you like it?" Her hot breath touched his face.

"I can smell your dinner."

He didn't struggle against the toned arms and legs holding him down. Her petite body wasn't heavy. When she lowered her lips to his he didn't resist either. It had been a long time since they'd been together, and he had to admit she hadn't crossed his mind much. She was a casual fling, and he'd decided it was better to keep it as such.

She kissed him hard and pressed his head into the mattress. He couldn't move and her lock on his mouth was too much. He wrenched his arms free and pushed her away.

"Hey!"

"You still kiss like a limpet mine."

"You say the sweetest things."

"Get your clothes off."

"Is that an order?"

"Don't make me tell you twice."

"You don't get the whisker biscuit so easy."

"The *what*?"

She laughed and tried to kiss him again. He turned his head. She bit his ear instead. He let out a cry and shoved her. She rolled away and landed beside him with her head propped on her hand.

"Still think you're giving orders?"

He grabbed her shoulder and forced her onto her stomach and delivered another solid smack on her plump behind.

"Hey!"

"You bit my ear."

"It was there!"

Another smack.

"Ouch!"

"It's big enough you'd think it wouldn't hurt."

"You ass!"

"No, yours."

She lunged at him, almost shoving him off the edge of the bed. She let up to let him scoot back, and he grabbed her again and pushed her onto her back. This time he straddled her.

"Now what, hot shot?" she said. Her chest rose and fell under her heavy breathing. Her lips were wet.

Raven grabbed for the button and zipper on her jeans. She didn't help. He tugged to get her pants down. She laughed.

"Lift your butt up."

"No."

"Dammit, Watson!"

She lifted her rear end and he pulled off the jeans with her underwear and then she helped him get the rest of her clothes off and his too.

38

OMAR TALMAN ROLLED BACK THE CUFFS OF HIS SWEATER. THE sleeves were too long. The rest of the sweater was also too big, but the cuffs bothered him more. He didn't want anything getting in the way of his gun hand should the need arise. At least the sweater was long enough to cover the selective-fire Glock 18C holstered behind his back.

He watched Tanya Jafari in the mirror. She fussed with the last of her luggage, struggling with a zipper, cursing. Omar went to help. She stepped back with another curse but Omar pulled the zipper closed. Then he reached out an arm and drew her to him. She leaned on his shoulder and sobbed.

News of her father's death in Berlin had reached them quickly. The "disappearance" of Hannah had accompanied the report. Tanya knew the truth. Hannah had defected to the Americans and the Americans had killed her father.

"We can mourn later," Tanya had said after the phone call. "Now we need to get ready to get out of Paris."

But a day later, when they had to pack and leave, she obviously couldn't keep her emotions at bay.

She sobbed without much noise and Omar said nothing.

There were no words necessary. Anything he said wouldn't help.

With a final sob, she pulled away. Tanya wiped her eyes. "I'm okay," she said.

"I know."

A knock at the door. Tanya ducked into the bathroom. Omar answered. Sila Kaymak, the Turkish assassin who had flown them out of Virginia, entered. He carried his two suitcases.

"All set?"

"Almost."

The toilet flushed. Tanya exited the bathroom. Her face was still wet from where she'd missed drying, but she no longer looked upset.

"Is the car ready?" she said.

"It's prepared," Kaymak said.

Tanya checked out of the room via the television, clicking through selections with the remote to mark the end of their stay. Kaymak took the lead as they departed. A large black BMW 740Li waited in the hotel parking lot. The trio loaded their luggage in the trunk. Kaymak took the wheel. Tanya and Omar sat in the back.

"Where to?" Kaymak said as he left the hotel property and merged into traffic.

Tanya gave him directions. She'd been keeping their departure point a secret until today. They were heading for a port on the edge of the Seine. A yacht waited for them. She explained they would board the yacht, follow the Seine to the English Channel, and meet a ship. The ship would take them the rest of the way to the Islamic Union's island compound.

From the compound, Tanya would wait for the results of Operation Triangle.

Her assets should already be in place. They knew their orders. They'd planned the operation to include a communications blackout. If the mercenaries faced any issues, they were on their own to solve the problems or abort.

Very soon she'd have her revenge. Not only for her husband, Ahmad, but Francesca and her husband, Tamal. And now her father too.

Tanya was glad to let Sila Kaymak do the driving. Paris traffic infuriated her. She liked the city, but the congestion of people, cars, and buildings took the joy away after a long day. It was as if the city designers had built a town full of buildings and other structures, suddenly remembered they needed roads, too, and cut narrow streets through the mass of buildings. Job done. Time for wine. Typical French bullshit.

She grabbed Omar's hand and squeezed. He squeezed back and offered a smile. She had to force her face to comply, but she smiled too. They held each other's eyes a moment. Omar had only required real sleep and real food to return to "normal" and they'd made up for lost time. Before the devastating phone call. But at least they'd had a proper reunion before reality intruded once again.

The drive took longer than she wanted, but soon Sila turned onto the Quai Andrei Citroen. She told him to follow the road all the way to Port de Javel Bas. The Seine sat off to their right side. Plenty of boat traffic crowded the waterway. Tanya shook her head. More congestion. More delays.

But they'd be out of France and on their way soon.

"We have a tail," Sila Kayak announced.

Omar Talman didn't look back. He leaned forward to pull the Glock 18C from behind his back. He held the gun low with his booger hook off the bang switch.

Tanya looked back. She said, "Which vehicle?"

"Blue van has stayed with us since the hotel."

"You're only telling me now?" she said.

"I wasn't sure till now."

Omar turned to look. He spotted the van four cars back

in one of the other lanes. He sat forward. Tanya cursed and twisted back too.

"Your sister?" Omar said.

"I doubt it. She knew nothing."

"Our people in Syria?"

"The CIA might have grabbed somebody, yeah."

Sila Kaymak said, "I'm open to suggestions."

Omar looked around. Seine on one side, the waterway full, the wharf crowded with workers and tourists.

Opposite side. More buildings. Restaurants, shops, pedestrians. The road. Nothing but traffic.

"We're in a box," Omar said.

"I know, honey."

Sila Kaymak said, "See the red brick buildings ahead?"

Tanya and Omar craned their necks to see. "What about them?" Tanya said.

"There's an alley in between we might find useful."

"Go."

Omar said, "They'll want us alive."

"It's our job to make sure they don't succeed, Omar."

From her purse, Tanya pulled out her own weapon. She racked the slide on the CZ 75B 9mm and flicked up the safety.

Sila Kaymak had the heavy firepower. Hidden in his smaller suitcase was a Swiss B&T APC9 submachine gun.

Omar glanced at Tanya. A grin pulled at the corners of her mouth. She licked her lips. He patted her leg. She took a deep breath. "Leave none of them alive," she said.

Traffic moved at a moderate pace. Sila swung into the left lane for the turn into the alley between the two red brick buildings. Signs out front identified the businesses, but nobody in the car paid attention. They needed a place to fight.

Sila cut left, crossing the opposing lane, and steered into

the alley. The BMW's engine rumbled as he pressed the accelerator, then hit the brakes. The car slowed to a stop in the middle of the alley.

"Out!" Tanya shouted.

Omar exited first. They had plenty of space between the car and either side of the buildings. Stacked pallets and dumpsters provided cover and concealment. Omar ran to a dumpster and dropped to one knee.

Tanya stayed by the car. It took a moment for Sila to get the APC9 from his suitcase, and he left the case open on the passenger seat. He moved to the hood of the BMW.

The surveillance van entered the alley and the tires screeched as the driver stopped. Tanya opened fire with her CZ 75. The 9mm pistol spat flame. She traced a line of slugs into the windshield. The man in the passenger seat jerked with each hit. A burst from Omar's full auto Glock blew the face off the driver.

Tanya ran ahead. Omar charged after her with Sila bringing up the rear. She reached the van first, smashing out the passenger window. Climbing onto the running board, she stretched her hand through, screaming as she fired more rounds. The CZ's action locked open, empty. Sila grabbed the back of her shirt, pulled her away, and assumed her place. He fired the APC9 into the rear, emptying the magazine in seconds.

Omar wrenched open the side door of the van when the B&T fell silent. There was no need for more shooting. Two dead in front, three dead in back. The three in back each wore handcuffs and pistols on their belts. They'd indeed meant to capture him and Tanya alive.

Tanya shouted, "Come on!"

They ran back to the BMW. Sila threw the car into drive and powered along the remaining length of the alley to the street ahead.

Omar, out of habit, reloaded his weapon, but he was the only one to do so.

"Don't go back to the quai right away," Tanya advised Sila. "Go right and let's work our way back."

"Will the yacht wait?" Omar said.

"They'll wait," she told him.

Sila reached the street and followed directions. Traffic was lighter so he drove faster.

Tanya turned to Omar. She didn't hide her grin. Her eyes were alight with excitement.

"The CIA will get the message," she said. "They can't stop me. They can't stop *us*."

"Indeed, they will," Omar said.

"And then we will send a bigger message," she added, "when we wipe out their team in Syria."

Omar only nodded.

"I want the other loose ends eliminated too."

"Stathoti and Horn?"

"Stathoti yes," she said. "Leave Horn. His men are carrying out Operation Triangle. We need him. Stathoti is replaceable."

Omar Talman said nothing more. He wanted out of Paris. He wanted to be on the open sea where the Americans couldn't find them. And once they reached the island compound, they'd be untouchable.

AT CIA HEADQUARTERS, Deputy Director of Operations Christopher Fisher entered the conference room. His number two, Layla McCarthy, followed. Neither looked happy about the urgent summons. Clark Wilson and Paul Heinrich were already waiting.

"What happened?" Fisher said. He didn't bother to sit down. Layla McCarthy sat and rested her arms on the table.

Heinrich used a laptop to put pictures on the big screen wall monitor. Police photos of the carnage in an alley in Paris, the shot-up van front and center. Other pictures showed the carnage within.

Wilson said, "Joe Hayden and his crew in Syria have been busy interrogating the two Islamic Union suspects they captured a few days ago. They learned Tanya and Omar Talman were in Paris. We sent a crew to grab them. The pictures tell the rest."

"Where did she go from here?"

"We don't know," Wilson said. "They were traveling along the Seine, so we figure they met a boat."

"With all the traffic there," McCarthy said, "tracing which boat she's on won't be easy."

"And it's a private craft anyway," Fisher said. "There won't be a record of departure." He began to pace. This was not the news he wanted.

He stopped with his hands on his hips and turned to Wilson. "Where's Sam Raven?"

"On his way to Greece."

"The gun lead?"

"Yes, sir. Shall I inform him about this?"

Fisher said no.

39

STATHOTI LOGISTICS OCCUPIED WAREHOUSE AND OFFICE SPACE at one of the many ports in Piraeus. A docking area behind the warehouse gave access to the Saronic Gulf and the Aegean Sea.

Raven and Misty sat in a surveillance van down the street from the Stathoti offices. The van's concealed rooftop cameras focused on the front gate and parking lot. The automatic gate was part of the fencing surrounding the property. It was still open as the clock ticked past six p.m. Two cars sat near the front door of the building.

Misty sat in the back of the van in front of two computer monitors and a keyboard. One monitor showed the parked cars. The second monitor was linked via satellite to MI6 and Interpol databases.

Raven stood behind Misty. He fastened his shoulder harness and slid the Nighthawk Custom .45 auto into the holster. Spare magazines rode under his right arm. He pulled on a long jacket to cover the rig.

They'd already run the plates on the cars to see who they

belonged to. Stathoti owned the silver four-door Lexus. The Honda sitting next to it belonged to his assistant manager, Amanda Liviakis.

"Do we wait for the woman to leave?" Misty said.

Raven put his hands on his hips and watched the monitor over her shoulders. "If she leaves first, yeah."

"He won't leave her behind to lock up," Misty said. "If he's working on any of his illegal activities after-hours—"

"I'll take that bet," Raven said. "Besides we don't want any witnesses."

Raven sat down next to Misty. The interior felt cramped, the roof low, and the glow of the monitors hurt his eyes. Misty had turned down the brightness level of both, but their glow still filled the space. The overhead light wasn't enough to cut down the glare.

They sat without talking for at least an hour. Then a tall woman with long black hair exited. She slid into the Honda and drove away.

"Exit the assistant manager," Raven said.

They waited ten more minutes. Stathoti did not follow.

Misty left the monitors and climbed behind the wheel. They wanted the van close for when they grabbed Stathoti and chucked him in the back.

"Let's pull up and make this quick," Raven said.

Misty started the motor. Raven said, "Wait."

"I see it," she called back.

A third car drove through the open gate. The driver turned the vehicle around. He backed into the slot vacated by the assistant manager's Honda.

Misty ran back to the console and pressed two buttons on the keyboard. The roof-mounted camera took a snapshot of the new car's license plate. The picture appeared on the second monitor. She used the mouse to drag the picture into the search box of the MI6 database.

"Don't bother, it's a rental," Raven said.

"How can you tell?"

"Gut."

Misty tapped the Enter key and ran the search anyway.

A lone man exited the vehicle. He was bulky with a thick mop of hair and wore a long jacket. He looked around as he eased the door shut but didn't close it all the way. The whites of his eyes stood out against dark skin.

"Misty—"

"You're right, it's a rental."

"Paid for by John Smith, right?"

"Edward Lewis."

"He doesn't look like a Lewis."

The man moved to the building entrance. He pulled on the door handle. The door didn't budge. The man removed something from a pocket of his coat and bent toward the lock.

"We gotta get in there," Misty said.

She grabbed the compact SIG Sauer P229 pistol from her belt and racked the slide. They exited through the back doors. Raven wondered if they'd brought enough firepower.

STAVROS STATHOTI HATED WORKING LATE.

But doing so was the only way to keep his legitimate operations going. The illegitimate took up most of the day. Done in secret, of course.

He wasn't a tall man. He wasn't a thin one, either. His hard-packed 280 pounds made him look like an upright bulldog. His puffy face almost swallowed his eyes.

His cramped office sat adjacent to a conference room with an open doorway between them. Another doorway in front of him led to the hallway where a left turn took him to the warehouse, front desk to the right. The walls needed a coat of paint, and the carpet had worn out a decade ago. Stathoti's priorities always lay elsewhere. The needed interior improvements remained on the bottom of the to-do list.

He sat at his desk filing paperwork for shipments going out over the coming days. The desk held several stacks of pink and yellow forms. He preferred to work in a quiet environment with no radio or television. Only the scratching of his pen on paper and his labored breathing filled the silence.

Buried under a small stack of forms on his right was his Dell laptop. The computer never left his side. Its hard drive contained details on his illicit affairs.

The front door squeaked open.

Stathoti stopped scribbling. He looked up. He could not see the front desk area from where he sat. He called out, "Amanda?"

No answer.

He scooted back from the desk and stood. As he stepped around his desk, a man moved through the conference room to his office. He held a suppressed pistol in his hand. Stathoti froze. His eyes widened and he opened his mouth to shout but nothing came out. The gunman lifted his pistol to arm's length and fired twice. The slugs slammed into Stathoti's big chest. A third shot smacked through his forehead. Stathoti fell over. His heavy body hit the ground with a thud.

The gunman slipped his gun back under his jacket.

From another pocket of his jacket the killer extracted a small thermite grenade. He pulled the pin and set the grenade on the cluttered desk.

He turned to leave but stopped short as the door swung open and a man and a woman entered. They both held pistols.

The gunman grabbed the thermite grenade from the desk and pitched it forward. It crashed on top of the conference table, exploding in a burst of blinding flame. The fire ate into the wooden table and thick smoke filled the room.

The killer moved for the hallway door. A quick step left and the doorway to the warehouse lay ahead. He ran.

RAVEN SHOVED Misty out of the conference room as the thermite grenade landed on the table.

They tumbled onto the floor near the front desk, Misty crying out as Raven landed on top of her with most of his weight on her right leg. He sprang to his feet and helped her up.

"Get him!" she said, leaning against the desk a moment.

Raven bolted after the killer. The assassin reached the doorway to the rear warehouse and Raven fired twice. Both .45 slugs smacked into the killer's back. He pitched forward into the dark warehouse and his face hit the concrete floor with a crack.

The fire alarm kicked on, a piercing blare attacking Raven's eardrums. He winced. Smoke filled the office. Overhead sprinklers kicked on and showered the fire with water, bringing some relief.

Misty joined him and they rushed into Stathoti's office. "Hurry!"

Raven covered his mouth and nose with the sleeve of his coat and ran into the office. He spotted the laptop. Lingering smoke stung his eyes. Raven grabbed the computer and ran out. Misty pushed the door open ahead of her and held it while she ran. He followed. It was a long dash to the van and Misty jumped behind the wheel while Raven settled in the passenger seat.

Misty started the motor and drove away. Raven set the computer on the floor while he buckled his seatbelt.

"She's tying up loose ends," Misty said.

"We might find something on the computer."

Misty turned onto the road.

"And if all we find is his everyday business stuff?"

"Then we're shit outta luck," Raven said.

40

"DO YOU EVER GET TIRED OF HOTEL ROOMS?" CLARK WILSON asked.

"Do you ever get tired of your office?"

"Yes."

"Ditto."

Wilson laughed. "I hope you have something."

Raven sat on the edge of the bed. Misty was across the room at the desk, scouring the files on Stathoti's laptop.

"We do and it's not good," Raven said.

"Tell me."

"The weapons Ben Doyle shipped to Stathoti went out on a ship to three different places. Los Angeles, Chicago, and New York City."

"Chicago is landlocked."

"I have no information of how they're transporting the weapons to any of the cities, Clark."

"Where's the ship?"

"Don't know. It's called the Sea Queen and I have the IMO number for you."

"Shoot."

Raven gave him the International Maritime Organization number. The seven-digit prefix would help Wilson's crew identify the ship's current location. Where it originated wasn't as important as where it was.

"We'll get on this," Wilson said. "Anything else?"

Raven sighed. "Yes."

"I sense more bad news."

"We have another player on the board."

"Anybody we know?"

"Unfortunately, yes. Dante Horn."

"Oh, no."

"Oh, yes."

Dante Horn, former Green Beret, special operations expert, now persona non grata in the United States. He owned a private military company called Black River. The CIA and Pentagon had once made extensive use of his services. Then they discovered he was taking taxpayer money while working counter to US interests. The government cut him off. He'd had an ax to grind against the United States ever since.

"Where did you find the Horn connection?"

"Stathoti's email."

"Why is the gun shipper dealing with the mercenary commander? You'd think they'd be separate from each other."

"Tanya made a mistake. She forwarded an email to Stathoti with a request from Horn regarding the shipment and left Horn's email connected with hers. I didn't need a database to tell me to whom the name *Horn* referred."

"Gotcha."

Raven said, "It's given a clearer picture of what we're facing with Operation Triangle."

"What?"

"Tanya and her father are using a combination of Doyle,

Stathoti, and Horn to organize the strike. They wanted us looking in the wrong direction and miss the real perpetrators who are *not* of Middle Eastern descent."

"You think you can identify the strike force via Horn?"

"I won't ask nicely."

"No holds barred at this point, Sam," Wilson said. "I'll make sure Fisher is aware."

"Horn is in Antwerp. We're heading there next."

"Good luck."

"Find that ship, Clark. We can assume the Triangle force is already in the US. All they need is their weapons and then the mission starts."

Raven ended the call. The clock was ticking closer to zero. And if the Sea Queen had already reached the United States, they might already be too late.

TIGER JOE HAYDEN, the CIA man in Damascus, making his twice weekly stop for a bag of cardamom coffee, missed the first assassin coming out of the alley.

He didn't miss the second.

A fight on a busy sidewalk wasn't what he wanted but the enemy wasn't giving him any choice.

The second assassin wasn't more than five feet tall but moved fast. He turned from a street vendor's cart and lifted the front of his shirt. Hayden saw the butt of his pistol before the man grasped it and drew the gun.

Hayden threw the bag of coffee. It struck the killer's face and broke open. The ground beans spreading across his face, falling onto his shirt. The killer let out a startled yell. Hayden closed the gap, filling his right fist with the concealed push-dagger he habitually carried. His hand gripped the T handle with the sharpened blade extending through his fingers. He slammed a fist into the killer's gut. The blade sank into his skin, ripping open his stomach. The killer wailed. Hayden wrenched the gun away with his left hand. Withdrawing the dagger, he pivoted behind the killer's back and slammed him into the nearest wall. The killer's head struck the stone surface and cracked. Witnesses screamed. Some started running.

As Hayden stepped back to avoid the killer's tumbling body, the second assassin, only a few feet away, lifted his gun.

Hayden's pulse raced as he brought the captured pistol to eye level. He was using his left hand, and years of practice firing with the non-dominant hand paid off. He fired twice. The recoil of the suppressed 9mm pistol snapped his wrist to the right. Both shots scored. The bullets punched through the second killer's chest. The man's face twisted in agony as his forward movement stopped, and then he fell.

Hayden dropped the bloody push-dagger and switched the gun to his right hand. He dropped into a squat. People were running, screaming. The street vendor behind him yelled for the police. Hayden scanned the scene quickly. No other threats came his way. Rising, he broke into a run. He ran two blocks without stopping and ducked into an alley. Stowing the pistol in his waistband, he grabbed his cell.

He called Colleen first.

Her phone rang four times, but Colleen didn't answer.

COLLEEN ANDREEV STEPPED out of the shower and dried with a big towel. She lived in a small one bedroom, one bath, and the place had seen better days. Everything in it carried the patina of age. She could handle not having all the comforts of home, but a big fluffy towel with which to dry off from a hot shower wasn't one of them.

She hung the towel on the wall rack and exited the bathroom. She'd laid out her clothes for the day on her bed and dressed without rushing. In the kitchen she poured a cup of coffee and relished the idea of a cup of the cardamom coffee Hayden was bringing to the office.

They'd been busy in the last few weeks. The interrogations of the two captured Islamic Union suspects had taken up the majority of their time. The Paris lead had been the only productive result. But it hadn't panned out and cost the lives of five good operatives.

She leaned against the counter in the small kitchen and sipped her coffee. Somebody knocked on her door. She frowned. She never had visitors unless it was Hayden and Freddy and they always called ahead.

She ignored the knock.

Then a heavy kick splintered the aging wood frame. A second kick sent the door crashing inward.

Colleen let the coffee mug fall from her hands as she left the kitchen for a desk. It sat in a corner near her dining table, and she kept her gun there. She grabbed the autoloader from a drawer and upended the table for cover. As the table tipped onto its side with a crash, she knew she couldn't get behind it in time. The two men entering the kitchen raised pistols of their own and opened fire. The rapid *phuts* of their suppressed handguns filled the room.

Colleen felt the slugs punching through her and she fell without a sound.

The killers ran out.

She'd left her cell phone on the coffee table on the other side of the room. The phone began to ring.

FREDDY LYMANN ARRIVED at work before Hayden or Colleen. It wasn't unusual. He liked being there early to get the computers booted and spend some time alone before the other two showed up.

He moved down the line of computers, switching everything on, then stopped at a printer to look at the messages sent through overnight. He shifted on his feet. His prosthetic wasn't treating him very well today. He'd awoken with an itchy stump, and still felt itchy despite the medicated lotion he'd rubbed on before attaching the fake leg.

It was another day in the windowless basement. Another day in the glamorous life of an American spy.

His cell phone rang. He carried it on his belt, and answered when he saw Joe Hayden's name on the caller ID.

"Good morning, boss," he said.

"Freddy!" Hayden shouted. He was out of breath. Freddy's pulse jumped. "Two guys tried to kill me, and I can't reach Colleen."

"She's not here."

"You're closer to her apartment than I am," Hayden said. "Get over there and check."

"Right."

Freddy hung up and started for the elevator across the room.

The doors started to rumble open.

A sense of relief came over him when he expected to see Colleen step out.

She didn't.

41

HE COULDN'T BREAK THE HABIT.

As Dante Horn parked his car in his reserved spot, he took a last look in the rearview mirror. He'd colored his hair the day before, and he ran a hand through his hair to make sure the color was uniform. He knew it was. He paid to make sure. But he was self-conscious about the process and always checked after each coloring session.

The pitfalls of getting older.

Horn left the car and locked it with the key fob. He was a few months away from 50 with a solid build on his six-foot frame. He still looked good. He could catch the 20-something babes if he wanted. The 40- and 50-somethings wanted a shot, but who had to bother with them when the younger ones lined up too? But the appeal didn't settle his anxieties.

His career in the US military had been stellar. Most of his service had been in special operations. Green Berets in the army, then the classified Special Missions Units of the Defense Intelligence Agency. He was too good for the CIA paramilitary units. Screw those guys.

The digital clock on the wall of his office read 8:59 when

he set his briefcase on his desk. Black River Headquarters operated within a multi-level steel and glass structure off Turnhoutsebaan. The building overlooked Rivierenhof Park in the center of the city. The sea of trees and grass from the wide window of his office always brought a sense of calm to a busy day.

His secretary entered with his coffee. She wore a blue suit with her blonde hair tied back and she didn't look at him as she set the coffee on his desk.

"Mr. Yarvis is on his way," she said, turning to exit. He said OK and picked up the coffee. There was no reason to sit until John Yarvis arrived. Horn stood by the window looking out at the park.

"Dante."

Horn turned. John Yarvis waited in the doorway. Yarvis' big bulk required tailor-made suits. The gray suit he wore fit perfectly on his frame. He always made Horn shrink internally. Yarvis didn't need to color his hair. He did fine with women. He was Horn's number two but could easily sit in the big chair if he ever decided to push Horn out of the way.

But they'd served together. Horn didn't truly think his friend would ever betray him.

"Sit down," Horn said. Yarvis eased into the chair in front of Horn's desk. Horn sat and put the coffee cup in front of him. "What's up?"

"She wants to talk to you."

"When?" He didn't have to ask who *she* was.

"Now. She's waiting on the secure link."

"Might as well get it over with," Horn said. He turned on the large screen monitor on his desk, which activated the web cam mounted atop. The camera was plugged into a small unit beside the monitor which scrambled the signal in and out.

Yarvis moved his chair behind Horn as the boss typed

commands into the keyboard. Then a box filled the black screen. A moment later, a woman's face filled the box.

Tanya Jafari.

"Dante," she said, "we have a problem."

"I'm listening." Horn sipped his coffee.

"The Americans know about Operation Triangle and they're taking steps to stop us." She explained about the tragedy in Berlin and how she'd eliminated Stavros Stathoti. She told him about the dead CIA people in Syria. She was confident the Americans wouldn't pick up further leads.

"What do you need from me?" Horn said. "I don't see what role I have other than what we've already done."

"Your people are in place?"

"Not only are they preparing as we speak, we have redundancies in place to keep the missions going should one team have to abort. You'll get your money's worth, Tanya. Even if you kill me." He forced a smile.

"I have no intention of killing you, Dante. We cannot complete this mission without you."

"I will set up defensive measures in case the Americans find their way here."

"There's only one you need to watch for."

"Who?"

"A man named Sam Raven."

Horn frowned. He exchanged a look with Yarvis. Yarvis only shrugged.

"Do you know him?" Tanya said.

"I know the name," Horn said. "But neither John nor I have met him."

"He's dangerous."

"Whatever you say."

"Do not take his presence lightly."

"If you've taken out Stathoti, there's nothing else linking us to you."

"Be ready in case."

"Is there anything else, Tanya?"

"I'll be in touch if anything else comes up."

Tanya vanished from the box. Horn turned off the camera and the computer returned to its default desktop display.

Yarvis moved his chair back to the front of the desk.

"We don't need a fight with the United States," Yarvis said.

"I wouldn't mind taking out a few US operatives," Horn said.

"You need to pour a bucket of water over your vendetta, Dante."

Horn scoffed and swallowed more coffee. His beef against the United States was well known to Yarvis and two other close associates. While accepting contracts from the Pentagon, Horn double-dealt with anti-US elements overseas. Via cutouts, he lent mercenaries to jihadist units in the Middle East. The mercs trained the jihadists on how to counteract US tactics.

He'd assured his freedom from capture or prosecution via blackmail of selected members of Congress. But the protection didn't keep the Pentagon from cutting him off and making him a pariah in his former home.

It didn't bother him much. Dante Horn didn't have a family, and he liked Belgium.

"Look up this Sam Raven fellow," Horn said. "Get a picture. I want people at the airport watching for him."

"You think he'll find his way here?"

"I trust Tanya took the required precautions," Horn said. "But you never know."

Yarvis promised to get a team to the airport right away. He left the office.

Horn sat with his coffee and stared into space. His deal with Tanya and her father put several million US dollars into his account. He hoped he lived long enough to enjoy the profits.

———

HORN'S MERCENARIES began preparing to put Operation Triangle into action.

They worked in teams of two in New York, Los Angeles, and Chicago. Weapons and explosives had been delivered, and each pair began scouting targets.

Los Angeles: a local television station.

Chicago: the Cloud Gate sculpture at AT&T Plaza.

New York City: a section of the subway.

The teams took photos and videos and reviewed the material carefully. They needed places to plant their bombs. They wanted the bombs to create mass casualties and push survivors in a desired direction. Into the muzzles of their automatic weapons. The plan called for bombs first, mass shooting second.

Escape routes were up to each team.

They worked independently, unaware of the others' assignment, and without connection to Horn, Tanya, or Berlin.

The plan had been Tanya's, refined with the help of her father, with instructions delivered to the mercenary teams by Horn and Yarvis.

The countdown to zero hour was on.

RAVEN AND MISTY LANDED AT ANTWERP INTERNATIONAL Airport. Clark Wilson at the CIA promised somebody Raven knew would meet them. He didn't want to waste time with silly contact protocols.

Raven's chartered jet taxied to a hangar not far from the main terminal. It was one of a line of private hangars, all of which were busy. The jet wasn't noticed. He glanced out one of the cabin windows. A black SUV with a man standing at the driver's door waited. Raven smiled. Wilson had sent an old pal named Mike Cutter.

Raven exited the plane with Misty and shook Cutter's hand. "Long time, Mike. Good to see you."

Cutter smiled back. The grip of his rough hand was strong. "Likewise. Glad I could be here to help."

Cutter matched Raven's height and looked wiry with a thin face. Raven and Cutter first met in the early years of their respective CIA careers. Both worked for the para-military branch. They'd never served in the same units, but Raven knew Cutter was a top operative. He had several intelligence awards in his classified file.

"Wilson pulled me from another mission to meet you," Cutter said.

"How much do you know?"

"Everything. And we have a team on the way too. Get your gear in the vehicle and I'll explain."

Cutter checked with Wilson at HQ while Raven and Misty took their luggage from the plane. The suitcases fit it in the back of the SUV with room to spare. Raven rode up front with Misty in the back.

The expanse of the runway and open green space beyond presented Belgium in its best light. Further in the distance, the city itself. Cutter drove off the airport property and through a cluster of quiet neighborhoods.

Cutter said to Misty, "Your chief wants you to check in. I guess you haven't been answering your phone?"

"No," she said.

"I think they want you to come home."

"Tough," she said. "I'm staying."

"Better call in anyway."

She said nothing more. Raven added nothing either. He watched the passing houses. He wouldn't say so, but he wanted Misty gone. She'd been a big help with Doyle and Stathoti, but they'd learned Operation Triangle didn't involve the UK. She didn't need to be there any longer.

He'd lucked out with Hannah. If he lost Misty, it would be a tough one to overcome.

Maybe her chief at MI6 would demand her return. Raven felt it was for the best.

He said to Cutter, "What's the plan?"

"Two teams on the way. The priority is capture and interrogation."

Raven laughed. "They don't want a repeat of what I did in Berlin."

"Correct."

"How long before the teams get here?"

"Tonight. I'm prepping the staging area. We'll hit his house. At the same time, we'll go for his number two, John Yarvis. I have a team covering Yarvis. I need you to keep an eye on Horn. Make sure he sticks to routine."

"Which is what?"

"He likes to party and go home with younger women."

"Who doesn't?" Raven grinned.

"Hey!" Misty said.

"If he deviates," Cutter said, "use your best judgement."

"And take him alive."

"Exactly. This won't be a walk in the park. And the clock is ticking."

Raven didn't argue. "What kind of security do they have?" he said instead.

"Horn has two bodyguards," Cutter told him, "and Yarvis is alone. Both are carrying sidearms."

"Odd Yarvis is alone," Raven said. "I don't know much about him."

"Former Marine," Cutter said. "Been in the mercenary community for decades. Plugged in with Horn a few years ago and became his second-in-command."

"What is it with Americans," Misty said, "who go on their own and end up on the bad side?"

"I could ask the same thing of Brits, Misty," Raven said.

"Touché."

"Way of the world," Raven said.

"It stinks," she said.

Raven agreed. But those inclined only toward wealth and power always found a way to achieve their goals. Such was the case of Dante Horn and John Yarvis.

But they'd crossed one line too many. Raven intended to make them pay for their choices.

No amount of money would save them.

CUTTER DROPPED Raven and Misty at their hotel and said he had somebody on the way to deliver their rental. He provided Raven with the office address of Horn's company and other pictures. Cutter reiterated Raven had to keep an eye on Horn until the strike force made their move.

Raven didn't appreciate the micromanaging. He said so to Misty as the elevator carried them to the hotel's fifth floor. They had adjoining rooms.

"Consequences of being a cowboy, Sam."

"If I didn't have a personal stake in this, I'd leave."

"No, you wouldn't."

"How do you know?"

"Because I know *you*, Sam."

Raven scoffed. "I suppose you're right."

She winked. "I know."

"Don't let it go to your head, Watson."

They reached their rooms. Raven suggested twenty minutes to refresh before they hit the street to find Horn.

MISTY WATSON DOUBLE-LOCKED her door and set her suitcase on the bed. It was a king and looked comfortable, but she didn't think she'd spend any time there. She pulled out her cell phone and called headquarters. After passing through the verbal confirmation checks, the HQ operator patched her through to her chief.

Sir Miles Montgomery said, "It's about time, Miss Watson."

Montgomery was a gruff bear of a man who ran MI6 with an iron fist. His grouchy tone told her all she needed to know. He wasn't happy with her.

Raven had no idea what micromanaging meant. He'd never met Sir Miles.

"Where are you?"

"Antwerp."

"Why?"

"Next lead, sir."

"Why haven't you called before now? I shouldn't have to have the CIA give you a reminder."

"I don't intend to be recalled from this assignment, sir."

"How do you *know* I'll recall you?"

Misty let out a quiet sigh. There was a time when his choice of words made her flinch. No longer. She said, "I've worked for you for six years, Sir Miles. We've determined Operation Triangle doesn't involve the United Kingdom. There's no official reason for me to be here."

"Yet you want to stay?"

"Because of Raven, sir."

"I've never understood your fascination with him," Sir Miles said. "The man is a rogue. Irresponsible. He has his own agenda and he'll let nobody get in the way."

"Anything else, sir?"

"Watch your tone, young lady." Sir Miles cleared his throat. "I am not recalling you. The Stathoti information you sent has proved invaluable. We now know how various terror groups are getting their weapons, through whom, and by what means. If you're determined to stay, I hereby order you to do so. I want to know what else you can find. Tell me about the new lead."

Misty updated Sir Miles on Dante Horn and what the CIA wanted to do in Antwerp.

Sir Miles said, "I'll call the cousins and make sure you're included on whatever they find."

"Thank you, sir."

"When this is over, I want you back in London. No argument."

"Yes, sir."

"We'll discuss this further then."

Sir Miles ended the call without saying goodbye. Misty cursed. She tossed the phone on the bed. They wouldn't welcome her home a hero. There'd be a price to pay for not checking in like a good employee.

Maybe, she thought, *I'll take off on my own like Sam.*

She laughed at the absurd notion as she stepped into the bathroom.

RAVEN STOOD at the hotel room window. A stretch of the N13 stood out against the backdrop of blue sky and more of the sprawling city.

Misty's words reverberated in his mind.

"Because I know you, Sam."

Did she know him better than he knew himself in this case? Because she did have a point. He'd rather work with a group of allies toward a common goal than take on the task alone. Going solo was usually his first and only option. This time, he had help. Maybe he needed help. Perhaps taking on as much responsibility as he did wasn't serving his cause.

He felt the locket hanging under his shirt. No. She was wrong. He didn't mind working with allies, but he preferred working alone. He'd made his vow alone; he pursued his cause alone. Nobody else understood. Often, he didn't understand himself. But he knew what he had to do.

This time, he had help. Thanks to the tightrope on which he found himself, allies were welcome.

Next time, he wouldn't allow the bureaucracy he'd left behind tie him down.

43

RAVEN AND MISTY BET EACH OTHER $20.00 US DANTE HORN would skip his nightlife routine and go home after work.

Raven lost.

Misty laughed as they picked up the Black River CEO's trail. He rode with two bodyguards and a driver and they drove into downtown Antwerp. Horn's car stopped in front of an Irish pub called Josie's. Horn and his bodyguards exited the car. The driver pulled away to park up the block. He remained with the car.

Raven parked the rental Ford on the street behind the pub. They walked around to the front. Halfway there, Raven smelled frying food and his senses perked. Whatever was cooking smelled delicious. A hostess greeted them at the door and the smells became stronger. Even Misty's eyes widened at the prospect of a good meal during a boring surveillance job.

The hostess escorted them to a booth of dark mahogany walls and a polished wood table. A light hung above. The circular leather seat hissed as they settled across from one another.

"I didn't come all the way to Antwerp," Misty said, "to sit in a pub."

"Whatever they're cooking doesn't smell like Brit pub food."

"What are you suggesting?"

"British cooking sucks, my dear Watson."

She sighed as she opened her menu. "So I hear."

Raven started to look at his menu but felt restless. He closed the menu and looked around. Tables and booths full. Long line of people at the bar drinking and talking. On the other side of the dining area, some played darts. Others leaned over pool tables. The noise and low light might have been cozy to the regulars, but Raven's combat senses screamed silently. He felt anxious, caught in a box, with only one way out.

And too many people around if the night went bad. Rule One was never far from his thoughts.

Worse, neither he nor Misty saw Horn.

"Private room?" Misty suggested. She made a show of examining her menu while examining the crowd.

"Nope," Raven said. "Corner booth."

"How do you know?"

"Because one of the bodyguards left and is crossing to the bar."

Their waitress arrived. She was a young woman with blonde hair and blue eyes and a sleeve tattoo of interlinked rainbows on one arm. Raven and Misty ordered drinks and food. The waitress departed. They looked at each other.

She smiled. "Let's see what Belgium pub grub is like."

"Sir Miles give you a hard time?"

"He was his usual self."

"A fussbudget?"

She laughed. "Exactly! With a touch of grumpy old man sexism."

"And you're staying?"

"The Stathoti intel proved valuable. Now they want to know how Horn's information might make it better."

"Fingers crossed he gives us something. I didn't tell you about my chat with Clark."

"When?"

"After we arrived at the hotel."

"Good news?"

"Very bad news."

"Tell me."

"Stathoti's ship came and went. Docked in New York City for two days. Now it's heading for South America."

"How long to get the weapons to Chicago and Los Angeles?"

"Depends if they're driving or flying," Raven said. "If it were me, I'm having them driven to Chicago and flown to Los Angeles by separate couriers."

"We're going to cut it close, aren't we?"

"The sooner we make Horn talk, the better."

"And if we're too late?"

"I don't want to think about it."

But think about it he did as they ate. The food was amazing, and their mutual glances of delight took his mind off the situation, but never for long. Misty's messy spareribs left her fingers covered in sauce. Raven didn't tell her some smeared on her chin. He ate his hot Irish stew slowly, savoring each swallow. The mix of lamb and fresh vegetables was rich indeed.

After dinner they sat with pints of Guinness because who doesn't drink Guinness in a pub? Misty excused herself but came back glaring at Raven for not telling her about her chin.

They were so full from dinner they drank slowly, and Raven decided as boring surveillance jobs go, it wasn't a bad one. Horn and his entourage presently made their job a little easier. Horn began throwing darts with a group of young women. The dart game then turned into a billiard challenge. By eleven o'clock Raven and Misty were getting tired, but by then Horn had made his choice. With a thin brunette in jeans and a pink tank top in tow, he paid his bill and the bill of the brunette's friends. She joined the entourage outside.

Raven and Misty paid and hurried around the block to their rental. Traffic wasn't too heavy, and Raven weaved through lanes to catch up with Horn's vehicle. Misty told him to take it easy. "A rookie could pick you out," she chided. When Raven finally had Horn's car in sight, he eased off the gas and settled back three car lengths.

"Better?" he said.

"I should be driving."

Raven scoffed.

Horn left the city limits for his home. Traffic thinned, but enough cars remained to provide cover for Raven's rental. Once Horn turned up a two-lane road into the hills, the situation changed. They were the only two vehicles on the road. Raven cut off his headlamps. He eased off the gas. Forest surrounded them and Raven kept to the middle of the road to avoid going off the edge.

Misty called Mike Cutter on her cell and put him on speaker.

"We've already spotted you, Sam," Cutter reported. "In 500 feet you'll find a turn-off. Take it. Follow the dirt road until we stop you."

"Copy," Raven said.

The turn-off appeared as advised and Raven slowed. He turned the wheel to the right and the Ford left the pavement. Turning the headlamps back on, he proceeded carefully. More forest all around. The dirt road was clear of overgrowth suggesting its use wasn't rare.

They drove almost ten minutes. When two figures in black stepped out onto the road, Raven stepped on the brake. The figures approached, one on each side. Raven powered down his window. The one on his side shined a blue light into the car.

The figure's combat fatigues and chest harness showed the man was ready for business. Flash bangs and high-explosive grenades rode on vest straps. Sidearm on his belt. Suppressed M4 carbine in hand.

Raven said, "Nice night for a walk."

The man examined Raven's face in the low glow of the blue light. Raven had no idea what the man looked like. A helmet covered his head, a balaclava concealed his face from the nose down.

"It's him," the man announced to his partner.

"Follow you?"

"We're not far."

The two CIA commandos turned and moved off at a trot. Raven drove slowly behind them.

"Here we go," Raven said.

"Our gear isn't as cool as theirs," Misty said.

Raven allowed himself a quiet laugh.

44

RAVEN STOPPED THE FORD IN AN UNEVEN CLEARING. HE FELT the car tilt a little on the slanted ground.

He spotted more armed CIA paramilitary operatives hanging around. Cutter spoke with a man Raven didn't recognize. Two black Jeeps sat nearby.

Raven and Misty exited. Raven frowned. His first impression was off. He counted only four shooters. We need more than this!

Cutter approached with the other man. Raven cut him off before he could introduce the fellow.

"Four shooters?"

"Plus, you, me, your friend, and this man," Cutter said. "Sam, meet Joe Hayden. We call him Tiger Joe."

Raven and Misty shook Hayden's hand. He and Hayden sized each other up with a prolonged look. He was shorter than Raven, but his grip suggested strength. He wondered what his background was. He turned back to Cutter. He wasn't going to let go of his train of thought.

"This is all we have?"

"Relax," Cutter said. "We have eight more coming in by

chopper. The choppers are armed with machine guns and rockets, if necessary. We're the ground squad."

"What do the locals think of this invasion?" Raven said.

Cutter let out a short laugh. "They want Horn gone. He's staying out of prison here the same way he stayed out of it in the United States. He's got dirt on everybody who might charge him with anything."

"Okay," Raven said. He looked at Hayden. "What's your story?"

Cutter excused himself. Hayden leaned against the Ford's fender and folded his arms. It was hard to make out his features in the low light. Electric lanterns lit the area, but their glow didn't extend far.

"I was in Syria," Hayden said.

"No kidding."

Hayden nodded.

"The drone strike?"

"Yeah," Hayden said. "And Paris. After Paris, the Islamic Union tried to kill me. They missed but murdered my two teammates."

"What happened in Paris?"

"You don't know?"

"No clue."

Hayden shook his head. "Ask Clark why he kept you out of the loop. We rounded up some IU players in Damascus and made them talk. They put Tanya Jafari and Omar Talman in Paris. The Agency sent at a team to get them and failed. She killed all of them."

"The body count keeps rising."

"And this may be our last shot," Hayden said.

"Glad to have you here, Hayden."

"Call me Joe."

"Sam." They shook hands a second time.

Hayden said to Misty, "What's the British interest in this?"

"Any attack on the US hurts the UK," she said. "If we don't stop Tanya Jafari now, she may hit London next."

Mike Cutter returned with a laptop. He put the computer on the hood of the Ford. "Here's the target."

Hayden moved away, explaining he'd seen the photo already. Raven and Misty stepped close to Cutter. Raven examined the daytime satellite picture of Horn's mansion. The kind of home only blood money could buy.

The layout of the mansion resembled one side of an octagon. Main house in the center, three stories according to Cutter. Sections extended at an angle from either side of the house like outstretched arms. They connected with tower structures. Each tower featured round tops and spires. The second level of each "arm" was topped with a canopy of curved glass. Through the glass, the walkway between the house and tower showed. Each tower had a wrap-around balcony. Concrete courtyard in the center. Hedges lined the front walls of the house.

Cutter pointed to a separate multi-car garage on one side. A tennis court/swimming pool combo sat on the other.

The forest continued up the hill until it stopped at the tall green grass surrounding the property.

Raven said, "Nice house."

"Shame to blow it up," Misty added.

Cutter checked his watch. "Black Hawks arrive in ten minutes. Let's get you geared up. We all hit at the same time."

Raven and Misty didn't get camo uniforms, but they did get the combat vest and associated gear. The weapon of choice for the assault surprised him. Cutter handed him and Misty a Haenel MK 556 automatic rifle. It was the latest and greatest from the German company with ergonomics and controls similar to the M16/M4. It felt immediately familiar to Raven. Each rifle had an optic sight mounted on top. The buttstock extended or contracted.

Misty preferred her stock short; Raven extended his all the way.

"It's a good rig," Hayden commented as Raven examined the weapon.

"You ask for this assignment?" Raven said. He slung the rifle.

"Yeah. I want payback."

"Do me a favor," Raven said, "and take it easy. We both have a score to settle, but we need to save American lives first."

"Not my first rodeo, Sam. I get it."

Cutter said it was time to get moving. The crew cleaned up the site and loaded into the Jeeps. The four CIA shooters climbed into one Jeep, while Raven, Misty, Cutter and Hayden piled into the other. Cutter drove. The engines rumbled to life. The off-road vehicles moved along the dirt road with four car-lengths between them.

Raven and Misty sat in the back. Even with Cutter driving slowly they jostled against each other at every bump.

Raven felt sweat on his palms. He wiped his hands on his pants. He didn't want to feel nervous, but he had no idea where they stood in terms of Operation Triangle's timetable.

Success or failure depended on getting information out of Dante Horn.

"HERE THEY COME!" Cutter shouted. He stepped on the gas and the Jeep surged forward.

Two Sikorsky UH-60 Black Hawk helicopters thundered overhead. As the two-lane road began to level out, the Horn mansion came into view. Raven saw the tips of the towers first, each one bathed by ground lights.

Muted machine gun fire hammered above. The first Black

Hawk made a pass over the courtyard and front of the house, strafing the exterior. The heavy slugs plowed into the stonework, shattering windows. The second chopper hovered at the edge of the grass.

Cutter steered the Jeep at the driveway. Horn didn't have a security gate, but Raven gave it no further thought as return fire smacked into the Jeep like dozens of enraged hornets.

Raven pushed Misty down and bent over her, Hayden shouting for Cutter to go right. A burst of fire shattered the front windshield. Cutter screamed once. The Jeep lurched left. Hayden shouted, "Hang on!" Steel crunched as the front end of the Jeep plowed into the left-side tower. The sudden stop rocked the vehicle.

Raven and Misty lurched forward as if shoved violently, their bodies whipping back under the strain of the safety belts. Raven looked up as Misty pulled away. Cutter's head leaned forward on his chest, his face a mash of blood and tissue. Hayden yelled, "Get out!" and Raven didn't waste another moment on the late Mike Cutter.

Raven slid out, yelling for Misty to follow. The Jeep covered them from the return fire, but all it would take was another lucky burst and they'd join Cutter in eternity. She dropped beside him. Hayden crawled over the front seat and scrambled out the back as well.

The three squatted at the rear fender. The second Jeep had stopped a few feet away. The four gunners had spread out in the grass, firing at the house. The Black Hawks disgorged more shooters who dropped on rappelling lines. The thunderous rotor blades and the chatter of automatic weapons fire forced Raven to shout.

"We can't stay here!"

"Up the tower!" Hayden shouted.

"On me!"

Raven ran from the Jeep as more slugs slammed into the body. A tire popped. Raven forced the sounds from his senses. The tower loomed large in front of him. He paused at a doorway, the MK 556 at his shoulder. The bottom of the tower contained no threats. A spiral staircase of stone steps followed along the wall to the upper level.

"Clear!"

Raven started up the steps. His shoes scraped on the stone, and he kept his head up. He had no idea what waited on the top level. Horn's defenders could very well be on their way to intercept.

Machine gun fire from the choppers and the crackle of small arms continued outside.

Raven focused on putting one foot in front of the other. A glance back showed Misty and Hayden behind, Hayden bringing up the rear with Misty in between. Raven pushed on. Another step, and another. He neared the top landing. He pressed the rifle stock deep into his shoulder and rested his finger on the trigger.

They had to get to Horn before the Black River CEO had a chance to escape.

45

RAVEN SET FOOT ON THE LANDING. AN ARCHED DOORWAY ON his right led to the balcony encircling the tower. He was steps away from the glass-canopied walkway.

He shifted left and stopped at the wall. "Clear." Misty and Hayden finished their climb.

The walkway ahead wasn't lit. Glare from the still-on outside lamps filtered through the glass. One of the Black Hawks roared over the top. The gunfire outside didn't let up.

"On me," Raven said again. He moved forward at a quick pace, stepped onto the carpeted walkway. Another large arch waited at the end. A second step—

Overhead fluorescent lights snapped on. Raven shouted, "Get back!" and hit the floor. Automatic weapons fire ripped through the glass. Panes shattered; glass dropped. Raven twisted around and crawled over the shards back where he started. He wiped blood from his left hand onto his pants. Misty and Hayden were already flat on the landing.

"See them?" Hayden said.

"Third floor balcony."

Tiger Joe lived up to his name in that moment. He jumped up. "Cover me, Sam! Misty, shoot the lights!"

Hayden ran for the first doorway off the landing, the one to the wrap-around balcony. Raven joined him as he squatted behind the iron rail. Raven had a clear view of the third-floor balcony where several gunners fired at the CIA ground force. Staying a foot back from the doorway, he opened fire with short three-round bursts.

Hayden kept his MK 556 on single shot and chose targets carefully. He fired with precision. Raven kept the shooters hopping between them and the ground force. Unaimed return fire peppered the tower with ferocity, tearing chunks out of the brick. Hayden's rounds knocked the gunners down, one after another, like bowling pins. A heavy machine gun salvo from one of the Black Hawks finished them off. The big steel slugs ripped into the balcony, shearing it from the house. Chunks of concrete and broken bodies crashed to the courtyard.

Raven and Tiger Joe ran back to the walkway. Misty had shot out the overhead light and remained on the landing to cover them.

Over the com units jammed in their ears, the commander of the CIA ground team gave an update. The falling balcony took the fight out of the defenders at the front of the house. The two teams were splitting up to enter. Raven radioed back they were approaching the second floor.

Raven, Misty and Hayden reached the entryway at the end of the walkway. Raven told his companions to spread out. The gunfire outside had lessened but sporadic shots crackled on the first floor.

Raven studied the room they entered. It looked like a large sitting/group dining area with furniture and tables throughout. Art on the walls. Raven hoped they weren't about to shoot up rare paintings.

Raven, Misty, and Hayden traveled the length of the long room but found no targets. Another wide doorway led to a hall overlooking the main entrance to the ground floor. Raven shifted left and right. Behind him, the hall continued with a line of bedrooms. Ahead, staircase to the third floor.

The three checked the bedrooms, easing open each door for a quick look inside. No hidden threats. No shooters under the beds or in the closet.

"First floor clear," reported the CIA team commander. The gunfire had stopped, but Raven hadn't noticed.

"Second floor clear," Raven radioed in return. "Any further casualties?"

"Two wounded."

"Copy."

"I'm sending two men up to you."

"We're expecting them."

Raven, Misty and Hayden went back to the open section of the hallway. Raven looked at the staircase to the third floor.

"What?"

"If Horn hasn't escaped and isn't upstairs, where did he go?"

Hayden said, "None of the choppers reported an escape. They were supposed to take out the garage to keep him from getting away."

"Yeah," Raven said. "So, where is he hiding?"

THE NIGHT HAD BEEN GOING SO well!

Dante Horn almost had perky Caroline out of her pink tank top thanks to a game of "strip darts" in his den.

Each had won a game and lost a game, so they were both sans pants. It was hard to focus on the target with Caroline standing in her tank top and white strawberry-dotted panties.

She stood with her hands behind her back, smiling coyly as he raised a dart. She thrust out her ample rack to further distract him. No. Uplifted round tits would not distract him. He had to score higher than her and get her out of those strawberry bottoms. He threw the dart and the projectile sailed across the open space to the dart board. *Smack.* An eight.

"Not enough!" Caroline said. She laughed and jumped and clapped. "Take something off!"

They weren't playing by any standard game of darts rules. They were both too drunk to follow the 501 rules and subtract to zero. Easier to base points on where darts landed. Three darts each round, and whoever came up short shed something.

Horn grinned sheepishly as he took off his shirt and draped it over the back of a leather chair. His slacks were already there. He knew of faster ways to get a 25-year-old doe-eyed DTF hottie naked and on her back, but the game made it more fun.

Getting Caroline out of the pub had been easy. The driver and bodyguards made her frown, but she stayed cool. The detached garage with his exotic car collection made her squeal with delight, but then she noticed the armed security force.

"I think I should go home," she said. "You're a drug dealer or something, right?"

Horn laughed and went into sales mode. Overcome the objection and get the sale.

"Nothing of the sort," he told her. "I do work for the American government."

"Is it dangerous?"

"Dangerous *and* secret, know what I mean?"

She arched an eyebrow. "You're like Jack Bauer or something?"

Another laugh. "Kind of. These men are here for my protection. This is the safest house in Antwerp."

"Well," she said, her pitch increasing the way young women often spoke, "okay, I guess."

He took her up to the third floor and his game den. It was a cozy room with dark carpeting and walls, various pieces of colorful abstract art, game tables, a sitting area of leather furniture, and a glass-enclosed floor-to-ceiling cigar humidor.

Sans shirt, Dante Horn plucked his darts from the board and stepped back. Another round. Caroline, with her three darts, wobbled in front of the board as she tried to aim and laughed. "I'll fall over as soon as I throw this," she said.

She threw the dart and indeed lost her balance. Horn grabbed her and held her upright.

"Hey," she said, laughing up at his face, "what's poking me?"

"Oops," he said. He didn't let go. She grinded her rear end against him. The soft plumpness of her rear end, with nothing between him and her bare skin but their skivvies, stirred desire in his lower region. He let her go. She licked her lips, then turned to address the board for her next throw.

At the end of the round, she lost. He told her to ditch the strawberries. She said no and reached up her back to unhook her purple bra. She pulled it out through one side and let it fall on the floor on top of her jeans.

The house shook with the unmistakable roar of large helicopters. Horn knew the sounds well. Caroline screamed and ran under a Foosball table. Machine gun fire hammered the house.

Horn jumped into his slacks but ignored his shirt. "Get dressed!" he shouted. Caroline stared at him with a blank face, but then it dawned on her it wasn't time to get caught in her knickers. She moved quick to her jeans and pulled them on. She bundled the bra in her left hand.

More gunfire outside. A *lot* of gunfire.

"What's going on?" Caroline shouted.

Flame flashed outside the wide window overlooking the detached garage. Horn dived at Caroline and forced her to the floor. He covered the back of her neck as the crack of an explosion followed. The window shattered. Chunks and glass *whooshed* into the room and peppered the floor. The heat from the explosion followed.

There go my cars!

"What's *happening!*?" Caroline shouted as she squirmed under him. "Get off me!"

He moved away. "Come on. Get up, I have a safe room."

"A what?"

"A safe room, come on!"

He pulled her to her feet and half dragged her to the other side of the den. A line of wainscoting divided the wall in half. Above, artwork. Below, blank space. He punched a combination into a small panel on the wall. A section under the center line slid open. He gave her a shove, but she dug her feet into the carpet.

"No!"

"You'll be safe, it's okay."

Another explosion shook the house. All argument stopped. She dropped to her knees and crawled through the gap. He hit the combo again and the section of the wall slid closed.

She'd be fine. The room was lit, and a button on the inside would open the door in the worst-case scenario.

Horn turned away with a grim set to his face. There was a war outside and no mistake. The helicopters above the house continued their passes. His cars were gone, and with them his means of escape. His only remaining option was to run. They'd cut him down for sure if he tried.

His two bodyguards entered, both out of breath. They carried automatic rifles. One of them held two and passed the spare to Horn.

"What's outside?" he asked.

Horn listened to their description and it meant only one thing. *The Americans.* And not Sam Raven playing solo. The entire CIA clandestine group was outside blasting their way in.

And he had no way out.

He faced a choice. He only had his bodyguards with him. The rest of his force wasn't going to turn the tide. He could make a last stand or choose another option.

Surrender.

46

No.

Horn knew many things the Americans would want to know, but they'd never make a deal after his previous subterfuge.

"Let's go," he said. He pushed through the two bodyguards and took the lead out of the room. He didn't care if he was shirtless. This was his endgame. He'd be blown to smithereens so it wouldn't matter anyway.

Horn stopped at the corner at the top of the stairs. A line of American shooters approached the staircase. He brought the automatic rifle to his shoulder and pulled the trigger.

Somebody screamed and fell. The other four spread out. Two ran for the stairs. He ignored them. The narrow hallway restricted the movements of those who remained. Like him, they had nowhere to go. He charged down the steps, keeping low, his bodyguards firing overhead. Return fire cracked. Horn's narrowing tunnel vision blocked most of the view, so he fired at the nearest threats. His weapon kicked and spat flame. He pivoted, fired, turned, fired another burst. One body fell. Somebody ran by on his left. He pivoted with the muzzle of his rifle tracking, then a series of punches smacked him in the back. They weren't from fists, but bullets. Horn felt his body hit the floor hard. Breath left him. He tried to move and couldn't. Then his darkening vision faded forever.

RAVEN ROSE from his squat and didn't take his eyes off his sights.

His MK 556 chugged some more, and he shifted his aim with each burst. The two men at the top of the stairs tumbled down and stopped in a heap atop each other.

"Clear!" he shouted.

The stench of cordite hung in the hallway. Hayden joined the two CIA men on the staircase. Raven heard an agonized wail. He spun around and saw Misty bleeding on the carpet.

He ran to her as Tiger Joe began calling for more help. "One down!" he shouted. Raven didn't think he meant the bad guys.

Misty rolled onto his side. Several of Horn's slugs had punched through her leg and stomach. Blood trickled out her mouth. Her face was twisted in pain.

"Hold still," Raven said. He slung his rifle and pushed her onto her back. She coughed and her body jolted, then settled. "Help is on the way."

She breathed hard and fast, but at least she was breathing. Raven wiped blood from the corners of her mouth with his thumb. "You'll be okay."

Her eyes moved up and down his face, but she didn't respond.

"Let me through, sir."

Raven stood up as one of the CIA shooters with a medical kit took his place. Two other CIA medics tended to the other wounded shooters. Hayden had moved to the landing between the first and second floors. He held his phone to his ear but wasn't talking.

Raven went over to Horn's prostrate form. He'd fired the rounds into Horn's back, and the little holes had opened up big holes in his front. The carpet beneath him was drenched in blood. And his eyes remained opened.

Whatever he knew had died with him.

Raven turned as the commotion continued. The remaining CIA crew from outside began carrying the wounded down. Hayden stood to the side to let them pass, then ran to Raven. Color had drained from his face. Raven knew the next words he spoke would contain bad news.

"Just talked to Wilson," Haydon said. "We were too late, Sam."

Too late.

The echo of the words in Raven's mind drowned out any other commotion.

EVERY NEWS NETWORK had cameras at each disaster scene.

Deputy Director of CIA Operations Christopher Fisher sat in his office. His number two, Layla McCarthy, sat in front of the desk. He felt numb all over, and Layla sat forward in her chair with her eyes locked on the television screens.

Fisher had three wide screens mounted on the wall to the left of his desk. They were always muted, each screen showing a different news network. Fisher often forgot they were there until a disaster happened.

Like today.

The attacks had occurred within minutes of each other. As anchors reported the first, the second took place, and the third. Reporters, stunned at the incoming information, struggled to keep up.

In Los Angeles, a truck bomb detonated outside a local television station. The explosion vaporized a chunk of the building, exposing every floor bottom to top. Debris and bodies covered the street and sidewalk as emergency crews arrived.

And then the ambush began.

Three gunmen emerged from hiding and opened fire with automatic weapons. They cut down the cops and firemen and any straggling civilians nearby.

In New York City, a subway car exploded as it pulled into Bay Parkway station. As steel and glass debris mixed with fire and flame, gunmen opened fire on anybody still on the platform.

In Chicago, the terrorists hit the Cloud Gate structure. The bomb blast lifted the silver ball off its base, cracked it in half, and opened a crater in the plaza in which it sat. Another mass shooting followed the blast.

Fisher watched as the news cut back and forth between each city. He didn't have the sound on. He didn't need to hear the large volume of conflicting information. His job wasn't to explain what happened. His task was to stop the attacks. Since he'd failed, his job was now to find those responsible.

He exchanged a look with Layla. Her usual pale features were more so now.

He wasn't sure what to do but wait for Sam Raven's report.

A knock on the office door stirred him from his stupor.

He called out, "Yes?"

His secretary opened the door and leaned in. "Clark Wilson to see you."

"Yes, please, hurry."

The secretary stepped back and Clark Wilson entered. A

flush of red filled his face and sweat dotted his forehead. He carried a notepad.

"Tell me you have something, Clark."

Wilson stopped before the desk. He took a moment to catch his breath and consulted his notes. "Horn is dead."

Fisher cursed. Layla rested an elbow on the edge of Fisher's desk and covered her forehead.

"Any good news?" Fisher said.

"Our second strike team captured John Yarvis alive."

"Which one was he?"

"Horn's number two, sir," Wilson said. "He gave us data we can use."

"What is it?"

"Longitude and latitude coordinates," Wilson said. "Heinrich and I checked them out. They point to an island in the North Atlantic, south of the Azores."

"Who's on it?"

"Our satellite scan shows somebody who built up a fortress and has plenty of troops."

"Tanya is there?"

"Her father owns the island," Wilson said. "He bought it fifteen years ago. Yarvis says if she vanished after we lost her in Paris, she's probably there. It's where the rehearsals for Operation Triangle took place."

"What does Raven want to do?"

Wilson shrugged. "Go there. Him and Hayden."

"I'll make the arrangements," Fisher said.

Layla looked up. She said, "Can we talk the president into sending bombers? A two-man crew isn't going to do the job."

"You read my mind," Fisher said. "But I'm thinking of a carrier strike group out of the Med." He picked up the phone to call the Director of Central Intelligence. They had to move fast.

47

TANYA JAFARI STOOD ON THE BEACH, HANDS IN HER COAT pockets. Waves crashed on the shore with more ferocity than daytime. Their thunderous soundtrack calmed her racing mind. Cold wind whipped at her face, but her heavy coat kept her warm.

Operation Triangle was a success. Hundreds of dead civilians and America terrified and confused. She could not have imagined a better outcome. The plan had carried with it a lot of risk. Her father's connections with Ben Doyle, Stavros Stathoti, and Dante Horn made it possible. And the Americans kept looking in all the wrong places for clues. Icing on the cake.

But it wasn't a victory. The United States would be out for blood. *Her* blood. And the blood of anybody associated with the Islamic Union. Wiping out the CIA agents in Damascus had sent a message, but others would soon take their place. The new crew, motivated by vengeance, would hunt her people to the ends of the earth. Somebody would talk about the island. Tanya Jafari figured she could count the number of days left to her on both hands. The island sanctuary, set up by her father decades ago, wasn't going to remain so very long. They'd find her. Only a matter of time.

The success of Operation Triangle didn't bring back her father. The death toll wouldn't change Hannah's mind either.

No plan survives the first five seconds of its implementation. Operation Triangle had been no different. Successful, yet unsatisfying.

What had started so innocently as her and Francesca falling in love with two Muslims turned into nothing but pain. Operation Triangle had been an attempt to relieve the pain, avenge their fallen husbands, and Francesca too, who hadn't been able to live with the loss.

I've been dedicated to righting injustice.

She didn't regret her chosen path. The west needed to pay for how they treated people like Ahmad and Tamal.

But what has it taken from me?

The only answer was *everything.* Tanya had lost all that was dear to her in pursuit of her goal. She hadn't planned on losing everything after already losing so much. But she had. It was a reality she needed to face.

No amount of spilled blood changed the situation.

But she had Omar Talman on the island with her. If she were entering her final days on earth, she'd spend it with the man she loved. She'd never expected to love another man again, but Omar had surprised her. Maybe life had other surprises in store as well. One could hope.

She tried not to find an analogy between her thoughts and the darkness into which she stared. The night sky met the pitch-black ocean. There was no way to tell where one ended and the other began except for twinkling stars. And even then, she wasn't sure of the divide.

Tanya turned around. The main headquarters building sat a short distance away. Only a few lights lit the exterior perimeter, and no lights shined inside. She was awake well beyond "lights out" and only a minimal security force remained awake. Sleep had eluded her, but not Omar, so she'd taken a walk. Right now, she needed solitude more than company.

Tanya glanced up as the echo of whipping rotor blades grew louder. One of her patrol choppers passed overhead. She wondered if the crew saw her. Besides the pilot, four troops rode in the cabin, ready to jump out and engage intruders while the pilot radioed for reinforcements.

She'd probably have to increase the number of patrols. During the day she had two flying, one at night. Maybe three daytime and two at night would be better.

Tanya moved to a nearby rock and sat. The chill of the stone bled through her jeans. She stared into the dark some more. Darkness was everybody's final destination. She had no idea what she'd encounter once she arrived, but it wouldn't be as peaceful as the darkness she looked into now.

It was time to savor however many moments she had left.

A FAST-MOVING arrow cut through the choppy waters of the North Atlantic.

The motorboat was standard SOCOM issue, a Combatant Craft Assault boat. The forty-foot craft tapered at the bow to resemble an arrow. An apropos description. Sam Raven and Joe Hayden stood at the controls of an arrow fired at the heart of Tanya Jafari and her organization.

They'd flown to the area of the North Atlantic, south of the Azores, where "Jafari Island" as Raven called it, in a C-130. When the plane reached the designated drop zone, the load master launched the boat first. Parachutes guided the CCV to the water. Raven and Hayden parachuted into the ocean behind it. After a few tense moments of climbing aboard and getting the engine going, they steered for the island.

Hayden drove. He had the experience necessary from his days as a Navy SEAL. Raven monitored the radar screen next to the pilot seat.

Both wore black combat suits, prepared for war with all the associated gear and weapons. If the island had radar capability, the CCV's composite body wouldn't show up. Enemy boats and planes not similarly designed would flash on the radar screen.

Another screen showed their progress to the island. Another fifteen minutes.

Raven bounced in his seat as the CCV cut across the rough water. He constantly wiped spray from his face. The cold water chilled his skin. The chilly temperature bit through their combat fatigues. He let his thoughts wander to take his mind off the discomfort. The fate of Misty Watson filled his mind.

She'd live, but Horn had hurt her badly. Her recovery would not be short or easy. But at least she'd live to fight another day in whichever manner she saw fit.

The hectic exit from Antwerp was behind them now. At least one of the two raids ended in success. Horn's number two, John Yarvis, had proven his value under interrogation. Raven doubted if they'd have found Horn as cooperative. Knowing what criminal charges he faced in the US, and how his previous blackmail scheme wouldn't save him this time, he'd have been tough to crack. But Yarvis didn't have the same baggage and wanted to save his neck. He sang like a canary.

Raven's mission of prevention and revenge had simply become *revenge*. And he felt defeated going into the final battle. His only recourse was to make Tanya Jafari feel the same sense of dread. Make her pay for what she'd done, and the lives she'd destroyed.

Raven hadn't bothered listening to any news of the Operation Triangle disaster. He didn't need to see the suffering or know the death toll. He'd failed to stop the attack. Tanya had won again.

And while she might have achieved victory, Raven would have the final word. Any sense of triumph she now enjoyed had a short time limit.

Raven and Tiger Joe studied several satellite shots of Jafari Island during their flight. The island looked like a mutated T, with one side of the T jagged and diagonal. All the facilities were at the top of the T, with everything south jagged rocks and hills with a little bit of grass. A cove at the southernmost tip might provide a suitable spot to leave the CCV and begin their infiltration. They wouldn't know for sure until they arrived. If the cove didn't work out, they'd improvise. But nothing was going to stop them from getting onto the island.

Nothing would stop them from showing Tanya Jafari the meaning of *payback*.

48

THE CRESCENT-SHAPED COVE LOOKED ABOUT TWO MILES across with no beach in which to run the CCV aground. The cove ended at a cliff face 50 feet high. Raven and Hayden did not have climbing gear. To the left of the cove was a rough patch of ground leading up to the top. They'd get a workout but there was no other way unless they found another entry point.

Ocean waves entered the cove at several angles. The waves rocked the boat to-and-fro as Hayden steered left. As the port bow bumped against the edge of the shore, Raven leaped out. He tied a nylon rope around a large boulder. Didn't matter if it held. They wouldn't use the CCV for escape. They only needed the rope to hold a few moments.

Fisher had arranged backup. Within four hours they wouldn't be the only Americans on the island. The USS Abraham Lincoln, from the US Sixth Fleet, was on the way from the Mediterranean. The carrier not only had F-18s on stand-by, but also two Black Hawks full of SEALs.

Raven and Hayden had a simple task. Locate Tanya. Terminate when the cavalry arrived. Hayden jumped off the boat and joined Raven. Each man carried a US M4 rifle, with suppressor, along with a combat harness containing a variety of grenades and spare magazines. Wireless com units fitted into their right ears. Spare magazines, combat knives, and their personal pistols completed the rig. Small packs on their backs carried more ammunition magazines. The packs also contained their night vision gear. Shedding the packs, they removed the Sinister 509 XL6s Hayden had scrounged before leaving Antwerp. The goggles fit over their eyes like a diver's mask and amplified the starlight. The darkness took on a greenish glow.

The surf crashed at high volume on all sides. Raven took point up the rise. The hard-packed volcanic soil gave way to a flat top. A clear stretch of soil provided a road to follow. On the opposite side, a line of lush trees. Raven spotted tire tracks. The wheelbase was too narrow for a pick-up. Tanya's crew used ATVs. The tracks went to the edge of the cliff and back.

"Stay by the trees and follow this road," Raven said.

"Gonna be a long march."

"We better get started."

Raven and Hayden crossed the open road to the tree line. They walked upright but with a ten-foot gap between them. Raven remained point man. They'd see an ATV patrol before hearing the vehicle. The rider would need his headlamp. But they had no idea of the patrol routine or how many troops they'd encounter.

They continued their advance. The road forked further on, the branch leading down a slope to a beach. They ignored the fork. The sea breeze ruffled the tree leaves above. It was almost too peaceful a place to have a fight. At any other time, Raven would have found the island the perfect place for R&R.

Not this time.

Presently a bright light flashed in the distance. "Down!" Raven said. He dropped behind a mound of grass while Hayden broke across the road to a small gully.

The ATV headlamp became larger as the vehicle approached. There was only one with a single rider. Raven readied his M4. He poked the barrel through the top of the grass. And waited.

The sound of the motor didn't overpower the ocean. The rider continued his approach, and once his torso filled Raven's gun sight, the M4 whispered once.

He never saw the rider's face but watched the man's body stiffen and pitch over the side. The back wheels rolled over the trooper's body. The ATV veered left, up a short rise, and rolled back. It stopped against the rider's body.

Raven ran to the ATV and started to turn it back the way the rider had come when Hayden told him to stop.

"Got another," the CIA man said.

Raven cut off the motor and pushed the ATV into the trees. He dropped beside it with the M4 at the ready.

The second rider stopped ten yards from Raven. He turned on a hand-held light and shined it back and forth. The light stopped at the body of the first rider. He started to get off the ATV but didn't make it. Raven and Hayden fired at the same time. The second rider collapsed and lay still.

"One for each of us," Hayden said. He left the gully and ran to the second ATV as Raven pulled the first out of the trees. They followed the tracks at a moderate speed.

They had a general idea of their final destination from the satellite pictures. A cottage sat on a hill on the upper left point of the T. The cottage overlooked a cluster of buildings in a small valley. Barracks, they assumed. Over a rise behind the buildings, level with the ocean, was an airstrip. A road twisted through the landscape connecting the strip to the cottage. The road they followed also branched off to connect with the cottage. They expected to find Tanya inside.

Bushy terrain near the cottage would hide them from the barracks in the valley. All they had to do was wait for the Navy and then kill Tanya Jafari. Two shots center mass seemed about right. Raven didn't want to waste time talking to her. He wouldn't miss. Hayden's target was Omar Talman, Tanya's lover, the man who'd slaughtered CIA personnel at the Blue Ridge black site.

They rode for several miles until the trees thinned out. Overgrowth and open soil replaced the trees. They stopped the ATV before the end of the trees and made the rest of the way on foot. When they found the branch leading to the cottage, they moved fast through the overgrowth. The downward slope of the road didn't slow them down, though Raven was careful not to slip on loose soil. On either side of the road, a down slope led to more grass and rocks. He stopped midway to take up a security scan while Hayden moved forward. They continued the leapfrog movement until they were twenty yards from the cottage. They found plenty of places to conceal themselves, but no solid cover.

Raven felt his black combat uniform clinging to his sweating body. He breathed hard. They rolled into the overgrowth and looked twenty yards ahead at Tanya's cottage.

The landscape around the little house had been cleared. Tall grass swaying in the breeze remained. Railed porch. No light behind the windows. Tanya and Omar were asleep inside.

Raven checked his watch. Three hours till dawn. Three hours till the Navy showed up.

A long way, but the goal was within sight.

And then Hayden jabbed Raven's left arm.

"Chopper incoming."

49

THE CHOPPER'S SPOTLIGHT SWUNG AROUND THE COTTAGE grounds. Raven and Tiger Joe yanked off their night-vision goggles.

The rotor wash whipped at the grass, exposing their position. The light flashed over them. A burst of automatic weapon fire crackled. Bullets tore chunks out of the soil as Raven and Hayden rolled away in opposite directions.

Raven shouted for Hayden to run as he rolled onto his back. There was no solid cover; he was in the open, exposed. He extended the M4 and fired two long bursts. The chopper drifted left, and the salvo didn't appear to cause damage. The carbine clicked empty. The chopper began to descend again as Raven rolled to his feet and ran.

Hayden raced up the road they'd followed to the cottage. He jumped off the edge into a crevice of dirt and grass. He braced the M4 against his shoulder.

The chopper landed near the cottage. Four troopers jumped out, two from either side of the cabin. Lights snapped on inside the cottage.

Hayden cursed as he started shooting. Everything was

going down the tubes and Raven had no cover. The M4 hammered against his shoulder. The troopers split into pairs as the chopper lifted off. The chopper's engine noise faded as it flew over the hill to the barracks. They'd bring reinforcements. He and Raven were toast.

But he wasn't going down without a fight.

Tiger Joe tracked his targets, but they moved too fast, and the 5.56mm stingers missed their marks. He dropped down to reload. Rising again, he fired. Two of the troopers broke off. The other two started crawling through the overgrowth toward him.

"Joe!"

Hayden dropped from sight. "Still kicking!"

"We go for broke!" Raven shouted over the com link. "If we die here, we take Tanya with us!"

"Copy!"

Hayden jumped up again and worked the trigger. His burst drove the two troopers into bushes. They were halfway to him. He was at a disadvantage without his NVGs. Return fire smacked the soil behind him. The crevice was no place to stay. Hayden plucked a grenade from his vest and pulled the pin. He tossed it toward the enemy. Springing from the crevice, he ran across the road toward Raven.

The grenade blast thumped and unleashed shards of metal at lightning speed. The two troopers' bodies broke apart like a dropped Lego toy as the force of the blast smacked them. They fell in dead heaps.

The remaining two turned their guns on Hayden as he ran. He fired back, driving them to concealment. He joined Raven on a down slope. The cottage lights snapped off again. What was happening inside?

One of the troopers jumped from cover, ran toward them, and dropped and rolled again. The two rounds Raven fired missed. He and Hayden ducked as the gunners fired back. Nobody could see anything. They were shooting at shadows on black backgrounds.

"Chopper will bring more bad guys," Hayden said. He grabbed for another grenade.

"It's a party for sure." Raven pulled one of his grenades. "On three!" He counted. They tossed at the same time and pressed into the ground. Debris rained overhead as the explosions tore up the terrain. Chunks of wet flesh and burning scraps of fabric fell with the debris.

Raven reloaded his M4 with one eye on the cottage. *Now or never.*

"Joe, put a grenade on the front porch."

The sea breeze brought them the sound of whipping rotor blades. More than one. *Getting closer.*

Hayden tossed. The grenade landed short, but the explosion gave Raven the desired effect. The explosion knocked the front door out of its frame and shattered the front windows. The concrete steps cracked and fell to pieces. The porch wood splintered and snapped.

Two more helicopters passed in a long turn behind the cottage. Troops fired from the cabins. The projectiles rained on Raven and Hayden. Raven waited for the choppers to pass completely behind the cottage. The firing stopped. He sprinted for the wrecked porch. One of the choppers landed and let off four more troops. It lifted off and executed a sweeping left turn over Hayden's position. The wind from the rotor blades kicked loose ground ash into his face. He shut his eyes tight.

The chopper passed over. Hayden fired controlled bursts, shifting his aim with each squeeze of the trigger. The suppressed M4 whispered death. One trooper fell, the gunman behind him tripping over his body and tumbling. The others found cover. Return fire forced Hayden down. The rounds zipped overhead.

The second chopper landed. Four more troops exited. Hayden tossed one grenade, then another. He hoped Raven was clear of the blast. One boom, then another. Pounding footsteps joined strangled screams. He'd killed some but not all. Shadows rushed him.

Hayden fired on instinct. The M4's near silent salvo brought down one shadow. He pivoted left and shot another with a triple-tap to the chest. The body fell, sliding across the ground to knock him over. He landed with a cry on his right arm. He pushed the body away, rolled, and jumped to his feet. Hayden swung the butt of the M4 into the head of another gunman. The impact rattled his body and the weapon. He spun right, the figure ahead shuffling to one side, then the other, as Hayden fired from the hip. A miss. He swung the muzzle to the target again, but another flash of flame filled his vision first.

Hayden remained standing but stopped moving. His body burned for a moment. He didn't scream. He collapsed near one of the dead troopers and moved no more.

RAVEN LEAPED over the wrecked porch and slipped through the cottage doorway.

He ducked and dived for the floor as guns barked. He rolled left and bumped into a couch. Scrambling over the cushions, he dropped over the back. Landing on the hard wood floor almost knocked the wind out of him, and he gasped as he rolled again. The legs of a dining table stopped him this time. He rose and started to shoot, shifting the M4 side-to-side, firing blindly. The weapon clicked empty.

Raven dropped the carbine and grabbed his pistol. He stayed flat on the ground.

He tried not to think of the sudden silence outside. A chill raced down his neck as men yelled from the porch. They spoke Arabic. A woman's voice from across the room answered their sharp exclamations. Raven rose to a squat and fired in the direction of the woman's voice.

Two troopers rushed in. Raven pivoted toward them with the .45 in both hands. The Nighthawk spat a tongue of flame once. Neither fell. And then they were on him.

They pounded him with rifle butt stocks. The first, against his forehead, sent him spinning. He lost his grip on the Nighthawk. The second impact smashed his right shoulder. His face hit the floor. More blows landed but darkness overtook him. He felt nothing.

50

RAVEN'S VISION SPUN, HIS HEAD HURT, AND HIS RIGHT shoulder throbbed.

Raven wiped his eyes and then frowned at his free hands and feet. They hadn't restrained him. He was on a narrow bed in a small room. Before he took in more of the environment, nausea overwhelmed him. He vomited onto the floor but stopped mid retch. He wasn't alone in the room.

They'd dragged Tiger Joe's body in with him. Hayden's body rested in the center of the floor. A neat bullet hole sat in the middle of his forehead, another dead center in his chest. His still-open eyes stared at the fluorescent lights above.

Raven let out a low wail and vomited more. When he stopped, he let his head dangle a moment to make sure he'd finished, then eased back onto the mattress. It hurt to breathe.

He looked around despite his shifting vision. Wherever he looked, things tilted left or right. Small room. Two beds on either side. Wall-length lockers behind him. Had they moved him into one of the barracks? The door to the room was shut. He tried to stand up and see if they'd locked him in but had no balance. He dropped back onto the bed.

They'd stripped him of his combat rig, pistol and knife. But a glance at Tiger Joe's body showed they'd made a mistake. They'd collected his rig and pistol too but forgot the knife. Hayden's K-Bar remained in its belt sheath.

How long did he have before the Navy showed up? His watch was gone too.

He lay there breathing steadily for what seemed like an eternity. Tried not to think of the corpse on the floor. After a while, he tried to move. With every ounce of strength he could muster, Raven rolled onto the floor. He remained on hands and knees a moment. He took deep breaths. His vision had stabilized a little, but he still felt dizzy. Inside his head, it felt like somebody was banging a drum.

He turned to look at Hayden. "Sorry, Joe," he whispered. He reached for the K-Bar, unhooked the safety strap and tugged out the knife. The lights above flashed on the razor-sharp stainless-steel blade. He tossed it onto the bed. He crawled over to Hayden and closed the CIA man's eyes with his fingers. "You were a good man to have in a fight."

Sitting up, he put his arms on the mattress and rolled back, drawing his legs close. He stayed on his side and kept the knife concealed behind his bent knees.

His gaze settled on Joe Hayden again. How many more lives would Tanya claim before her reign of terror ended? What if the Navy failed? No. Raven pushed doubts away. Hold fast. He wasn't dead yet.

With a jerk of alarm, he grabbed for his neck. Raven sighed with relief when he felt the locket secure around his neck. A favor from Tanya? Or had they missed it?

Time to make a plan.

His mind wouldn't cooperate. The dizziness stayed with him. He lay in a daze and wondered what was coming next.

Tanya Jafari had won every battle so far.

How much longer would luck be on her side?

THE DOOR LOCK SNAPPED.

Raven rolled onto his back. The dizziness had subsided. His head and shoulder still hurt, but he thought he could manage.

Tanya Jafari stepped into the doorway. She wore jeans and gray loose shirt with a Beretta pistol on her belt. Her hair fell onto her shoulders. She folded her arms and looked stoic.

Raven glimpsed a man behind her but didn't see his face.

"You found me," she said.

Raven sniffed. "You left a few threads uncut." He spoke low, his voice cracking. His throat felt raw from the vomiting.

"Horn?"

"Yarvis."

She shook her head. "Somebody always slips through."

"Your whole life is a lie, Tanya."

"No." Her face flushed red. She straightened and pointed a finger at him. "My life is based on bringing justice to oppressed people. We're the same, Sam. Only different sides." She lowered her finger but still glared at him.

"Your father started this, Tanya. No random mob in Berlin is responsible."

"What do you mean?"

"He had goons attack the families of your boyfriend and Francesca's boyfriend. Then he groomed them to start the Islamic Union in the aftermath. They were tools to him. Means to an end. He manipulated all of you and you fell for every trick."

"Who said this?"

"Your sister," Raven said.

"She's a liar. And since you killed my father, we can't ask him, can we?"

"You know I'm right. Has part of you ever been suspicious?"

She flinched. Stoic became defiance and turned to doubt. She shook her head and laughed.

"Poor Sam Raven," she said. "In your last moments, you're grasping at straws."

"You can kill me. When I'm gone, you'll spend the rest of your life wondering if I was right."

"Stop."

Raven raised his voice. "You'll wonder how your life might have been different."

"*Stop!*"

"Or what, Tanya?"

Somebody reached for her through the doorway. She shook the hand away with a curse. She took one step forward.

"Aren't you curious why I've kept you alive?" she said.

"We meant a lot to each other for a short time, didn't we?"

"It was all an act."

"You deserve an Oscar."

"It was a performance only for one."

"What do you want, Tanya?"

"I want your locket, Sam." *Another step forward.* "I want you to watch me open it as I kill you. Your secret will be mine forever."

"Come and take it."

She snatched out her Beretta as she reached him, clawing with her free left hand for his neck. He batted her reach away and she slammed the gun into his head. Raven's eyes rolled back, and another wave of dizziness took over. He felt her hand on his neck. She grasped the chain. The chain dug into his skin as she began to pull.

Raven's right hand flashed beneath him and he grabbed the hilt of the K-Bar. Her eyes never left his and she didn't see the movement until it was too late.

"Remember what I said I'd do to you if you lied to me, Tanya?"

He slammed the knife forward. The sharp blade penetrated her belly with a tear of fabric and flesh. She gasped, eyes widening. Raven didn't blink as he pushed the knife all the way in, then shoved upward. Her body jerked with the movement as the blade tore through her guts. Her mouth opened to scream but nothing came out but a line of saliva.

"Tanya?"

Raven grabbed the Beretta and fired over her shoulder. The man in the doorway stopped short as the first bullet hit him. His head snapped back as the second delivered its impact. Omar Talman dropped.

Another man leaped over Talman's body. This one carried a submachine gun. His identity registered in Raven's mind. His was Sila Kaymak, the man who pretended to try and kill Tanya in Stockholm the night she and Raven met.

Kaymak lifted the SMG as the Beretta barked again and again from Raven's rapid fire. The 9mm slugs punched through Kaymak's chest and he joined Talman on the floor.

Raven dropped the empty Beretta and shoved Tanya away. She flopped onto the floor. She still had some life left in her and grabbed uselessly at the K-Bar's hilt. Then her hands slipped and rested at her sides. Her eyes remained open.

Raven rose from the bed. He breathed hard from the exertion but stood long enough to stare at her. He burned the image of her dead face into his mind.

A roar in the distance grew louder. Raven snatched up

Kaymak's submachine gun and grabbed a spare magazine to stuff into a pocket. Alarms outside blared. A panicked voice began shouting over a loudspeaker.

And then the first bomb landed.

The building shook with the blast. The walls swayed and the lights popped out. Raven was in darkness once again. He dropped to the ground and crawled over bodies, ignoring the blood smearing his clothes, to the doorway. Emergency lights in the hall lit the way ahead.

Jets thundered above. The F-18s, on schedule. SEALs on deck for mop up. Another bomb blast shook the ground. Windows shattered and glass flew inside. Raven covered his eyes with an upraised arm as he advanced and felt bits of glass hit him. A third blast crumbled part of the wall, and the ceiling collapsed behind him in a heap of sheet rock. Dust choked the hallway and stung Raven's eyes. He ran for his life.

51

THE NAVY DOCTOR TURNED OFF HIS PEN FLASH AFTER SHINING it above Raven's eyes and asking him to follow the light.

"You have a concussion for sure," he said. "Plenty of abrasions. Nothing broken. You got off easy compared to these other guys. Rest while we head back to Italy."

"Right. Where's my—"

"Your personal effects are on the nightstand."

Raven turned his head. His locket sat where the doctor said in a clear plastic bag.

The locket he almost lost.

The one thing he couldn't bear to be separated from. His reason for being rested inside.

The doctor moved to the next bed. Several wounded SEALs lay in the sick bay with Raven. Nurses hurried about. He ignored the commotion as he looked at his hands. Dried blood remained on his right hand. Tanya's blood.

Another man came over.

"You all right?"

Raven lifted his head. The man was Greg Macedo, one of the CIA agents who'd helped him get Hannah Schrader out of Berlin. He and his partner Mitch Storey had landed with the SEAL team because they knew what Raven looked like.

"I'll live," Raven said.

"Glad we found you when we did. You didn't look so good."

Raven had exited the burning barracks only to collapse near a tree. His head barely missed a large rock. He'd decided to lay there and wait. Either the SEALs would find him, or the last of Tanya's forces would finish him off. In that moment, he hadn't cared if he lived or not.

But then Macedo and Storey found him and dragged him out of the fight.

"What did you get?" Raven said.

"Plenty of prisoners, for one," Macedo said. He stood with folded arms. "We took a bunch of stuff we hope will provide more information, too. With any luck we'll shut down the Islamic Union once and for all."

"Good."

"We'll have Germany's help."

"Really?"

"We took Hannah back to Berlin so she could provide the BND with a statement. They found the information in her father's safe tying him to the Islamic Union and various other groups. The guy who ran his servers, somebody named Phillip Dassler, is also cooperating."

"And?"

"They've agreed to help us wrap things up as long as we keep them out of anything related to Operation Triangle. They're embarrassed Schrader was operating under their nose and they missed the signs."

Raven nodded. "I suppose it's a good thing."

"Is it?"

"Until the next terrorist comes along."

"I'm sure the president will make a wonderful speech taking credit for everything."

Raven laughed without humor. "Yeah, if he can remain lucid enough." He let out a heavy sigh. He sagged against the soft pillows propping him up.

"I'll let you get some rest," Macedo said. "We'll be back in the Med in a day or so."

"How many people died in the attacks, Greg?"

Macedo looked sad. "Too many." He walked away.

Raven closed his eyes. He'd recover and live to fight another day. Tanya Jafari was dead, the Islamic Union with her, but they'd lost so much in the fight, he still felt a sense of defeat.

There was no victory. Only pain and regret. If he'd been a little sharper in the beginning, maybe the disaster could have been avoided. Or maybe he was fooling himself. Deep down, nothing would have stopped her plan. If she hadn't reached out to him, she'd have found somebody else.

But now it was time to rest.

When he felt better, he decided to go to London and check on Misty Watson.

Perhaps together they could share some desperately needed R&R.

A LOOK AT: THE WAR BUSINESS: A SAM RAVEN THRILLER

BY BRIAN DRAKE

Raven Returns – and this time, a friend will betray him …

Sam Raven and Aaron Osborne forged a warrior's bond in the toughest covert battles of the Iraq War. Now, Aaron is desperate for Raven's help. He owes a debt to the kind of people who don't take IOUs and plans to rip off a pair of French drug dealers to get the money fast.

Raven thinks the plan poses too many risks, but Aaron saved his life once, he can't let a friend down. The best way to make sure Aaron gets away clean is to help him pull off the heist.

But when Raven discovers Aaron has lied to him, and the stolen money is actually financing a war profiteering conspiracy to ignite a conflagration in Europe, he'll chase his old friend from one side of the world and back again to prevent the deaths of millions of innocent people.

From the author of the Scott Stiletto series comes a new hero. Sam Raven is grittier, deadlier, and you better not stand in his way.

AVAILABLE JULY 2025

ABOUT THE AUTHOR

A twenty-five year veteran of radio and television broadcasting, Brian Drake has spent his career in San Francisco where he's filled writing, producing, and reporting duties with stations such as KPIX-TV, KCBS, KQED, among many others. Currently carrying out sports and traffic reporting duties for Bloomberg 960, Brian Drake spends time between reports and carefully guarded morning and evening hours cranking out action/adventure tales.

A love of reading when he was younger inspired him to create his own stories, and he sold his first short story, "The Desperate Minutes," to an obscure webzine when he was 25 (more years ago than he cares to remember, so don't ask).

Brian Drake lives in California with his wife and two cats, and when he's not writing he is usually blasting along the back roads in his Corvette with his wife telling him not to drive so fast, but the engine is so loud he usually can't hear her.

briandrakebooks.com